MOONLIT MAGIC

THE THORNE WITCHES BOOK 9

T.M. CROMER

Cover art: Deranged Doctor Designs
Editor: Trusted Accomplice

BOOKS BY T.M. CROMER

Books in The Holt Family Series

FINDING YOU

THIS TIME YOU

INCLUDING YOU

AFTER YOU

THE GHOST OF YOU

DEDICATION

To Deb & Lissa:
You are two of the most selfless and giving people I know. Your
constant support has enriched my life. Thank you for all you do.

CHAPTER 1

1828 – The Natchez, somewhere along the Mississippi River

"*W*e've been summoned."

Nathanial "Nate" Thorne cracked an eyelid to peer at his younger brother Andrew. He grunted and shut his eye. His booted feet were unceremoniously shoved off the table they rested upon. A deep, weary sigh escaped him. "By whom?"

"Father."

"*Shit.*"

Drew let out a humorless chuckle. "You sound like an American. Mother would be so proud."

Nate experienced a small pang of homesickness, but not for England. No, only for his mother. Ten long years he'd been away, and he missed the unconditional love she'd showered upon him.

Giving up all pretense of napping, he stretched and straightened. "What's the emergency?"

The severe expression on his brother's normally mellow countenance told Nate all he needed to know. He wasn't going to like what Drew had to say.

"The Enchantress needs to be contained."

"By us?" His incredulity caused his voice to crack.

The Enchantress was bloody bad news any way you looked at it. In her quest for power, she was known to enslave men, women, and children alike, mostly all magical with a few innocents getting caught up in the madness. It was why he was stuck in America with his siblings. Their parents wanted them as far away from that insane bitch as they could get. Rightly so, since Isolde de Thorne didn't care if she stole magic from her kin. That was obvious when she'd cornered and killed Nate's brother Jonah.

There was no way Nate wanted a damned thing to do with corralling the most powerful witch alive. She was an Aether. A keeper of magic, and the balance between good and evil. The one person able to give or take away a person's abilities based on a whim. Only one Aether could rule at a time, and when one died, another would take his or her place.

Unfortunately, this particular one had gone mad over the last twenty years.

"We won't be the only ones to subdue her, Nate. Isis has called forth the strongest from the Six. I'm afraid that's you and me from our family, brother."

The Six he referred to were the original bloodlines. Each descended from the gods and contained limitless power but were subject to the caprices of those same gods. If they were being called to action, they had no choice but to answer.

"Chance and Lottie? What's to become of them?"

"Father's suggested Chance and Charlotte hole up here in America until we return."

"You mean *if* we return." Unease tickled the fine hairs on the back of Nate's neck. "This is suicide, Drew."

"Father will be with us for the fight."

"You think the great Jonas Thorne will be able to prevent the Aether from obliterating us where we stand?" He made a scoffing noise and rubbed the heels of his hands over his face. "Bloody hell."

"I'll leave instructions with Chance should the worst happen." Drew tugged at his cuffs and cleared his throat. "But we need to go."

"How do we explain our disappearance from the boat?"

"Technically, we'll be gone, so there will be no need."

"Come on, Drew. If we survive, we'll want to return. Or at least, you and Chance will."

"You don't?"

"I don't know what I want." Yes, he did, but he wouldn't voice it yet. Nate didn't want to risk cursing his luck. What he did say was, "We've made our fortunes at the tables. We could walk away and invest in any enterprise that captures our fancy."

"It's all neither here nor there, big brother. We've been recalled home."

"The least we can do is compel the Captain to pull into the nearest dock. Our departure won't be as suspicious."

"Fine. I'll take care of it. You teleport and make arrangements for the twins."

Chance and Charlotte would be irate at being ordered to stay behind, but to leave those young'uns to their own devices on this vast side of the world would be foolish to the extreme. Lottie had a wild streak longer than the Mississippi River and twice as wide. Chance indulged his twin at every turn.

"Nate?"

He glanced up and met his brother's solemn jade eyes. No words needed to be spoken. They both knew what they faced when they returned to England. "The strongest of the Six, huh?" he asked with a half-grin. "This should be interesting."

"Father said Isis intends to pull from the Otherworld. This ceremony promises to be a treat."

Drew's sarcasm regarding the upcoming attempt to defeat the Enchantress wasn't lost on Nate. With a resigned sigh, he clapped his brother on the back. "I'll be back soon."

Closing his eyes, he mentally pinpointed their location and calculated the distance to the closest town. *Baton Rouge*. The city was always on his radar. They usually stayed at a small, clean boarding house not far from the port. At this time of night, only the drunks would be awake and not many of them. Most likely, they'd be in an alley somewhere, sleeping off the night's excess.

Nate's cells warmed as he visualized the narrow access road behind the boarding house. Within seconds, he was at his destination and scanning the area for any witnesses to his teleport. Finding none, he strode up to the building's kitchen door and tried the handle. With a quick look behind him, he murmured, *"Recludo."*

The metal bar securing the door from the other side released and allowed him entry. Nate replaced it and silently made his way to the second floor, stopping at the first bedroom on the right. This time, he didn't speak as he disengaged the lock.

He stood at the foot of the four-poster bed and stared at the woman lost to her slumber. The clouds outside the window parted —with a little help from Nate—and moonlight shone down on her pale, classical features. His heart turned over in his chest. For years, they'd been dancing around their feelings, with Nate too much of a coward to tell Evelyn he loved her. Now, he might never get the chance. For sure, informing her just before running off to confront the deadliest witch in history was bad form.

Nate sat on the edge of the bed. "Evie."

She smiled in her sleep.

"Evie, I need you to wake up." He trailed light fingers along her temple, stroking her silver-blonde hair. "Wake up now, love."

Her lids lifted, and her stunning amber eyes focused on him. "Nathanial? What are you doing in my room?"

"I have a favor to ask, and I hope you won't refuse me."

Heat flared in her cheeks, and she lowered her gaze to the coverlet she gripped. "I'll not lay with you, Nathanial. I've told you that."

"I've no doubt I'll wear you down one day, love, but it's a different favor I'm after."

Concern clouded her face as she turned more fully toward him. "What's wrong?"

"Drew and I need to return to England. Will you keep an eye out for the twins while we're gone?"

"Of course." A handful of heartbeats passed as they stared at one another, each unable to break the spell surrounding them. "H-how long will you be gone?"

He couldn't lie. Couldn't flirt and tease his way through a bullshit answer. Not with Evie. Not right then. His tone was solemn as he said, "I don't know, love. With any luck, a few days at most." *Maybe never,* the little voice inside said. But he didn't want to scare her. He didn't want to turn what might be their last moments together into a sober, sad affair.

Nate forced a grin. "The Thornes will be out of your beautiful hair soon enough, Evie, my love. Never fear."

He started to stand, but she grabbed his hand. "Nathanial? You'll be careful, won't you? Despite whatever harebrained scheme you've got going, you'll come back?"

The desire to weep was strong. He stared at her so long, she became uncomfortable and squirmed under his steady regard.

"Nathanial?" Her voice was a mere whisper, caressing the exposed skin at his throat. He very nearly swore when he realized he wasn't properly dressed. No wonder she acted like a shy maiden. What was she supposed to do when she woke up to find a man with his shirt half undone, lurking over her?

"I'll come back, Evie."

She closed her eyes and nodded, her lips in a tight, thin line.

"I'll always come back to you, love. *Always.*"

Her eyes flew open and locked on his tortured features. Tears shimmered, and one escaped down her cheek. "You'd better, Nathanial Alastair Thorne."

This time, his wide grin wasn't forced. It had only taken her fierce order to make his soul sing. He threw caution to the winds. "I believe it's well past time I told you I love you, Evie. Don't you think?"

She nodded.

"Don't promise your heart to another while I'm gone."

"Then you best hurry home to me," she retorted, sassy as ever.

He pulled her to her feet and tucked a lock of hair behind one small, delicate ear. "Count on it." His lips settled on hers, and her soft gasp of pleasure ricocheted through him. He pulled back and ran a thumb along her damp upper lip. "Soon."

Nate tapped the leather packet he'd placed on the bedside table. "This is everything I have in the world. Use what you need."

"I'll keep it safe for you."

"Use what you need," he said firmly. "You have a business to run and two ruffians to support now."

As he turned to go, she latched onto his forearm. "Nathanial." He gazed down into her beautiful face. Her lips moved as if she wanted to speak, but no words tumbled forth.

"I know, love."

With one last light kiss, he teleported back to his room on The Natchez. He had an Enchantress to conquer.

Eythrope, Aylesbury, England

ISOLDE DE THORNE WATCHED HER SON PLAYING IN THE GARDEN THREE stories below. Even through the distortion of the glass, she could see the strong aura of magic surrounding the boy. One day, he'd possess more power than she. On that day, her hunger would outweigh her love for him, and she'd steal what he had—or die trying.

Most people believed her heartless, and they would be ninety-nine percent correct. But that remaining one percent was for the black-haired boy below. He deserved a better life than the twisted, dark one she had to offer. He deserved to grow up normal, with love and laughter surrounding him. A small part of her, the only human percentage left after four hundred years, wanted that for him. The larger, non-human part laughed at her foolishness.

Power. It had to be consumed at any cost to feed the beast within.

She closed her eyes and rested her forehead against the cool windowpane. Sending him away was the only option. But who to trust? Who wouldn't take advantage of his innocence for their own?

Alastair Thorne will be his savior.

A vision of a blond man with sapphire-blue eyes appeared in her mind. Those eyes held knowledge, confidence, and good humor. Yes, he'd be the perfect man to care for her son.

While they'd never met, she knew of the Thornes. Rumor had it, the family patriarch was a decent man and a good father. He was the only trustworthy warlock she could recall. As a distant cousin to her son, he might be inclined to care for the boy and see he had a proper upbringing.

Unlike yourself, a little voice taunted.

Her eyes popped open, and she bunched her hair into fists on either side of her temples. "Shut up!" she hissed. "Shut up! Shut up! Shut up!"

Her son paused in his play, startled like a deer sensing danger on the wind. Slowly, he inched his head up and met her gaze. Isolde could detect no fear from him, only concern for her. A single tear formed and fell. The trail of wetness mocked the snarling beast inside her, enraging it further.

Today. She had to send him away today if she wanted to save him. Already, she could feel the hold on her sanity slipping. Soon, she'd strike against him, an innocent boy of only eight years, and he'd be defenseless against the monster she'd become.

Belatedly, after years of consuming magic at an alarming rate, Isolde realized she'd made a mistake. She had thought by feeding the beast, she'd keep it happy, but in its greed, it only wanted more and more. Now, that horrid creature wanted her son. She could hold out. She must.

With a simple snap of her fingers, she woke the writing tools on her secretary. The pen scratched out her convoluted thoughts, pausing now and again when her brain stuttered over her request. Finally, it swirled her name at the bottom and dropped to the polished wooden surface.

A wave of her hand dried the ink.

"Deliver yourself to Alastair Thorne," she instructed the parchment.

It rolled itself tightly and disappeared in a light puff of black smoke just as a shockwave rocked the countryside.

Adrenaline and an odd anticipation thrummed through Isolde's veins. If she wasn't mistaken, a goddess was about to pay her a visit. The beast stopped clawing at her insides and lifted its head to sniff the air.

"Yes," it purred. *"More power."*

Her cells warmed as she thought of the garden and her son below. Within mere seconds, she stood ten feet away from him. Although wary, the boy stared at her calmly, his obsidian eyes prepared for the news she had to deliver. It was as if he'd expected her to come to him.

"Come here, boy."

Because he was wise beyond his young years, he obeyed and trudged forward, stopping only a foot away. He didn't touch her. He knew better than to trust she wouldn't absorb his magic. She'd warned him only two years before—hugs were forbidden between them.

"I've made arrangements for your care, but you must hide now. There, over the ridge, about a hundred yards to the north. Don't return, boy."

He opened his mouth, but she held up a hand to forestall his words of protest. Out of a sense of obligation, he'd stay to try to protect her, and he'd be killed or wounded in the process.

"My darling, you'll do as I say," she commanded past the knot forming in her throat. "Promise me you'll cloak yourself as I've taught you and come out for no one but Alastair Thorne. Can you do that?"

Once, they had been as a mother and child should be, and the remembered love flared in his eyes for a brief second. He nodded, tears welling, but not falling. "I can do that, Mama."

Mama.

Not "Mother" as he'd called her for the past few years, but "Mama" as he'd done when he first learned to speak and would run to her on chubby little legs without reservation, knowing she'd sweep him into a fierce hug and rain kisses on his lovely little face.

"I love you, Damian. I need you to remember me how I was, not how I've become." She squatted to make them eye level. "It's possible for one such as us." Isolde placed a hand on her heart. "I feel it here. You'll find a great love one day. And when you do, you'll be a far better parent than I ever could be."

"I love you, Mama."

"Good. That's the one thing I was unable to destroy." She tapped a finger to his adorable nose. "Go now, son. I'm out of time."

Damian broke her steadfast rule and flung himself into her arms. The beast within her snarled and snapped, straining at the flimsy chain holding it in place. Isolde allowed her son only two seconds to embrace her before she forcefully set him away.

"Do as I say, boy."

"Yes, Mama," he whispered, staring at her face as if to memorize every feature. "We'll meet again. Try to remember this." He gestured between their hearts. "Please, Mama. Don't forget."

Her vision blurred, and she swiped the back of her hand along her damp cheeks.

"I'll remember," she lied. If she survived today, the one percent would be snuffed out. They both knew it as surely as they drew breath.

"Please do."

She smiled at his formal tone. "Goodbye, my precious boy. Remember to cloak yourself, and don't come out for anyone but Alastair Thorne," she reminded him.

Then he was gone.

The grass muted the sound of footfalls, but Isolde sensed the crowd forming behind her. Slowly, hands in the air, she turned to face the dozen or more people who'd come to destroy the Aether.

Fools.

Her attention was caught by the blond man in front. She tilted her head to the side as she focused on him. The man looked slightly different from her earlier vision. Thinner and a bit taller. Less elegant, somehow.

"Alastair Thorne?" she asked curiously.

He shot a quick look at the older warlock next to him. "Nathanial Thorne."

"You'll not set your sights on my son," the auburn-haired man beside him said gruffly.

She laughed.

Sauntering forward, Isolde kept her gaze locked on Nathanial Thorne, ignoring his father completely. "You're incredible. All fierce and proud. Your magic…" She closed her eyes and inhaled the warm scent of cinnamon. "Your magic is *divine.*"

Her eyes snapped open, and she released the seductive energy she used to reel in her victims. "Come to me, Nathanial," she purred. "I want to taste you, lover."

"Shit!"

Her magic was met with resistance as he shook his head and jerked backward.

"Evie," he said under his breath.

A vision came to her of a pale-haired woman with amber eyes. Her gaze held love for the man standing before Isolde now.

"She's lovely. I've never seen anyone with her hair color before. So silver as to be white," she said, taking another step toward him and lifting her hand to beckon him forward. "If you join me now, I shall spare her life."

The blood drained from his face, leaving his skin a sickly shade of gray. But he stood his ground.

Suddenly, a bright gold light flared between them, and Damian ran through the rift, placing himself in front of Nathanial. Shock held her immobile as Nathanial's father raised his arm, a flaming ball of energy directed at her son.

"Noooooo!" she screamed. She surged forward, prepared to decimate the entire group if it meant saving Damian.

Nathanial caught his father's arm before it descended, and he shook his head. Wrapped in his other arm was her boy. "We don't make war on children, Father. You taught me that."

"He's her son, Nate. He'll grow to be evil like *her*." In desperation, he added, "Did you forget what she did to your brother Jonah?"

Nathanial's cold-eyed stare collided with his father's. "He's a boy, now under my protection. You'll not harm him."

Isolde's shock held her immobile, and she met Damian's sad, knowing eyes across the short distance. He'd seen the future, and it was Nathanial Thorne who would see her son to adulthood. How or what part Alastair from her vision played, she didn't know. She only hoped her son didn't descend into insanity as she had.

"Go," she mouthed to him.

He shut his eyes tightly and teleported himself and Nathanial away.

"What the bloody hell—!"

"Our sons have saved each other, Mr. Thorne. You should do the same and teleport to safety. I won't be taken today." Isolde lifted her hands, and the wind picked up around them. The sturdy oaks bent and swayed under the force of her power. Fire flared to life in the stone urns bordering the garden, dancing up and outward, as it threatened those closest.

The twelve remaining witches and warlocks surprised her when they parted and encircled her. She'd have thought they'd have run for the hills at her casual show of force.

A warlock with light brown hair and a face similar to Nathanial's captured her attention when he stepped forward. "We're here to stop you, Aether." Determination shone brightly in his jade-green eyes.

"You can try, child. But between all of you, there isn't enough magic to do so."

"Perhaps not, but *she* has plenty."

An atmospheric change occurred, and the air crackled around them. Blinding light flooded the garden just as the goddess appeared through a rift in space, followed by twelve of the most powerful witches of the Otherworld.

Isis had arrived, and she didn't look thrilled to be calling.

CHAPTER 2

Modern Day – North Carolina

*V*acation at last!
Elizabeth Thorne stepped through the double doors of Thorne Industries and inhaled a deep, cleansing breath. The newest artifact her boss had been so all-fired to acquire was safely disposed of, and now, the family could rest easy for a bit. Surely, there weren't that many more threats to their kind left out there, right? Fourteen days of relaxation—mixed with a few nights of margaritas and Karaoke—were just what the witch doctor ordered. She sniggered at her internal joke.

With a spring in her step, she walked at a fast clip toward her Jeep. Just as she reached the vehicle door, an atmospheric change lifted the hair on her neck, the air around her becoming highly charged.

Incoming!

She whirled, ready to strike, but her hand was caught in a vice-like hold. Acting on instinct, she brought her knee up, only to have her balance threatened when she was released as quickly as she'd been detained.

"You should be more careful, *qalbi*. Deserted parking lots aren't safe for beautiful women such as yourself."

The grave expression on the man's dignified face was his standard trademark whenever she saw him these days. But once upon a time, he'd relaxed enough to let his guard down. When he had, those dark, seductive eyes of his filled with sparkling mischief.

"Rafe. I should have known." She clicked the remote in her hand. "Other than you, no one would dare accost me on Thorne property. What are you doing here?"

"Accost? You struck first." He shrugged and answered her question. "I was in town. I thought perhaps I could persuade you to dine with me."

Goddess, she wanted to, but starting something with a man who had serious commitment issues and disappeared on a whim went against good sense. *And* she'd started a new relationship less than two months ago, so there was that. Although, to be honest, if she believed for one second Rafe wanted something more than a convenient lay, she'd toss old whatshisname over in a heartbeat. Not great girlfriend etiquette, but the heart wanted what the heart wanted. Hers wanted Rafe Xuereb. Had for nigh on four years. *Damned Thorne curse.*

"Sorry. I have plans." She cast him a cool, dismissive smile over her shoulder.

"No, you don't."

No, she didn't, because her new boyfriend, Franklin, was out of town—*again*. But she'd be damned if she'd admit to being abandoned for the fifth time in as many weeks. He was the fourth guy in a year who seemed to find matters other than their budding relationship more important. She was beginning to develop a complex.

Swinging open the door, she tossed her purse across the console to the passenger side.

"Liz."

When he said her name in that soft, compelling way, her insides turned to liquid heat. She froze in place as if he'd cast a containment spell on her. He hadn't. Rafe was far too noble and forthright to do anything dastardly. No, that was his appeal.

"Don't."

She closed her eyes against the remembered pain of the morning he'd left her. She'd believed they started something, and when she woke to find him gone after three days in her bed—no note, no message of any kind—she'd been devastated. Family legend held that Thornes only loved once. They tended to recognize their soulmates instantly and become completely enamored. It had been no different for Liz when she met Rafe that one sunny spring day in Paris.

"*Qalbi,* why won't you talk to me and let me set the misunderstanding to rights?"

Suddenly furious and tired of it all, she whirled to face him. "Misunderstanding? Rafe, you left me without bothering to say goodbye. Without bothering to leave a simple note with your phone number. How is that a misunderstanding?" She smacked his hand away when he would have touched her. "Look, I get it was a casual fling for you. I should've realized that from the start. But for me..." She trailed off and shook her head.

He shifted closer, ducking his head to meet her eyes. "For you, what? Finish your thought, Liz. Tell me what it meant to you."

"Why? So you can laugh at my naiveté?" she snapped.

"Never that."

"It doesn't matter now. I'm seeing someone."

His mouth tightened into a thin white line. "He is a bastard and doesn't deserve you."

"Regardless, I don't cheat."

"I'm not suggesting you do." He paused for a heartbeat or two. "You should break up with him."

Of all the arrogant—! "Why? Other than the fact he's dating me, why do you hate him so much?"

"Isn't that enough?" He met her gaze with such intensity and directness she nearly gasped.

"I don't understand you, Rafe," she managed from her suddenly

15

parched throat. "You disappear for weeks—sometimes months—on end, doing Goddess knows what, and then return to say things like this. Please, stop. Franklin is good to me. He may even love me." She couldn't quite state the lie and say she loved him in return, but she was growing fond of him. A life could be built on that type of affection, right?

Rafe's face became an inscrutable mask. "Of course. I have no wish to disrupt your life. Good night, Liz. I'll see you tomorrow."

"Actually, I'm on vacation for the next two weeks." She wasn't quite certain why she felt the need to blurt the information. Possibly because her last true vacation was the one she'd taken to Paris. Or maybe she wanted to test him in some small way.

The hot look in his eyes seared her. Seemed he, too, was remembering their time in France. Or rather, in the swanky *hotel room* in France. Once they'd met, they didn't leave their suite.

"Alone?" The timbre of his spine-tingling voice deepened. It set off all sorts of alarm bells in her head.

"Franklin will eventually join me. Right now, he has business elsewhere."

"I'm sure he does."

Rafe's contemplative gaze slowly ran the length of her body. She was positive he missed nothing and, like Superman, could see beneath her form-hugging pencil skirt and white button-down top. Or perhaps he was remembering her nude. Neither of them had been shy during their brief interlude as lovers.

A flush started somewhere around her toes and worked its way up her neck. Her face started a slow burn—pretty much like her libido, which had been on a four-year hiatus unless Rafe was around. *Ah, hell!*

His tongue swiped along the part in his lips, and Liz swallowed hard. It wasn't an overtly sexual gesture on his part, not meant to be sleazy at all. It was more like an unconscious movement or muscle memory. An act he'd performed after kissing her most private areas, as if he wanted to taste her again.

"Are you going somewhere… exciting?"

16

She might have released a small meep, but if she did, they both purposefully ignored it. Wanting nothing more than to give him the exact location of her first stop so he could join her, she closed her eyes and shook her head.

"That's a shame, *qalbi*. You should have adventure in your life."

"I have adventure," she sputtered. "Plenty of adventure. Every day is one big adventure." *Christ on a cracker, she was babbling!*

A slow, amused smile turned up the corners of his mouth and crinkled the olive-toned skin on the sides of those magnificent midnight-colored eyes. "I'm sure it is. The Human Resources department has to be thrilling most days," he teased.

Scowling, she whirled away.

As Liz reached for the door handle of her Jeep, Rafe stepped to within inches of her back. She could feel his warm breath on her neck, and the sensitive skin at her nape raised with goosebumps.

"*Qalbi*, I can show you all the excitement you'll ever need. Just say the word, and I'm yours."

Paralyzed with want and a major case of indecision, Liz stood breathing like she'd just ran a mile, *and she wasn't a runner*. Hated any type of exercise if the truth be told. Well, any but sex. That was her favorite form of workout. Thank the Goddess her magical genetics kept her in shape.

The ringing of her smartphone jolted her out of the sensual spell Rafe had created. She dove headfirst into the vehicle to retrieve her cell.

RAFE RELEASED A LOW GROAN. LIZ WAS BENT OVER THE DRIVER'S SIDE seat as she scrambled for her bag. It was at moments like these, with her perfect, round ass prominently displayed in this manner, he wished he could permit his inner neanderthal to take hold. He wouldn't, because his father had raised him to be a gentleman, but oh, how he wanted to throw aside social niceties and claim this woman for his own.

She'd been rejecting him in one form or another over the last year, right after she tracked him to Thorne Manor to deliver his dismissal papers from the Witches' Council. He was at his wits' end.

She continued to cling to the excuse of a relationship with whatever guy she happened to be dating. Currently, that evil sonofabitch Franklin Moore. Rafe considered her relationships shams because she never truly committed to a single one. That would require more than the occasional dinner and end-of-date kiss. Liz's frustration in that department would continue to grow because he happened to have placed a spell on old Franklin, and all of the men before him. Whenever she kissed one of her companions, the guy would suddenly remember he was needed elsewhere, leaving both parties supremely frustrated.

"Franklin! Hi!"

Her voice sounded too chipper for a guiltless woman.

Rafe leaned back against the Jeep, crammed his hands in his front pockets, and waited.

"What do you mean you can't make it? *At all?* Why?"

For a brief moment, Liz's downcast expression triggered Rafe's guilt. He'd found out from her cousin that Liz was planning a holiday. His intent hadn't been to ruin her vacation, only to get Franklin the Weasel out of her life.

"No, I get it. Are you sure you don't have time... no... I understand." She disconnected her call and stared morosely at the screen.

"Everything okay?" Rafe knew it wasn't. He'd dabbled in Franklin's business affairs to make sure he fouled up any chance the guy could get away.

"Nothing important."

He hated her defeated tone. Her sadness caused an answering pang in his own heart.

"Liz..."

"I've got to go. I need to pack."

"Pack? You're a witch. You could conjure anything you might need."

"How will it look if I show up without a suitcase?" she snapped.

He shifted closer and bent his knees to meet her furious eyes. "What do you care? The woman I knew—"

"But I'm not the woman you knew. She's long gone, if she even existed. I'm different now. More staid and predict—er, dependable."

Pressing his lips together to stem off a smile, he nodded. Yes, to a large degree, she was staid and predictable. Dependable, even. But she had the potential to be much, much more.

"Those plans you had for dinner. Do they still stand?" he asked softly. "If not, I know a great Italian restaurant only two blocks from where I reside."

"Do you live close?"

"Within a few minutes of you."

Her head came up, and she glared. "You know where I live?"

"I've made it my business to learn everything there is to know about you, *qalbi.*"

"That's *stalking,* Rafe!"

"You say tomato, I say tomahto."

"Not funny."

He shook his head. "You need to learn to have fun again. You are much too uptight."

"Fine. I'll go to dinner with you. I'll show you exactly how fun I can be."

"That would be my fondest wish," he said with feeling. "Care to drive? I teleported."

Liz's teeth snapped together, and Rafe was sure he heard her molars grind against each other. Jerking her head toward the passenger side, she climbed behind the wheel.

They drove in silence, and Rafe imagined he could hear the gears of her brain shifting from one topic to another at a rapid rate. Was she putting two and two together? He hadn't been subtle about his machinations, but he wouldn't care for Liz to be angry with him this soon in the game.

"Make a left at the next light," he directed. "It will be a quarter mile on the right-hand side. Calabresi's."

"Oh, I love that place. I've only been one other time, with Nash."

Had Rafe not known Liz and her cousin were close, the soft smile she wore would've given it away. "How is he going to survive without your services at Thorne Industries while you're on vacation?"

"His IQ is off the charts. I have no doubt he'll figure it out. Besides, he has Ryanne to help him if need be. She can run the entire world with one hand tied behind her back."

"She's impressive."

"And taken," she reminded him.

Rafe fought a grin. "No one could be left in any doubt. Nash can't keep his hands off her."

"They always think they're being sly." Liz's light laugh shot straight to his groin. It was going to be a long night. He had to continually tell himself he was in it for the long haul and not for the sprint.

Once they parked, he escorted her inside the restaurant. They were seated in an out-of-the-way area, overlooking the street. None of the outside noise filtered in, or if it did, it was drowned out by the overhead sound system that piped Italian love songs.

The ambiance of this particular place reminded Rafe of his second home in Italy. He hadn't been back in many months, and he was feeling a little homesick. While this part of America was beautiful, nothing beat his adopted country of Italy, or his father's country of origin, Malta. He'd give almost anything to take Liz there and to see the sights through her eyes.

For now, dinner would have to do. As they reviewed their menus, he silently debated the merits of filling her in on Franklin's shady business dealings. He could use her help to bring that bastard down, but the idea of placing her in danger rankled. And there was no doubt Liz would dive headfirst into the fray. She was a Thorne, and it was encoded in their DNA to get involved.

"What are you thinking about so hard?" she asked.

"You."

Her shiny blonde head whipped up as she stared at him with suspicious eyes. "Why?"

An involuntary smile curled his lips. "If you have to ask…"

A becoming blush stained her cheeks, and she ducked her head back behind the menu.

His Liz had become shy around him. Sadness rolled in. Over the years, he'd called himself ten kinds of fool for walking away in the early morning without her number. But back then, he'd been arrogant. He'd believed an elder of the Witches' Council would have no problem obtaining the number for Elizabeth Thereaux. Except she'd used a false name, and locating her had been impossible.

"I looked for you," he said suddenly, feeling it was important for her to know the truth.

For the second time in as many minutes, her head popped up to stare at him.

"I did." He sipped his wine then released a heavy sigh. "I know now why you changed your name—because the Thornes had powerful enemies in those days—but you were impossible to find under the fake alias." He met her stark amber gaze. "I did search," he finished softly.

"My cousin Alastair was adamant that no one who traveled used their real names. With Zhu Lin and Victor Salinger on the loose…" She pulled a face and shook her head helplessly.

"You don't need to tell me about Zhu Lin. That evil bastard shot me and tried to bury Zane Carlyle and me alive in Egypt."

"Winnie's husband?"

"Yes."

Winter Thorne. Who knew she was cousin to Liz and that ultimately through her, Rafe would find the woman he'd fallen in love with in Paris?

"I'm glad you all made it out okay."

Rafe thought back to that day last year when he'd trailed Winnie to Isis's temple in an effort to retrieve the Goddess's Uterine amulet. How Lin had tracked Winnie to the temple was anyone's guess. Perhaps he'd simply calculated the original location and had gotten lucky. Perhaps, like Rafe himself, Lin had put a magical spell on Winnie in hopes she'd lead him to the artifact. Regardless, that horrible excuse for a human being had taken Winnie, Zane, and Rafe hostage to get what he wanted—Winnie's never-ending source of power.

Absently, he rubbed his shoulder. Sometimes the healed wound still ached. Thanks to a bullet laced with a substance toxic to witches, he'd been critically injured. If it hadn't been for Winnie's quick thinking and the general kindness of the Thorne family, Rafe would be dead.

"Thank you."

"So, you and my cousin… how did you meet?"

He heard the hesitation in her voice along with a hint of another emotion. Jealousy? Goddess, he hoped so.

"I was in Malta, visiting my father's family. She happened to be in the hotel room next to mine. We shared a balcony, a cup of coffee, and a kiss."

She fumbled her wine glass, righting it before she spilled a drop.

"I didn't know she was your cousin at the time, Liz," he said gently.

"It doesn't matter. I don't have a claim on you." She turned her head and looked around the restaurant as if she'd never been there before.

"Don't you?" he asked silkily.

Her eyes cut sideways to lock on his face. "What's that supposed to mean, Rafe?"

"What do you want it to mean?"

"Jesus, you sound like a damned therapist in a B-grade movie."

He laughed. Her irritation had expanded into full-blown snark. Here was the woman he desired above all others.

"I'm in a relationship, or have you already forgotten?"

He sighed his frustration at her stubbornness and took a long drink. "How could I forget? You throw it in my face every five seconds."

"That's not what I'm doing, Rafe." Suddenly, she reached across and squeezed his hand. "I'm reminding *myself*. It's too easy to be around you. Too easy to forget Franklin."

Surprised by her honesty, he shifted to study her face more fully. Her discomfort showed in the slight flush of her cheeks and her avoidance, her refusal to look at him.

"Good."

Mouth agape, she stared. "What?"

"Good. I want you to forget Franklin. He isn't for you."

"And you are?" She snorted her skepticism and withdrew her hand.

"And if I said I was?"

"Come on, Rafe. Aren't we a little old for games?"

"I think it's important you understand one thing, *qalbi*. I don't play games. I never have." He covered her hand and rubbed his thumb in small circles over her silky skin. "I want you, Elizabeth. That will never change."

Her sharp indrawn breath clued him in to the fact she wasn't immune to him despite her proclaimed relationship status.

The ringing of her smartphone interrupted anything she might've replied. She dug it out of her over-large Coach tote and checked the screen. With a soft groan, she answered. "What is it, Nash?" She frowned and met Rafe's silent inquiry. "We'll be right there."

"What's happening?"

"All he would say was that it was urgent you and I head to my cousin Alastair's estate."

"Me? I'm curious to know how—"

She cut him off with a raised hand. "Scrying. It's what my family does best." She cast one last regretful look at the bread basket on their table. "Let's go."

Rafe bundled up the bread in the red-checkered cloth and stuffed it in her tote. Then he threw a twenty down on the table as a tip for their server. "Come, *qalbi*. There's a backroom we can use to teleport." He guided her to Gianni Calabresi's small office. "Hold tight."

He pictured the exterior of Alastair Thorne's home, and his cells warmed for the teleport, but nothing happened. With a frown, he tried again. They were landlocked. Only Blockers could prevent a witch or warlock from teleporting. Blockers were other mercenary witches previously hired by the Désorcelers Society to make the lives of the Thornes hell. The last of their ilk should've scurried into hiding after the final confrontation between the Thorne family and their age-old enemy. Apparently, they hadn't. If Blockers were present, then he and Liz were in deep shit.

"Liz, try to teleport us and do it now."

She closed her amber eyes in concentration. When they flew open, an edge of panic could be seen there.

"As I thought," he muttered. He engaged the lock on the door and turned back to examine the bookshelves behind Gianni's desk.

"What are you looking for?"

"Calabresi's cookbook. He changes its position on the shelf after every use. If you locate it, pull the spine down toward you."

Rafe found it first and tugged on the book. The closest bookcase swung outward to reveal a secret passage. "Time to go."

CHAPTER 3

*T*hey raced down the steps to a dark and narrow tunnel. With its dark brick walls and single-bulb lighting, the place had an overall creepy-ass atmosphere. Liz shuddered, and her hand spasmed within Rafe's grasp. He paused their descent and raised his brows in silent question.

"Where does this lead?" Her soft words sounded overly loud in the enclosed space. She sent a nervous glance backward at the bookshelf door as it swung shut to hide the tunnel.

"To a warehouse two city blocks away. We should be out of the range of the Blockers by then."

He led her forward again at a quick, steady pace.

"Rafe? How did they know to target us in the restaurant?"

"I couldn't say, but we'll find out when we get to your family's home."

They each remained locked in their own thoughts on the short journey to the warehouse. Once they reached the tunnel opening, they paused to listen.

"I don't hear anything," she whispered. "You?"

He shook his head and cast a frowning glance behind them. "I didn't hear anyone pursuing us through the tunnels either. This is all a bit odd."

"You can say that again," she muttered.

"This is all a bit odd," he deadpanned.

A giggle of disbelief bubbled up and out. "Funny."

"I'm glad you think so." He inched the bolt back and slowly lifted the floor panel to look around. "It appears to be all clear. Come."

He assisted her through the opening, then closed the trapdoor. He waved a hand over the top to reactivate the charm disguising the tunnel's entrance from this side.

Curious now that they appeared to be out of immediate danger, she took stock of her surroundings. They were standing in the center of a modernized warehouse. The entire floor was designed to function as a loft-style home. The industrial space, with its pale gray brick, large glass walls, and refurbished wooden floors, was warmed by paintings and comfy furnishings.

"I love it. Who lives here?"

He smiled slightly. "I do."

She whipped around to stare. "You?"

"I'm a silent partner in Gianni's restaurant. One of the perks is having an all-access pass, night or day, to his kitchen."

She shifted to take in more of the apartment's layout and trailed a finger over the butter-soft leather of the sectional. Had he always planned for them to end up here tonight? A small part of her yelled, *"hell yes!"* at the thought. She told that little voice to shut the fuck up.

"What is it you wish to know, *qalbi?*"

His silky, seductive voice spoke directly behind her and made her jump. "I, uh… nothing. We should go."

"Of course."

He held out his hand, and she tentatively placed her palm atop his. Their eyes met, and within those midnight depths, she saw understanding. Inside, she cringed, hating he could read her with so little effort. Hating that her confusion regarding their situation was so obvious.

Before her mind could twist itself in knots of angst, Rafe drew her close and wrapped an arm around her back. She ignored the rightness of being held by him as her cells began to ramp up. Heat danced along her body, and Liz held her breath for a teleport.

It never happened.

"What the devil?" Rafe swore.

"Why can't we teleport? Surely any Blockers couldn't prevent our magic this far from the restaurant?"

"I don't believe it's a Blocker issue. But either way, it looks as if we are driving to our destination."

He ushered her to his vehicle. A short while later, they were on the highway, cruising toward Alastair Thorne's private mountain estate. In the quiet of the car's cab, her stomach's growl sounded overly loud.

"May I eat in your car?"

Liz opened her purse at his nod. The smell of fresh-baked bread and garlic-butter goodness made her mouth water. Rafe's stomach roared, putting the sounds hers made to shame. He laughed and held out his hand for a breadstick. Soon enough, they had consumed the entire bundle, and Liz rooted around in her purse in the hopes of finding an escapee. It was not to be had.

"I'm sure your cousin will have food readily available should you ask," Rafe assured her with a low chuckle.

It went without saying that Alastair would indeed have a meal set out, but Liz figured the family would be consumed with finding out why their teleporting abilities were on the fritz and not be too concerned with dining.

"I should simply conjure us something now." She held out her hand, palm up, and visualized an apple. A tingling started at the base of her fingers, but then suddenly stopped. Her hand remained empty. "What the hell?"

Rafe's dark head whipped in her direction. "What?"

"I can't even conjure an apple!"

"Seriously?"

"Rafe, I'm worried."

He intertwined his fingers with hers and squeezed. "*Qalbi*, if I know anything about your family, I know they are brilliant—both individually and as a whole. You will all figure this out in short order."

Goddess, she hoped so.

They arrived at her cousin's estate and were ushered into the dining room where Alastair, Nash, and their respective fiancées gathered.

As predicted, platters of food ran the length of the long dining table.

"Help yourself, child." Alastair nodded his regal blond head toward the food. "We've done away with formalities. It will be at least two more hours before your cousins arrive."

Liz hugged Alastair's soon-to-be wife, Aurora, and took a seat.

"What's going on? Initially, we thought Blockers, but I wasn't able to use my powers even after we were a safe distance from the restaurant," she said as she plated her salad and grabbed a yeast roll.

"That's the question of the hour," Nash said. His expression was dark with worry when he met Ryanne's concerned gaze. "It seems to have affected the entire Thorne line."

Liz paused between bites to say, "Rafe was unable to teleport earlier. Have the Carlyles tried to perform magic?"

Alastair sent a sharp glance Rafe's way. "You were unable to teleport?"

Rafe explained they had both tried.

Sapphire eyes narrowed in contemplation, Alastair asked, "Did you try on your own, without touching Liz?"

"No."

"Will you be so kind as to do that now?"

Rafe stood, closed his eyes, and disappeared only to reappear a moment later. "It seems I'm not having a problem."

"Try again, please. This time, try to take Nash with you."

Rafe once again complied, but was unable to leave the room.

"Again without," Alastair ordered.

Rafe was able to leave and return.

"So, the conclusion to this little experiment is that Rafe can come and go at will as long as he isn't dragging along a Thorne," Nash said, with a grim look toward his father.

Alastair nodded. "Indeed."

Liz set down her fork. "Does this mean we are the target of another attack? If so, who the hell could be behind this? I thought Victor was the last of our enemies."

Rafe rested a warm hand upon her shoulder. She took comfort from the gesture. Most likely, he was only being kind, but she welcomed his touch. Without magic, her family members were helpless against whoever might want to take the powerful Thornes down a notch or two.

"As far as I know, he was. But that doesn't mean there isn't someone who knew him and who now has an ax to grind because of his demise."

"Serqet?" Nash asked quietly.

The Goddess Serqet had had a falling out with Isis many years ago. She began making life difficult for the sister's descendants, with the Thornes being at the top of her hit list. Victor Salinger had been her tool along with a whole host of previous baddies she'd randomly sent their way from time to time. It stood to reason she would find someone to replace Victor in her quest to make the Thornes' lives hell. And Liz dreaded discovering who. It meant her much-needed vacation just went bye-bye.

Alastair rose and drained the glass of brandy in front of him. "Could be. While we are waiting for the others, I'll head to the clearing and see if I am able to summon Isis. She may have the answers we don't."

"Not alone, you aren't." Nash stood and joined his father. "From here on out, everyone takes another family member and a guard with them. Safety in numbers."

A half-smile tugged at Alastair's lips as he studied his son. "Fine. Let's go." He brushed a kiss to Aurora's temple. To Liz and Rafe, he said, "Alfred can make up a room in case you care to rest until the others arrive."

"Thank you, sir."

· · ·

Rafe waited until Alastair and Nash cleared the room before he pulled out a chair and sat down. Without preamble, he said softly, "It's a dangerous time to be a member of your family, *qalbi*."

Irritation flashed in the amber eyes she turned on him. "You don't have to stay. Feel free to leave and protect your own ass."

"That's not what I meant." Because he understood fear was the root of Liz's agitation, he fought back a reactive response. He leaned forward to capture her gaze. "I intend to stick to your side until this issue is resolved. You'll need someone who has your best interests at heart."

Her eyes softened, and she nodded. "I'm sorry. Nerves are getting the better of me."

He imagined she was mentally running through all sorts of future scenarios should she not recover her abilities. Clasping her hand, he gave it a light tug. "All will be well. I promise."

"You can't promise that, Rafe. We don't even know who, if anyone, is behind this. For all we know, the Goddess has decided to make us all non-magical mortals."

"True. But I will always protect you. No matter what."

"You don't owe my family or me anything. You know that, right?"

He shook his head at her obtuseness. "There, you are wrong. I owe your family a great deal." He kissed her smooth cheek. "You, most of all."

Anything else he might've said was interrupted by the arrival of Alastair's butler. Aurora directed him to fix up rooms for their expected guests.

"I hope you'll consider staying with us until we have a handle on all of this," she said to them. "Do you intend to share a room?"

Perhaps Rafe should have been offended by Liz's blustering indignation, but her blush and downcast eyes told a different story.

He met Aurora's humor-filled gaze. When she winked, he almost laughed aloud. She knew very well what she was doing when she asked about their sleeping arrangements, the wily minx. Everyone but Liz knew he was crazy about her. He could appreciate that the Thornes were on his side and that they could recognize the situational humor of Rafe's unrequited feelings.

"A connecting door should be sufficient." He winced when Liz socked his shoulder. Who knew such a tiny woman packed that type of punch? "What? I want to be there should you need assistance..." He dropped his voice for her ears alone. "...in any capacity."

She lightly pinched his side, and he grinned. Yes, she was warming to him. Liz tended to get touchy, both in affection and in aggression, whenever her emotions ran high. He adored that about her. Of what concern was the occasional shoulder shove when her loving touch was so sublime?

He sobered, and his emotions swung to the dark side. The question was whether Liz would put aside past hurts and her pretense of boyfriends to give him a second chance or whether she would continue to keep him at arm's length for fear of betrayal?

"I should call Franklin to let him know what's happening," she said. "He'll want to know."

Rafe nearly blurted a derisive response. Forcing a calm he didn't feel, he asked, "What do you gain by sharing this matter with him? How will he be affected at the moment?"

"Excuse me? You don't think, as my boyfriend, Franklin would want to know what is happening in my life?" With each word, the volume and pitch of her voice rose. "Just because you cut and run, doesn't mean he will."

"I see." And he did. Liz had clearly answered the question as to whether she would continue to cling to past hurts. "You may wish to hold off relaying the Thornes' immediate circumstances until you are more sure of your current paramour, Liz. Not everyone has your best interests at heart."

Suspicion clouded her lovely eyes.

Rafe imagined her misgivings were about his motives and not Franklin's. With a deep sigh, he rose and crossed to a wall of windows to stare out at the stunning landscape. For the better part of a year, he'd been trying to get back into Liz's good graces. Most days, he wondered if he was fighting a losing battle. Rarely did she spare him a passing glance.

He rubbed a hand across the back of his neck in an attempt to ease his tension. He was feeling every one of his seventy-two years. Yes, he was older than Liz by nearly three decades, but in the whole scheme of things, age never mattered between witches and warlocks. Magical genetics meant a slowdown of aging. Physically, he looked and felt thirty-five. Mentally? Well, at this moment in time, he felt ancient.

"If you know something about Franklin, I wish you'd share it with me, Rafe."

He shifted to stare down into her worried eyes. They'd darkened to a golden-brown due to her turbulent emotions. The changing of irises was a witch's tell. Right now, hers revealed a lot.

"You wish so badly to be close to another person, you sometimes forget they aren't worthy of your time, Liz," he said softly. "I have no facts to provide to you at the moment, only a feeling. Perhaps my experience urges caution in matters such as these, but I would not be as trusting as you."

He turned on his heel and exited the room with a nod of acknowledgment to Aurora.

CHAPTER 4

"Why are you determined to shove Rafe away?"

Liz twisted slightly to address Ryanne. They stood roughly the same height, but where Liz's figure was more svelte and sporty, Ryanne's was pin-up worthy. She had curves for days and knew how to use them. More recently, Ryanne had added amethyst highlights to her dark hair. With the shoulder-length bob, it gave her a chic, modern vibe. It always amazed Liz her friend was so down-to-earth and caring. She'd grown up without magic but still could've used her looks to rule the world.

"I'm not," Liz denied with a shake of her head.

Ryanne snorted and rolled her eyes as only a good friend could. "You certainly fooled me."

"I don't want to talk about it." Liz turned to stare out the window Rafe had been staring out of moments before. The summer sun had set, and the beauty that had framed his tall, muscular figure earlier was now gone. Nothing but inky blackness stared back at her.

"Well, we damned well are going to talk about it. You basically told me to get my head out of my ass when it came to Nash, and now I'm telling you the same about Rafe." Ryanne placed a hand on

Liz's upper back and rubbed small circles. "He's crazy about you, Liz. You're the only one who refuses to see it."

"I can't trust him."

"Bull. Try again."

Aurora's reflection showed in the glass an instant before she added her two cents to this ridiculous conversation. "She doesn't trust herself."

Both Liz and Ryanne faced her with a soft gasp.

A gentle, understanding smile graced Aurora's face, lending to her delicate English beauty. "When I first awoke from my stasis, I pushed Alastair away. Because of his solicitous, reserved manner, I also believed he only cared for me out of obligation. As if I were a burden to him and everyone around me." She ducked slightly to make the two of them eye level. "I don't imagine it's much different for you, is it, child? Rafe left for business purposes and lost contact. Now you are trying to convince yourself he only wants to reconnect with you for convenience's sake because you are afraid to care for him again. If he leaves a second time, it will devastate you."

Tears threatened, but Liz ruthlessly suppressed them. "I don't love Rafe. We had a brief fling four years ago. It was nothing," she lied. Perhaps if she repeated it to herself enough, she'd eventually believe it.

"It wasn't 'nothing' if the longing gazes he sends your way are any indication. You're fooling yourself if you believe otherwise, dear girl." When Liz would have protested, Aurora held up a hand. "We won't badger you, but do keep your eyes and mind open. I think you may eventually see what the rest of us do. Now come. Let me show you to your room so you may freshen up."

Liz followed her hostess in silence. If she could teleport, she'd be thousands of miles away. Remaining in close proximity to Rafe for an extended length of time wasn't good for her head nor her heart. No, he had only to look at her with that wicked twinkle in his midnight eyes—the one that said he'd seen her naked and wanted to again—and she turned to mush. It was too easy to recall the way he'd touched her as if she were the only woman on the earth who made him burn—just as he made her burn.

Aurora paused inside the door of Liz's room. "There are fresh linens on the bed. The bathroom is through there. I'm afraid you'll have to share the *en suite* with Rafe, but you can work out an arrangement to use the shower or bath. Each room has its own toilet and sink."

"Would it be too much trouble to get a different room?"

"I'm afraid it would. The rest of the family will be arriving shortly. Alastair feels it's for the best if we all reside under one roof until this issue is resolved. The other rooms allow a little more privacy for my children and their spouses." She squeezed Liz's hand. "I'm sorry."

"It's perfectly fine. It's only for a few days, I'm sure."

"Precisely."

As her hostess glided toward the door, Liz called to her. "Aurora?"

"Yes, dear?"

"How did you let go of the past to trust again?"

A soft light entered Aurora's sky-blue eyes. "Who could resist Alastair Thorne? Not me." She smiled, and the beauty of it was breathtaking. "Never me."

Alastair was a force to be reckoned with, his charm and power legendary in the witch community and beyond. The air of danger surrounding him was like nectar to hummingbirds, and he fascinated the women who entered his sphere.

Just like Rafe.

Perhaps it was why she'd asked Aurora in the first place. The similarity between the men was great.

"Will you wake me when the rest of the family arrives?"

"Of course. Rest now, dear. It will be all right."

───────────

RAFE ENTERED LIZ'S ROOM WITH THE INTENTION OF WAKING HER TO

join her family's discussion about the diminishing of the group's magic. When he saw her curled up on the mattress, lost to her slumber, his heart hiccuped in his chest. The last time he'd seen her so relaxed and peaceful was their final morning in Paris—the morning he walked away.

He wanted nothing more than to take them back to that day. To crawl into bed with her and never leave her side. But he didn't possess the powers of a Traveler witch, so time travel was out of his hands.

He squatted by the bed and touched her shoulder. "Liz? It's time to wake up, *qalbi.*"

"Rafe," she murmured on a sigh. He caught his breath when she blinked and blessed him with a luminous, happy smile. She reached a hand toward him, but immediately dropped it and glanced around with a frown. "What are you doing in my room?" All the sleepy sexiness was gone, and in its place was suspicion.

"Nothing sinister, I assure you," he said dryly. "Aurora sent me to wake you. The rest of your family has arrived."

"Oh."

She looked confused and more than a little embarrassed.

"I'll wait for you in the hallway," he said gently.

"Rafe?"

He faced her from the doorway.

"I didn't mean to insinuate you were up to no good," she assured him. "I was simply surprised to see you in my room."

He nodded his understanding and left.

Liz joined him a few minutes later, and they walked to the dining room in silence. Before they entered, she stopped him with a hand on his arm. "I'm sorry. You've been nothing but helpful to us. To me." She grimaced. "I'm screwing this up. What I'm trying to say is that you could leave at any time if you want to. This isn't your problem."

Once again, she'd hammered at his honor and integrity. The desire to rail at her was strong, but he bit back his sharp retort and mentally counted to ten. When he could speak without giving away

36

his anger, he said, "I could leave, yes. But I won't leave you or your family defenseless against an attack." He waved his hand toward the door. "After you."

"Rafe—"

"Liz, if it makes you feel better, tell yourself I'm doing this for Winnie and Zane. I owe them for saving my life. Now, I believe we've delayed enough." For once, he did away with his ingrained manners and entered a room first, leaving her to find her own way to the table. If he spent another second in her presence, he might strangle the stubborn wretch.

The only remaining empty seats were right next to each other, and Rafe wanted to teleport home so he didn't have to be tortured by the subtle scent of Liz's perfume as he sat through the discussion. He changed his trajectory to the sideboard for a cup of coffee then propped a shoulder against the closest wall. It still allowed him to take part, but kept a good distance between him and the woman determined to torment him with her indifference for the remainder of his days.

"You're welcome to join us," Alastair gestured to the chair next to Liz.

"I'm good standing," he said.

The knowing glance from Alastair set Rafe's teeth on edge. In order to hold his tongue, he sipped his coffee.

"Right. Let's get to it, shall we?" Alastair tilted his chin toward Nash. "My son phoned early this evening to tell me he'd experienced a disruption in his magic."

"As you all now know, it isn't just me who's been targeted," Nash added. A deep frown tugged his dark blond brows together, and concern was evident in his jade eyes. "What we don't know is who or what may be behind this magical blackout. Isis had no news to impart other than a fun little riddle and to say a greater evil is rising. One we've not encountered before."

"Currently, this appears to be an attack on our family. Ryanne, Quentin, the Carlyles, Ryker, and Aurora have all retained their power. Because of this, if you are a Thorne by blood, it's imperative you stick with your significant other as a safety precaution until this is resolved. Rorie and I have opened our home to all of you. My security team won't allow anyone through the main doors." Alastair focused on Liz. "As a favor to me, I'd like you to keep Rafe by your side, child. He's intelligent and powerful with plenty of experience. He'll keep you safe."

Liz cast Rafe a sideways glance. She opened her mouth in what he assumed would be a protest.

Unable to withstand another rejection, he shook his head and offered up a rueful grin. "I'm afraid my company is too much for Liz, Alastair. I'm sure she'll be safe under your care while I search out who might be behind this attack."

"Don't presume to know what's best for me, Rafe," Liz snapped.

"Are you trying to say you *want* me to play bodyguard?"

The flush on her cheeks darkened, but she didn't look away. Rafe's heart picked up speed, and he straightened from the wall.

"I'm simply saying don't presume. I'll do what's best for the good of the whole," she stated primly.

"Of course, *qalbi*, you know it all and are wise beyond your years."

It was doubtful anyone missed his sarcasm. Liz, for sure, didn't. The tightening of her lips spoke of her pique.

"Liz." Although Alastair spoke softly, he commanded attention. "Please call your mother, brothers, and any other family members like Piper, who you may have a number for. Have them come here or get to the closest Thorne stronghold. I can provide three locations for their use."

She nodded, took his written list, and left the room.

Rafe fought the urge to race after her. He hated to leave her virtually powerless and vulnerable for one second of one hour of one day. Across the distance, he met Alastair's contemplative sapphire gaze.

"You must have some suspicions, Alastair. In the forty years I've known you, you've always had your pulse on what's happening in the magical community, even if you *were* on the outside in most cases." Rafe sipped his coffee then carefully set the cup in the saucer. "So tell me. Where do you believe this is stemming from?"

Alastair was the Thorne family patriarch. He was easily one of the most crafty warlocks in existence. There was only one other who had even a remote chance of going head-to-head with him—Damian Dethridge, also known as the Aether. No one else held the power to neutralize an entire family of witches.

Alastair narrowed his eyes and stared off into the distance. Clearly, he had his suspicions but was hesitant to voice them. Rafe was curious as to why he'd be so reserved when it came to the group as a whole. He had never been before.

"What constitutes a great evil? A person? A group like the Désorcelers? It's impossible to tell. If our magic was functioning properly, we could scry, I suppose. Currently, we are blind."

"I could be your eyes. Tell me what you wish me to do."

"First, we should make a list of potential enemies," Alastair said.

Autumn Thorne-Carlyle snorted. "That will take weeks, Uncle. And Goddess knows we'll likely miss fifty or so."

Rafe fought a grin. "Is there a prize for the family member who disgruntles the most people?"

"If there is, Uncle Alastair would win hands down," Winnie inserted with a cheeky grin at her uncle.

The dry look he shot his niece caused those seated to laugh. "If we never regain our powers, the lot of you could open a comedy club." He addressed Rafe. "The Champeau family might be one we should watch. I know you've had dealings with them in the past. Would you be willing to see what you might find?"

"Of course." Rafe's lower back began to sweat and feel sticky. He imagined Alastair knew the exact moment his nerves kicked in. Rumor had it, he had the ability to discern emotions through an empathic gift. Since Rafe had witnessed Nash utilize the same ability, it wasn't hard to imagine his father had passed it down through his bloodline.

Although Alastair narrowed his eyes on Rafe, he held his tongue.

39

There was no doubt he was being toyed with, but he'd be damned if he gave himself away.

"Why did you mention Champeau, brother?" GiGi Thorne-Gillespie shot a concerned look toward her husband, Ryker. "I thought my darling husband made peace with Marguerite months ago."

Marguerite Champeau had visited Ryker during the time he was incarcerated by the Witches' Council to lay their quarrel to rest. To say there had been bad blood between the two was to put it lightly. Ryker, as an agent for the Council, had been tasked with seducing Marguerite and stealing important documents. The only things he received for his trouble had been a poisoned bullet to the gut and an estranged wife.

Marguerite also happened to be cousin to Franco Moreau, aka Franklin Moore, aka Liz Thorne's current beau.

"Simply a feeling, GiGi," Alastair replied to his sister's question. "Nothing more."

But Rafe wasn't so easily convinced Alastair was going off a "feeling." The warlock was as wily as they came.

CHAPTER 5

" *R* afe, do you have a moment?"

Although his desire to escape was strong, Rafe waited for Alastair to catch up to him.

"Join me in my study for a drink, won't you?"

"How can I refuse?" he asked dryly.

Alastair chuckled as he clapped him on the back. "You can't."

When they were ensconced in the study, each with a tumbler of scotch in hand, Alastair got to the point. "I don't trust Franklin Moore."

"Join the club."

"I suspected as much. You already know he has shady business dealings both in and outside of the witch community?" At Rafe's nod, Alastair grimaced. "How long have you been watching him?"

"Since the first time he came in contact with Liz."

"You love her?"

The question threw Rafe. It shouldn't have, because the Almighty Alastair knew all, but still he hadn't been prepared for so blunt a query. "I do."

"Why don't you simply tell her? She'd dump that worthless excuse for a man in a second."

"No, she wouldn't. It would make winning her heart even more difficult because she wouldn't believe me." Rafe gave him a half-smile and took a sip of his drink.

Alastair chuckled. "Most likely." After downing some of his own scotch, he said, "We need to find a way to discredit Moore."

"I'm working on it."

"Good. In the meantime, keep Liz away from him if you can."

Rafe tried to hide his involuntary grin with his glass.

"What have you done?"

Had it been anyone else, Alastair's tone would've made them crap their pants. But Rafe understood the dangerous quality wasn't directed at him.

"I may have performed a small spell."

"Do tell."

"If Franklin attempts to kiss her, he feels the pressing need to be elsewhere."

"How's that been working out for you?"

"Like a charm. Old Franklin didn't know what hit him."

In all their acquaintance, Rafe never saw Alastair laugh so long or loud. "Brilliant!" he gasped. "Sheer brilliance. Thorne-worthy, in fact."

"Yes, well, Liz will have my ass if she ever finds out." Rafe shot a warning look his way. "I'd appreciate it if you kept this to yourself."

"It goes no farther than this room."

"Alastair, why *did* you mention the Champeau family at the meeting?"

"You know Franklin's true identity, do you not?"

"Yes. But I wasn't aware you did."

"I've been around a long time, Xuereb. There isn't a lot I don't know about the remaining families in the witch community."

Rafe suspected as much. If one wanted answers, they rarely needed to look much farther than Alastair Thorne. "Why have you never called him out or told Liz he's lying about his name? She'd believe you."

"There are many reasons for a person to use an alias. If I'm not mistaken, Liz used a different name when you first met. Regardless, without proof against Franklin, our soft-hearted girl will give him the benefit of the doubt." Alastair took another sip of scotch. "You and I know we can't afford to do the same."

They drank in companionable silence for a while.

"I should go to France," Rafe finally said.

Alastair lifted a brow. Rafe was sure it was his way of encouraging an explanation.

"The Champeau and Moreau families all come from the same region. I have an in. It will allow me first-hand spying and help me discover if they're behind this mess."

"That's one option."

"The other?"

"What do you know of the Aether?"

"Damian Dethridge? Not much. For the last twenty years or so, he's kept to himself." Rafe met Alastair's curious gaze. "My understanding is that he hides a source so powerful, he'd die to protect it. As far as I know, he never leaves his estate. I can't imagine he's behind this, but he's the only one strong enough to conjure the type of spell to drain the entire Thorne family."

"That is my understanding as well. I'd like to pay him a visit at Ravenswood. Will you join me?"

"Of course, although how we will get to his estate from here is questionable."

"I'll go the old-fashioned way and fly first class."

Rafe laughed at the idea of Alastair on a commercial flight. "It might be better if we charter a private plane."

"No. If someone has it out for our family, my hope is that they are principled enough not to murder hundreds of innocent people to get to me. A private plane is too easy to target. Any witches or warlocks flying with me would be vulnerable because their magic might be void."

"They could always teleport as long as they aren't touching you."

Alastair gave him a sour look, and Rafe laughed again. Who knew teasing Alastair could be such fun?

"I'll have Alfred make the arrangements."

Rafe placed his tumbler on the side table and rose to his feet. "I'll be ready."

LIZ WAS ABOUT TO KNOCK ON ALASTAIR'S STUDY DOOR WHEN IT opened to reveal Rafe. Her breath caught in her throat. His sheer beauty always stole the oxygen from her lungs. A lock of his thick black hair fell across his brow, and she had the strong urge to brush it away. Would her desire to touch him ever leave?

Their gazes locked as he shifted to allow her entry into the room.

"Rafe."

Alastair captured his attention, and Liz was able to restart her lung function. She also had an unobstructed view of his classic profile. The romantic, girly part of her heaved an internal sigh. Because of her distraction, it took a second for her cousin's words to sink in.

"I'd like to leave first thing in the morning if it can be arranged. The sooner we speak to Damian, the better."

"Damian?" she asked. "Damian Dethridge, the Aether?" Her voice had risen with each syllable, and she attempted to moderate it for her next question. "Why the hell are you going to see him?" Okay, so that didn't work.

Both men wore identical expressions: brows lifted in surprise and mouths forming a small O. Alastair was the first to recover.

"What do you know about Damian?"

"What don't I know?" She looked from Alastair to Rafe and back again. "He's dangerous as fuck. Why are you going to see him?"

A slight smile quirked Alastair's mouth, and Liz wanted to hit him because of its mocking quality. Her cousin knew she was freaking out on Rafe's behalf. No way in hell did she want him to catch the Aether's attention. Damian was all things dark and dangerous. He was the boogeyman of the witch community. Want to keep your children in line? Threaten them with Damian Dethridge.

"He may be the key as to why the Thornes have lost their magic," Rafe said.

"I don't want you to go," she blurted.

Again, his brows shot up in surprise.

"He's dangerous," she reiterated helplessly.

Understanding lit Rafe's dark eyes, and a soft smile curled his full lips. "It will be all right, *qalbi*. I've met Damian before. I'm no threat to him, so I have nothing to fear."

"And if you go charging in where goddesses fear to tread, accusing him of stealing our powers, you don't think he's going to view you in a different light?" She really needed to get control of her emotions, or the pitch of her voice would injure the eardrums of any dogs in the vicinity. "Also, let's face it. There isn't a person on the planet who would take one look at Alastair Thorne and not feel threatened." She cast an apologetic look at her cousin. "Sorry, but you know I'm right. You exude threatening, and you enjoy the chaos you create."

Alastair opened his mouth as if to defend himself, but Rafe cut him off.

"Liz, we need to discover what the root cause of the magical blackout is for your family. Dethridge may be able to provide answers."

"Then I'm going with you."

Goddess, she was an idiot. She didn't want to face off against Damian, but she didn't trust Rafe and Alastair to play nice either. They needed a moderator, and she was the calmest, most level-headed Thorne in existence. Or she was when Rafe wasn't involved.

"No." Rafe crossed his arms.

"Perfect." Alastair spoke over his objection.

She paid no attention to her cousin and remained focused on Rafe. "I'm going."

"I said no, *qalbi*. No way in hell am I putting you in harm's way."

"You aren't. I'm doing it to myself." She frowned and cut a side glance toward Alastair. The fool sat grinning as if vastly amused. "I meant to say, I... oh, screw it. I have a bargaining chip."

"Do tell," Alastair invited. He crossed his legs and took a slow sip of his drink as if he had all the time in the world.

"It's a magical artifact Damian asked me for." She held up her hand. "And before you think to bypass me and go to Nash, he doesn't know what it is. Only I do."

"Are you seriously going to hold back the information on the artifact to muscle your way into this situation?" Disbelief and some other fleeting emotion flashed in Rafe's eyes. She dare not think it was admiration.

Liz lifted her chin and met his gaze squarely. "Yes."

"I think the important question is, why did he approach you and not Nash?"

"Nash was out of the office at the time. I knew better than to give the Aether a powerful object to boost his ability."

"And you never told Nash?" Alastair asked. His casual air was false. One had only to look into his intense sapphire eyes to see he was hyper focused on the subject at hand. The man missed nothing.

She shrugged. "I did, but he was preoccupied with other family matters. We never discussed the object Damian needs."

"Needs?"

"I'll tell you everything if you promise to let me come with you. No tricks."

Rafe swore at the same time Alastair laughed.

With one elegant finger, Alastair crossed his heart. "Promise."

Liz looked to Rafe. His scowl told her he didn't care for her ultimatum.

"Fine. I promise."

She couldn't prevent her smug smile. "Like I said, Damian came to me looking for a special decanter. He knew we store artifacts for the Council. But we didn't have what he was looking for, so I couldn't help him."

"This decanter, what was special about it?" Alastair looked intrigued.

"It was a rare thirteenth-century Japanese jar that could transform any liquid into a toxin. I didn't question exactly *why* he wanted it. The man scared the bejeezus out of me."

When Alastair suddenly grinned, Liz developed the sinking sensation that she knew precisely where the object was. "You have it. It's the jar you took from the storage room when you helped Ryanne regain her powers, isn't it?"

Alastair rose gracefully to his feet and set his glass on the sideboard. "The good news is we need look no farther than Alfred for Damian's desired object."

"And the bad news?"

"We go tomorrow to meet the Aether."

CHAPTER 6

*D*amian Dethridge was an imposing individual. Even across the expanse of a room, his power could be felt, like tentacles reaching out and testing the waters around him. He wasn't overly tall, probably no more than six feet, but he was built well for an ancient warlock who looked no older than thirty. Mouthwateringly well.

He moved toward them in slow, measured steps, his eyes never blinking. A panther in human form. Liz's heart was hammering, and it wasn't just from nerves. Their eyes met—his so dark brown they appeared black. She found it impossible to look away. The man had a seductive quality. Hypnotic.

Rafe stepped in her path, and his tapered back blocked her view. She wasn't sure if she was grateful or disappointed. Damian was poetry in motion. The urge to shove Rafe aside to get a better view of the Aether was strong.

"To what do I owe this pleasure?"

A shiver danced along Liz's spine. His voice was like warm honey, sticking to all the right places.

Unable to help herself, she popped around Rafe and held out her hand. "Mr. Dethridge, it's a pleasure to see you again, sir."

"Ms. Thorne."

She suppressed a shiver at the warmth in his tone. With a wrist-flicking gesture toward the men somewhere behind her, she introduced Rafe and Alastair.

Damian leaned in close and whispered, "May I have my hand back?"

"Oh!" She squeaked and dropped her arm to her side. "Of course. So sorry. My bad."

Rafe sighed heavily and embraced her with a single arm around her waist. "She doesn't get out much."

Damian winked, and Liz was grateful for Rafe's support; otherwise, she'd surely be a puddle on the floor.

Alastair shifted forward. His gaze and tone were hard as steel when he said, "Dethridge."

Damian copied his arrogant pose, chin in the air, eyes narrowed and cold. "Thorne."

Their stances remained locked for all of three heartbeats before both men laughed and man-hugged with a hearty pounding on the each others' backs.

"It's good to see you again, my friend."

"You too, Al. What brings you here?"

"Wait, *what?* You know each other?" Liz tilted her head back far enough to look up at Rafe. She didn't feel as foolish when she saw his dumbfounded expression.

"Damian and I go way back," Alastair confirmed. He shifted and raised the duffle bag he'd been holding, presenting it to the Aether. "I hear you were looking for a very specific artifact."

"Is that the Kamakura moon flask I was looking for last year?"

"It is."

The gaze he settled on Liz was noticeably cooler. "I thought you said you didn't have it."

"She didn't. I did," Alastair replied smoothly. "I learned last night you were in the market for one."

"One? Try the only charmed flask in existence." Damian chuckled. "Now, tell me. What do you wish to trade for it?"

"It can't simply be a gift?"

"From you, Al? No." Damian's grin softened the sting of his reply. "But I'll take it." He shifted to shake Rafe's hand. "Mr. Xuereb. Good to see you again. Come, have a seat."

A light shuffling sound could be heard from behind the curtain. Damian cut his eyes toward the noise and placed a finger to his lips. Ever so carefully, he crept toward the floor-to-ceiling drapes. With great fanfare, he whipped back the curtain. "Aha! I caught you, you little miscreant! Begone, or I'll turn you over a spit and feed you to my guests."

The little girl he'd exposed was a tiny replica of his dark good looks. With her obsidian eyes as wide as saucers, she screamed, "No, Papa!" and darted for an exit.

"Teleport, love," he hollered after her.

The girl disappeared halfway to the door, leaving a smiling Damian in her wake.

"She's still a bit skittish," he said by way of explanation.

"How's Vivian?" Alastair asked, not unkindly.

It was as if shutters came down over their host's eyes. His expression became carefully blank. "I'm sure you're not here to discuss my wife." He gestured to the sofa and chairs in the center of the room. With a simple snap of his fingers, there were four teacups and a steaming pot on the coffee table. "Tea?"

"I'd love some," Liz gushed, eager to change the subject and get rid of the hard-eyed stranger who'd taken the place of the congenial Damian of minutes before. "Shall I pour?"

He gave her a nod and a bland smile.

Alastair perched on the arm of the sofa. "I won't beat around the bush, my friend. The Thornes seem to be under attack. Our powers are no more."

"Goddess!" Damian sucked in a sharp breath and glanced from one to the other. A calculating expression settled on his striking face. "You thought I was behind this?"

Alastair accepted the teacup from Liz. "As the Aether and someone who has the ability to collect another's power with ease, you are the most likely suspect. However, I believe we're being targeted by another."

"And you need me to discover exactly who is behind this," the Aether concluded.

"Something like that."

"The moon flask is in exchange for information, then?"

"Yes."

A devilish gleam lightened the dark void of his eyes. "You know, it *would* benefit me to take your power, right?"

"I do. But you're far too honorable," Alastair countered.

"Perhaps."

Damian stared into his teacup as if all the answers of the universe could be found there.

Liz wasn't aware she held her breath until Rafe ran gentle fingers along the nape of her neck. "Breathe, *qalbi*," he murmured.

Damian's attention was caught by the soft words. He studied the two of them as if he were conducting a science experiment, head slightly tilted without any discernible emotion. "Okay. I'll help you. I'll reach out to a few old contacts and should have answers within twenty-four hours. Two days at most. In the meantime, you can stay in my guesthouse."

RAFE'S FIRST INSTINCT WAS TO REJECT ANY OFFER MADE BY DAMIAN. The man radiated strength and power with a whole lot of menace. The ripple of his magic could be felt in every glance or wave of the Aether's hand. He was currently the only one of his kind, able to absorb the powers of others with little to no effort. Other than Knox Carlyle, who had been gifted with magic directly from the Goddess Isis, Rafe had never truly considered there would be anyone more powerful than Alastair Thorne. But across from him was the stuff of nightmares. Damian Dethridge could level a city block with a simple thought.

It had initially shocked Rafe when Alastair embraced Damian. He hadn't realized the two men were friends, although he shouldn't have been surprised. They were both the black sheep of the witch community: Alastair for his rebelliousness and Damian for his ability to drain an individual dry.

"How does your power work, Mr. Dethridge? How are you able to steal magic?"

Liz gasped at Rafe's boldness, and Alastair cast him a sharp glance. Damian merely smiled. There was coldness in the twist of his lips, but his eyes held grudging respect.

"There's no special skill, Mr. Xuereb. A mere thought can do the trick. Shall I show you?"

"*No!*" Liz practically threw herself in front of Rafe. "Please, don't. I… we… need him. He's all we have for protection."

"You are like a little kitten, Ms. Thorne. All sweet and docile one second, but fierce and spitting the next." Damian turned the full wattage of his charm on Liz, and Rafe bristled.

Color crept into her cheeks, and she ducked her head. Rafe's jealousy monster came out of hibernation. The need to challenge Damian was in every fiber of his being.

The Aether seemed amused by Rafe's behavior. "Because I like her and I respect Alastair, I'll leave your powers intact, Mr. Xuereb. However, I urge caution. Don't make the mistake of getting on my bad side."

"I wouldn't dream of it," Rafe replied. He'd be damned if he would poke the bear in the cage. Certainly not one so dangerous.

Once again, Damian's gaze coasted over the two of them, summing up the situation. "There are only two bedrooms in the guesthouse. I hope you don't mind sharing?"

The color in Liz's cheeks darkened to an alarming shade of red. "Oh, no. We're not together. Not in that way."

And the trapdoor closed. Damian grinned, and even Rafe blinked at the sudden change.

"Excellent. Then you shall be my guest here in the manor, Ms. Thorne."

"Not going to happen," Rafe growled. "She stays with me until she regains her abilities."

Liz began to protest, but he clamped a hand across her mouth, careful not to cut off her air. "Not another word," he warned. "We stick together."

Damian laughed as if the whole scene tickled him. "As I suspected."

"WHAT THE HELL WAS THAT, RAFE?" LIZ DEMANDED WHEN THEY WERE alone in the master suite of the guesthouse.

"That was me protecting you from Damian Dethridge," Rafe snapped. "What were you thinking by admitting we aren't lovers? It's like an open invitation to a man like him."

"You're wrong. He's actually very nice."

"He's a shark, Elizabeth. And not just any shark. He's a fucking Megalodon who eats innocent girls like you for breakfast."

"You're overreacting."

Rafe rubbed the back of his neck and prayed for strength so he didn't wring her lovely neck.

A knock sounded on the door to their suite. He jerked the door open with enough force to remove it from its hinges and only remembered in time to temper his magic and muscle.

On the other side of the opening was an older gray-haired woman in uniform. In her arms, she held a sequined gown the color of natural imperial topaz—almost the same shade as Liz's incredible eyes.

"Mr. Dethridge sent this along for Ms. Thorne with his compliments to the lady."

Liz rushed forward, gushing at the beauty of the dress. "Thank you so much. It's stunning."

A light brush of color tinted the maid's cheeks. "He said any undergarments can be conjured by Mr. Xuereb, if you need them at all. He also said he personally wouldn't ruin the line of the dress."

Rafe ground his teeth in an effort to restrain his inner beast.

What he really wanted to do was tell Dethridge to go fuck himself. He began to pace.

"Be sure to tell Mr. Dethridge the dress is lovely, but Rafe will take care of my future needs," Liz told the woman in a soft, polite voice.

"Dinner is at six o'clock sharp. I'll be back at ten minutes to the hour to escort you to the dining room."

"Thank you."

After Liz shut the door, she held the dress in front of her, twisting her hair up with one hand and admiring herself in a full-length mirror. "Stop letting him provoke you, Rafe. I suspect it's all a game to him anyway."

"It isn't him provoking me, *qalbi*. It's *you* provoking me."

"Me?" She tossed the dress on the bed as if she weren't just fawning over it. "How do you figure?"

"You hang on his every word. It's as if he is the moon and stars in your sky." And wasn't that the problem? Rafe wanted to be the most important part of her universe.

"That would be Franklin," she snapped.

He jerked as if she'd struck him, and the air left his lungs. Perhaps she did love that fuckwit Franco. If she did, Rafe had set her up for heartache in his desire to uncover the other man's dubious business practices and endless lies.

"My apologies, Elizabeth." He turned his back to give himself a minute to compose himself, trying to channel his inner actor.

"Rafe—"

Because he couldn't stand to hear her litany of excuses, he asked, "Do you wish me to conjure undergarments and shoes to match your gown?"

"Rafe, please. I—"

"While you decide what you want, I'll pop next door to see if Alastair needs me to whip him up a suit."

He strode into the hall without a backward glance. After he shut the door, he leaned against the wall and closed his eyes against the pain. Why did it feel as if his heart had been ripped asunder? Would she ever forgive him for his abrupt departure that morning in Paris? Goddess, he hoped so. In all his years, he'd never loved another woman as fiercely as he loved Liz.

"Woman troubles, Mr. Xuereb?"

Rafe's eyes popped open to see Damian leaning casually against the opposite wall, hands in the pockets of his trousers and his legs crossed at the ankles. He straightened and glared at Damian. "Not at all." The mocking smile on the Aether's face said he knew Rafe to be a liar. "I thought dinner wasn't until six?"

"I came to see if Al needed a suit."

"Seems we both had the same idea."

"Hmm." Damian studied him for a long moment. "Don't be disheartened, Mr. Xuereb. Ms. Thorne is yours for the taking."

Rafe snorted his disbelief. "If you don't mind seeing to Alastair's clothing needs, I need some air."

"Of course."

As he moved to pass Damian, the man clamped a hand on his arm. A surge of electricity transferred from the Aether to him. Calmness, not his own, settled in his mind.

"Consider it a magical Xanax. It will help you get through the evening without losing your cool."

Rafe snatched his arm away. "I don't care to have my mind altered against my will."

"Your mind is your own. All intact to torture yourself when the lovely Liz smiles my way."

"Fuck off."

CHAPTER 7

"*T*aunting Liz's young man again, Damian?"

Damian continued to watch Rafe as he stormed out the garden door. "He makes it so easy, Al."

"Yes, men in love are the easiest targets, it seems."

"Those two are destined for heartache if they can't get out of their own way."

"Lucky for them, I have vast experience as a matchmaker."

Damian laughed until he realized Alastair was serious. "Come keep me company. I get so little of that these days."

"I'll need an assist if you don't mind."

He sized up his blond friend and snapped his finger. In the time it took to blink, Alastair was clad in an Armani tuxedo, with onyx and diamond cuff links to complete the look. "By the way, I like the new hairstyle. I'd hoped you'd come into this century."

"Stuff it, Damian."

He grinned, enjoying himself for the first time in many years. "Come on. I still have a bottle of your favorite scotch in stock."

In his study, Damian poured them both a dram, handed a tumbler to his friend, and sat in the leather wing-backed chair by the fireplace.

"Care to tell me what's really going on, Al?"

"I can only tell you what I suspect."

"I'm all ears."

"Isis imparted her wisdom in the form of a riddle. 'A new threat rises from the old' was the way she phrased it."

He shot Alastair a frustrated glance. "What the devil is that supposed to mean?"

"I'll be buggered if I can figure it out. Other than the Dethridge line, there isn't another family older than the Thornes. So if you aren't the threat, that means one of my own may be the cause of this mess."

"You forget the Six."

"Of which, you and I are two. But no, I didn't forget. I simply can't see anyone among the other four families willing to make an enemy of me."

Damian could've contradicted him, but he didn't see the point. Alastair was arrogant, but he'd earned his reputation. There were many young, stupid witches looking to make a name for themselves, but they would need to be hellaciously powerful to steal from the Thornes. No one quite fit the bill. "You can't go around without your magic, Al. It's too dangerous for you, to say nothing of your kin."

"You aren't telling me anything I don't know."

Damian drained his drink and set the glass on the side table. "I'm assuming you've scryed for the source?"

"Not me personally, but yes, I have Knox Carlyle and my son-in-law, Quentin, on it." Alastair crossed to the fireplace, rested an arm on the mantle, and stared down into the flames. "It's the darnedest thing, but it seems all they get for their troubles is a black film over their scrying mirrors. They've literally tried every spell in the book."

"Knox has been gifted the power of a God, has he not?"

"He has. As Zeus's descendant, Quentin is just as strong."

"It makes no sense. Who could possibly hide from them?"

Alastair faced him, his expression troubled. "Only you, Damian. Only the Aether."

"If you believe nothing else in your life, Alastair, believe I would never start trouble with my oldest friend." He cast Alastair a wry smile. "Even without magic, you'd be a formidable opponent."

"I need you to scry for me. The sooner, the better."

Alastair would never ask for a favor from him without a damned good reason. He'd never want to be deep in anyone else's debt. Damian opened his mouth to agree when the fine hairs along his neck stood on end and a chill swept his spine. The flames in the hearth were doused at the same time the lights flickered.

"What the hell was that?" Alastair demanded.

Damian waited for the sneeze that always accompanied Alastair's swearing. It was a curse his friend had been saddled with upon his return from the Otherworld. If he swore, he sneezed, and the force would unleash a swarm of locusts.

Yet this time, it didn't happen. Damian imagined the shock on his face mirrored Alastair's. "You're truly powerless," he said, stunned.

Alastair's face turned a sickly shade. "I am."

"I thought perhaps it was hit-or-miss magic, but not a total loss. Fuck, Al. You can't be unprotected."

A gust of wind swept throughout the room. It shook lampshades, ruffled papers, and swayed curtains, plunging the two of them into darkness. Another chill gripped Damian. "I don't know what's causing this little haunting, but it can't be good," he muttered. He didn't mention it was the sixth attack against him in as many weeks.

"Book of Shadows?" Alastair looked around the study with a wary eye.

"It's in my private room behind the bookcase. Let's go."

He held up his hand and visualized a flame. His fingers acted as a torch to guide the way through the darkened room. The light was more for Alastair than for himself. Damian was blessed with night vision in addition to his other abilities.

A twist of his wrist triggered the lever for the hidden passage. He looked at his friend. "Are you going to be okay in a room with no windows?"

Alastair had been imprisoned during the Witch Wars by the Désorcelers Society leader, Zhu Lin. Although he'd never spoken of it, he went through hell. Enclosed spaces made Alastair sweat like a sinner in church.

"I'm good. Thank you for your consideration, Damian."

Damian pointed the way to the altar containing his spellbook. Although magical families had grimoires containing generations of spells, there was only one Book of Shadows, and that book belonged to the Aether—the strongest and most magical elemental in existence. "I'll let you search while I check on Sabrina. I'll be back shortly."

A COLD DRAFT SWEPT THROUGH THE GUEST ROOM, CAUSING LIZ TO shiver in her filmy sequined dress. She'd been sans undies since Rafe took off before she could ask him to conjure a pair. When the lights flickered and cut out, she grew nervous. And when the phantom appeared in the corner of her room, she knew something was terribly wrong. Not that she was skittish by nature, but ghosts showing up in the modernized English estate of Damian Dethridge didn't seem right.

Liz wouldn't call herself a coward in normal circumstances, but the truth was she had no way to defend herself against this new threat. And without a doubt, it was threatening because she could feel the ominous air. There was almost a hatred vibe coming off the thing.

With no idea where she intended to go besides away from whatever the hell was in the room with her, she hightailed it to the door, yanked it open, and promptly shrieked.

"Liz! It's me!"

"Rafe? *Thank the Goddess.*" She placed a hand to her thundering heart. "You scared the bejeezus out of me. Get me the hell out of here, please."

He peered around her into the dim recesses of the room. *"Qalbi, are you all right? What happened?"*

She cast a frightened glance behind her, but the spirit had vanished. "The power's out."

"I can see that."

"No, you don't understand. Even if a transformer in the area blew, Damian would have at least one backup generator for an estate this size. Probably more than one. Rafe, we need to find Alastair. Something's seriously off."

"Okay. Take a second and breathe while I conjure a pair of shoes for you. You can't run around barefoot." He frowned and ran his eyes the length of her dress. "I can see you didn't need my assistance for lingerie."

She shifted a little self-consciously. "I feel naked underneath this thing."

He smiled and wisely remained silent. With little effort, he conjured her a pair of four-inch, pointed-toe pumps with an ornamental topaz leaf that wove up the heel.

"Oh, Rafe! They're gorgeous!" And didn't a part of her turn to goo because he just seemed to inherently understand the girly part of her needed things like drool-worthy shoes?

"I've added a spell to make them comfortable. Shall we try your shoes on, Cinderella?"

Her heart longed for him to be her Prince Charming, and she wanted nothing more than to kiss him in that moment. Summoning all her willpower, she held herself back. She wouldn't go there if she wasn't sure of him, because if Rafe walked away again, Liz would die a thousand deaths.

She braced her hand on the doorframe and slipped on the heels he'd conjured. When a knock on Alastair's door went unanswered, they traversed the hallway leading to the main house. Without the lights, the whole place had a cold, menacing feel

"I don't like this, Rafe. It's creepy as hell."

He squeezed her hand, and Liz nearly jumped out of her skin. When had she latched onto him? She must've reached for him without conscious thought. If she were any braver, she'd remove her hand from his, but she wasn't, and Rafe didn't seem to mind.

A child's scream pierced the eerie silence. "No! No! Stay away from me! No!"

Liz reacted without pausing to consider the danger. One minute, she was the frightened damsel, the next, she was a warrior woman ready to do battle to protect a child. Call it motherly instincts, but she'd be damned if she cowered in the hallway. She ran toward the sound of the hysterical little girl. Right before they reached the opening to the sunroom, Rafe took the lead, hands raised at the ready to defend them.

A thick blue-black mist circled the child, swirling around her and lifting up here or there as if poised to strike but falling short roughly a foot from contact. Again and again, the darkness slammed against the child's invisible forcefield. Whatever the source, it was desperate to reach Damian's daughter.

"Get the hell away from her!" Liz charged forward, hands lifted to blast the threatening fog away. Only when Rafe swore did she remember she was helpless to fight it.

His strong arms encircled her as he barked, *"Tarka!"*

Rafe's quick action most likely saved her life. The mist slammed against the barrier he'd created and rocked them backward a step. He maneuvered them closer to the little girl, positioning their shielded bodies in front of hers.

"Where's your father, sweetheart?" Liz tried to keep her voice calm and reassuring, but the darkness whipped around the room, and the howling noise it made was near deafening.

Tears were gathered in the child's obsidian eyes, and her lower lip trembled. Despite the signs of distress, the girl shrugged as if she were uncaring.

Liz squatted and opened her arms. The girl ran through Rafe's barrier as if it didn't exist to bury her face against Liz's neck. The child's ability to step through their shield spoke volumes in regards to the strength of her powers.

Liz picked her up. "Let's head for Damian's study."

"Papa doesn't like me to go in there."

"He'll make an exception this time. I promise."

"I don't like it when he's mad."

She kissed the child's temple. "No one does, sweetheart. But he'd want you to be safe, no?"

Slowly, as if unsure, the girl nodded her dark head. Her insecurity broke Liz's heart. She intended to discuss Damian's neglect the second she had him alone.

"What's your name, little one?" Rafe asked as he shuffled them toward the hallway.

"Sabrina."

The mist doubled its attack on their shield.

"What a lovely name!" Liz tucked Sabrina's head against her shoulder and cast a worried glance Rafe's way.

They'd almost made it to the door when Damian skidded to a halt in front of them.

Liz doubted the man missed a thing as his gaze swept the room and landed on their small group.

Damian raised one hand toward the darkness. "Come to me."

The mist resisted his pull. It twisted and strained away as it emitted a screech. The darkness was no match for the power of the Aether. The lights flickered once, then the mist surged forward with an echoing pop.

Liz blinked against the sudden brightness of the room.

"Are you all right, beastie?" Damian addressed Sabrina.

He held out his arms, but his daughter burrowed closer to Liz, a clear rejection of her father.

Liz didn't miss his anguished expression. "I…" She didn't know what to say. "We heard her scream. I imagine you did, too?"

"No. I felt the pull of the evil surrounding her." He placed a hand on the child's upper back. "It can't hurt you, Sabrina. Others will continue to try because of who you are, but they can never touch you. Do you understand?"

Sabrina's haunted, tragic eyes lifted to stare at Liz. "He's a bad man."

Liz's heart seized, and she looked at Rafe.

"Not him," Sabrina whispered. "The other one."

"Your father?"

Sabrina shook her head.

"Alastair?"

Again, the girl responded with a negative shake.

"I don't know who you're talking about, sweetheart."

"Your boyfriend. He's a bad man."

Her arms must've tightened because Sabrina squirmed within her embrace. "Sabrina, can you tell me how you know?"

Frightened dark eyes turned to Damian.

He nodded. "It's okay, love. You can help her."

Sabrina placed her tiny hand over Liz's heart. A small bead of warmth touched her skin and grew exponentially until Liz's extremities were close to burning. Her skin tingled and felt close to melting as her magic flooded back into every cell of her body. She gasped and did her damnedest not to drop the little girl. Just as she was about to beg for relief from the fire under her skin, it stopped.

"Now you can see, too," Sabrina said.

"What the hell just happened?" Rafe demanded.

"My daughter restored Ms. Thorne's magic. If I'm not mistaken, she also gave her the added gift of sight."

Sabrina nodded and gave Liz a tentative smile. "Don't be scared. He can't hurt you now."

Liz swallowed past the dryness in her throat. "Was he trying to?"

"Yes." Sabrina shifted and held her arms out to Damian. "I'm tired now, Papa."

As he gathered the girl against his chest, he trailed a hand over the crown of her dark head. A halo of light sparkled above her before being absorbed by her body. "Rest now, darling girl. When you wake, you will be stronger yet."

Liz blinked in wide-eyed wonder. Did the Aether just super-charge his daughter?

His gaze locked with hers. "Yes." He rested his cheek on the girl's silky curls. "I'll explain everything after I tuck her into bed."

CHAPTER 8

"I don't understand. How does a six-year-old child have the ability to restore magic to the extent she did?"

"We'll have to wait for Damian to explain." Liz casually sipped her wine. She had no real answer for Rafe. Hell, she was still reeling inside from the news that her current boyfriend was evil. Had she sensed it? *No.* What did it say about her ability to read people? Depressed by the thought, she drained her wineglass.

A shadow crossed her path, and she jumped. Only when Damian touched her shoulder did she calm. "Thank you. I didn't realize I was still so on edge. What was the black mist?"

"I'm working on finding out. It's been after Sabrina since she came here."

She blinked her surprise. "She didn't always live with you?"

"I prefer not to discuss the past." His entire being turned chilly. The shift was subtle but strong, and extremely off-putting. He became all business. "What is it you wish to know about what she did for you?"

"Am I at full capacity?"

Damian's lips twitched. "I feel as if one of us should make a reference to Scotty and Star Trek."

Liz snorted and visualized a glassful of sweet red wine. She almost cried her relief when she saw the liquid fill the crystal wineglass. There was one thing to be said for her returned magic, it would keep her in enough booze to drown her sorrows.

"Was it so terrible without?" Damian asked softly, for her ears alone.

"It really was. Even though the loss only lasted a few days, it seemed like forever." She met his dark gaze and wondered how she ever thought him cold a moment ago. Dangerous, yes. Cold and dispassionate, not so much. "I grew up with the assumption I was an all-powerful witch. A Thorne. Untouchable to a large degree with a never-ending source of magic. I now know differently."

"Sabrina didn't just restore your power, Ms. Thorne—"

"Please, call me Liz."

"Liz. Sabrina didn't just restore your magic," he said again. "She gave you the ability to see into men's hearts. She also made it impossible for anyone to remove your power again. Even me."

She sat up straighter. Had they misjudged him? "You? Why would you want to?"

"I have no plans to do so. I'm simply stating how difficult it will be for anyone who tries. Blockers included."

She fumbled her drink and saved it just shy of ruining her beautiful gown. "Why would Sabrina do that for me?"

Damian smiled, and the harsh angles of his face softened. Liz felt uncomfortably warm. This man put off a sexual magnetism impossible to ignore.

"You put your own life at risk to help her, Liz. Neither of us will forget that."

"Is she safe here, Damian?"

"Safe enough. Probably safer than she'd be anywhere else. This is the first time the darkness has gotten that close to her. I'm not sure how it happened, but I enforced my wards around her and my home before joining you tonight."

"Good. She's a darling girl."

"She's a hellion. Don't let the innocent face fool you."

"Like you? I shouldn't let you fool me either?"

Damian gave a slight nod in Rafe's direction. "I'm not the one with secrets, my dear. But you'll see them if you look hard enough. Now, let us enjoy our dinner."

He rose to his feet and crooked his elbow. Liz locked her arm around his, feeling the pulse of his magic just below the surface.

"Is it frightening to hold so much power, Damian? Do you worry you'll lose control?"

"It's all I've ever known."

Did she imagine his sadness? She didn't believe so. Liz gave his arm a small squeeze. A gesture of understanding and compassion. Other than a single, light pat on the back of her hand, he gave no acknowledgment of her action.

"Mr. Xuereb," Damian called. "I've placed you to Ms. Thorne's left. Alastair, you'll be across the table, there." He pulled out the high-back parson chair and waited for Liz to sit before scooting it forward.

The meal was delicious, and the conversation flowed freely, as did the wine. By the time Rafe escorted her back to her room, she was buzzing.

"I don't know if this is baby-Aether magic or the booze, but I feel great." She twirled in place and laughed up at Rafe. "Woozy, but *alive*, you know?"

"Perhaps it's a combination of both, *qalbi*."

"What does the nickname mean?" For the first time, she braved the emotional landmine of the past. He'd called her *"qalbi"* since their first night together, and she'd never had the opportunity to ask about it. They were always surrounded by others, or her timing was off.

"My heart."

Her skin went cold then hot, and her pulse kicked into over-drive. "Am I?" she managed to croak out. "Your heart?"

"From the first moment I saw you." He unclipped her hair and spread it across her shoulders. "You were staring, lost in the beauty of the Eiffel Tower at night. Wonder in your incredible eyes. And *I* was lost in the vision of you."

"You approached me that night." She remembered the sensation of being watched and had turned to search the crowd. Rafe had stood to one side, arms crossed and head cocked slightly. A warm smile had played upon his full lips, and the gleam in his eyes sucked her in like a tractor beam.

"How could I not?" The corners of his mouth turned up in remembrance and made her warmer still. "The moon was full and glinted off the gold of your hair."

The memory of their brief interlude was still fresh after all this time. Regret hit her hard. They'd lost four years because he left her without a single word. No whispered goodbye. No brush of his fingers across her lips. Nothing to indicate he'd ever been there but a feeling of fullness between her legs and his scent on her skin.

A lump formed in her throat, and she swallowed hard to disperse it. "Why did you leave me the way you did?"

"I was stupid. As I said, I believed finding you again would be a simple matter. My resources seemed endless. They weren't, and I never discovered your name. But I never stopped looking. Every year, I went back to our hotel, hoping beyond hope you would return to me."

"I couldn't. I assumed it was only a fling for you. But for me, it was much more. I was emotionally broken for the first year afterward. Revisiting the place where I'd experienced such passion and such grief… I couldn't do that to myself, Rafe."

"If I had the opportunity to go back to the morning I left, I never would've. I'd stay and wake you with the brush of a rose's petals along your smooth skin so we might make love again." He lost all pretense and allowed her to see the truth in his eyes. The raw emotion. Or maybe it was Sabrina's gift. But either way, Liz could recognize the love he felt for her.

"I love you, Rafe. Your light shines brighter for me than any other."

His smile started slow, but blossomed into a wide grin. "I love you, Elizabeth." Then he kissed her.

His lips warm and firm against hers. Not aggressive, but not entirely innocent either. His touch set off a spark within her, along with a feeling of wrongness. Not about the two of them together, but about Rafe's association to a situation he shouldn't be connected with. Damian was right; Rafe had a secret. The knowledge blew through her mind with an assuredness she'd never experienced before. Liz pulled out of his arms.

"What aren't you telling me, Rafe?" she asked softly.

Wariness clouded his eyes, and he looked away. "I'm not sure what you mean."

Disappointment settled in her breast. She was tired of half-truths. Throughout her life, it seemed as if everyone around her had collectively decided she needed to be sheltered from the ugliness of the world. She hated being coddled.

"I mean you're hiding something from me, and I want to know what it is."

He crossed to the bed and sat down on the edge, his elbows resting on his thighs. His head hung low, and he stared at the floor as if he wished to be anywhere but where he was.

"You're not going to tell me, are you?" Her question was actually more of a statement. She already knew the answer. Whatever Rafe's secret, he had no intention of sharing it with her.

"I'm sorry, *qalbi*. I can't."

"Does it have something to do with Franklin?" Why she suspected as much, she couldn't say, but the impression of distrust and nefarious spell casting danced about in her mind. Was this Sabrina's gift, then? Because it was not what Liz would've chosen for herself. It brought nothing but suspicion and hurt.

"Whatever it is, Rafe, you can tell me."

He remained quiet.

"Right. I guess there's nothing left to say." She walked into the *en suite* bathroom and shut the door behind her. Tears burned the back of her lids, but she refused to give in to the disappointment and sadness she was experiencing. She'd cried enough in the early days after he left her in that Paris hotel room.

All that was left for her to do was find out what Franklin was involved in. Alastair might know, but she questioned the wisdom of asking him. He'd made it obvious he wanted Rafe to play bodyguard.

But what was it Damian had said? Her powers couldn't be taken away again?

She met the gaze of an extremely determined and pissed off woman in the bathroom mirror. Liz was done being played. Closing her eyes, she visualized her living room. Her cells warmed to almost burning. When she was cool again, she opened her eyes, happy to see the teleport had worked. Not so happy to see strange men in her home. Obviously, her wards had failed when she'd been powerless.

"Fuck."

FRANCO "FRANKLIN MOORE" MOREAU HAD BEEN IN THE MIDDLE OF A locator spell when he experienced a massive pull on his energy. The elements he called to him never manifested, and the magic he attempted fell flat. Only one thing could cause the fizzle of his amped-up power—*Liz Thorne's magic had been restored.* She'd been his continuous source and the tool he'd used to drain the rest of her family.

He'd shown up at her home within a half hour of his failed spell, hoping to find her and figure out what had gone wrong. For close to three hours, Franco waited, hoping like hell she'd return, but knowing she wasn't stupid enough to go anywhere without backup.

"Boss, why are we waiting here? It's obvious she's not coming home tonight."

Franco was damned tired of Petey questioning his every move. "If you want to keep your fucking tongue in your mouth, you'll shut the hell up."

The air grew charged, and Franco, Petey, and Chet all went still.

When Liz appeared, Franco almost sent praise to the Goddess. Now, did he play it off as if he was worried, or should he simply attack?

"Fuck," she muttered.

He had his answer. She knew something was amiss.

"Grab her!" he yelled.

Before his two hired mercenaries could jump into action, Liz lifted her palms and blasted them with category-five hurricane-force wind. Petey slammed into the wall, creating a man-sized hole in the drywall. He sunk to the ground in a daze. Chet was thrown into the entertainment center. The crack of his head against the oak cabinet was a sickening sound. Blood pooled on the floor around him. Franco didn't bet much on Chet's chance of survival.

Franco held up his hands in surrender. "Liz, sweetheart, I can explain." The room turned as arctic as her expression, and he shivered.

"Explain? What's to explain, Franklin?" Her full lip curled into a sneer.

He dropped his arms and inched his right hand toward the Glock tucked into his waistband. He'd taken the precaution of lacing his bullets with a cocktail of Witchbane, Wolfsbane, and arsenic. Killing her was his last option if he couldn't talk her down from her anger. Allowing her to run back to her family with the news he was not exactly who he said he was, wasn't an option.

"I brought Petey and Chet with me in case there was trouble. I teleported to the hotel, but you weren't there, and I was worried when you didn't answer your cell."

"Uh huh. And the 'grab her' part?"

She wasn't buying what he was selling, but Franco didn't get to where he was without knowing how to tap dance around sticky situations.

"Strictly for protection, Liz. To take you someplace safer than here."

Liz held out her hand and conjured a flaming ball of energy.

"Want to try again? Oh, and if you reach for your weapon, I'll toast your ass."

"Sweetheart, I don't know why you've become so aggressive. I'm trying to help you."

"I'm not your fucking sweetheart!"

The air crackled around them, and Franco knew it was his last opportunity to save himself. With a curse, he ran for the back door. Fire engulfed the opening as he ducked through. He ran as if that devil Alastair Thorne was after him because, in all likelihood, he would be if he wasn't already.

CHAPTER 9

"What the hell were you thinking?" Rafe shouted as Liz doused the flames licking up the wall by her back slider.

"Go away, Rafe."

"*What?*"

"I said, *go away*," she snapped. "I have this all under control."

He glared at her, and the urge to rail due to her recklessness overwhelmed him. He clenched his hands to curb the impulse.

"There is a dead man on your floor. I wouldn't call that under control, Liz."

Her stricken gaze locked onto the body by her entertainment center. Rafe could tell she didn't have time to process what she'd done. Liz had been in a reactive, self-preservation mode. She'd obviously used her magic to protect herself, and the result was the death of Franco's minion. Once she had time to register her part in the death, she'd blame herself.

"*Qalbi*, let me help you," he said gently.

"I can't trust you." She drew in a ragged breath, and Rafe's heart thunked in his chest.

The gorilla of a man, who was slouched against the wall,

groaned. He took one look at Rafe's threatening countenance and promptly scrambled to his feet. Liz was faster to react and slammed her would-be attacker against the wall. His head connected with a wooden stud, and down he went—*again*.

"I guess it's true what they say. The bigger they are, the harder they fall." Rafe shot her an admiring look. "Nicely done."

"Tie him up. Maybe we can get some information out of him. We'll let him catch a glimpse of Alastair before we ask questions. He'll spill his guts from sheer terror alone."

He grinned his appreciation for her vicious tactics. They could've used her when he worked for the Council.

A deep frown puckered her brows.

"What is it, Liz?"

"How were you able to teleport into my living room? I understand the wards were down with the loss of my magic, but you've never been here. You wouldn't have known what it looked like or where the furniture placement was. You could've injured yourself."

"I've known the exact layout of your home for some time. Nash gave me photos and an address in the event he couldn't get to you should you require help."

Rafe conjured a set of charmed handcuffs and clasped them around the unconscious man's wrists then covered the deceased guy with a throw blanket.

Liz inched forward. "How did you know this was where I'd come? For that matter, how did you know I left Damian's?"

"I knocked on the bathroom door after you hid away. When you didn't answer, I knew you'd run away from me."

"I didn't run away!" she denied hotly.

He raised his brows.

"Okay, maybe I did, but you... you..." She jabbed her index finger in his direction. "You're a damned liar!"

"You want to know what I was hiding?" He surged to his feet. "This! The fact Franklin Moore is really Franco Moreau. The fact he targeted you because he believes you're the weak link in the Thorne armor. The fact I love you and couldn't stand to see that bastard touch you so I created a spell to prevent it."

She stared at him in wide-eyed amazement, her mouth agape.

"I've been hiding the fact I've been protecting you from afar, *qalbi*, because the idea of you getting hurt was like a hot poker to my heart."

As he spoke the words, he moved forward until he was standing in front of her, staring down into her beautiful, stunned face. He wanted to pour out the rest of the truth, but now wasn't the time. That required a longer conversation, and he was a little less certain of her reaction. Franco could come back with reinforcements at any second.

Her surprise left, and in its place was a soft understanding. "I'm sorry I overreacted."

"I'd never intentionally hurt you."

Liz placed her palm flat over Rafe's hammering heart. "I know you wouldn't."

"I love you, Elizabeth Thorne. If you believe nothing else, please believe that." He ran his fingertips over the arch of her brow.

"Tell me how the spell worked."

He couldn't prevent the smile twisting his lips. "If he felt amorous towards you, he'd get an overwhelming urge to be elsewhere."

Her eyes flew wide, and she snorted a laugh. "Of all the sneaky, underhanded... it's genius!"

"Yes, well."

He joined in her laughter. They sobered when their prisoner moaned his pain.

"Why don't you go back to Damian's? I can take care of this."

"No. If Franklin, er, Franco returns, I don't want you to deal with him alone." She rubbed a hand along the back of her neck. "Do you think Damian can teleport Alastair here?"

"*Qalbi*, what do you know about the Aether?"

"Admittedly, not much. I know he's the strongest magical being on the planet next to a goddess."

"The question isn't *can* he. The question is *will* he. It's doubtful he'll leave his daughter without protection."

"So what do we do now?"

"I'll reinforce your wards. You call Alastair. The man is a superior strategist."

———

LIZ HUNG UP THE PHONE WITH A GRIMACE.

"What did he say?"

"He's displeased with us and suggested, quite strongly, that we return."

Rafe chuckled. "Yes, I can almost hear him now. What did he *suggest* we do with our prisoner?"

"Dropping him out of a plane without a parachute was mentioned."

The prisoner in question protested loudly.

They turned to stare him down.

"I know a guy with a plane," Rafe said casually, as if they were discussing the weather.

"Awesome. I say we fly directly over Franklin's estate and dump him in the pool."

Rafe frowned down at her. "Franklin doesn't have a pool."

"Someday, I'm going to ask you how you know that, but in the meantime, our friend here will probably make a decent-sized indentation in his lawn. I'll suggest a pool to fill the hole when next I speak to him."

"You Thornes are a bloodthirsty lot."

"Yes, we are. And these jerks had the nerve to provoke all of us at once. Stupid, *stupid* move."

"I agree." Rafe grinned and addressed their tied up guest. "You might want to start talking. It could save your life."

"W-what do you w-want to know?"

Liz rolled her eyes. "Firstly, do you always squeak like a boy going through puberty?"

75

Rafe's choked laugh almost made her smile, but she was trying to maintain a semblance of seriousness for their interrogation.

"Are you Petey or Chet?" she asked.

"Petey."

"Tell me, Petey, why did Franklin target me specifically? What did he hope to achieve?"

"He didn't tell me anything. I swear."

Rafe stepped forward, menace in every line of his body. "Nothing at all?"

Liz placed a restraining hand on his arm and shifted to stand in front of him. "I'll tell you what, *Petey*. If you don't start talking, I'm going to teleport your ass to my cousin, Alastair Thorne." Her prisoner paled. "Ah, I can see his reputation precedes him. Let me tell you, he's twenty times more ruthless than any rumors you've heard, and he absolutely despises anyone who threatens his family."

"In case you don't understand what Liz is telling you, let me drive home the nail. You threatened her by signing on as Franklin's minion. You're screwed." Rafe crossed his arms and gave Petey a casual shrug as if his welfare didn't affect him one way or the other.

"I m-may have overheard s-something," Petey ventured, casting a hopeful look between them.

"I'm listening." Liz's tone was hard as diamonds.

"They—"

"They who?"

"The Moreau and Champeau families."

Liz heard Rafe's sharp intake of air and glanced over her shoulder. "What's up?"

"Nothing."

His uneasy expression said differently, as did her new internal lie detector, but Liz decided to save the questions for later when they didn't have an audience who might use the information for his own purposes. She turned back to Petey. "So Franklin's family and the Champeau family, what was their intent?"

"To drain the Thorne witches of their power. They needed it for another source."

"What source?"

"I don't know. I really don't."

She eyed him, searching for any hint of deceit. "Do you know how Franklin intended to use me?"

"He believed you were the key to the Thornes' destruction. I don't know how he was siphoning off your magic."

"If he could do it from afar, why did he attack me here?"

Petey shook his head. "All I know is that he started to lose his own power tonight. He believed it was because yours was restored."

She met Rafe's thoughtful gaze. "Do you think I'm the conduit? Like once I got my powers back, it hurt his link to the others?"

"If that's the case, why hasn't your family's magic been restored?"

Liz didn't have an answer. This whole situation was beyond her scope of comprehension. What the hell type of "source" needed so much magic that it required an entire family's power?

"What do we do with him?" she asked Rafe quietly.

"Pack a bag of things you'll need. We'll turn him in to the Witches' Council before heading back to Damian's. I think it's important for the family to continue to stick together for a while longer. Just until we get a bigger handle on this thing."

"It's a solid plan." She looked back at Petey and raised her voice to be heard. "Maybe the Aether can get to the bottom of this. Since he and Alastair are such tight friends, I'm sure he won't mind helping out."

Petey started to sweat profusely.

Rafe leaned in to whisper, "Goddess, I love you and your sadistic tendencies."

She hid her smirk against his lips when she gave him a light kiss. "Remind me of that later when we're in bed."

"Oh, *qalbi*, you are playing with fire."

CHAPTER 10

*A*t midnight, Rafe and Liz arrived back at the Dethridge estate. They found Alastair and Damian in the study, discussing the darkness plaguing little Sabrina.

"I thought you'd be asleep by now, cousin," Liz said as she kissed his cheek.

"Not at all. I wanted to hear how it went with the Council."

"Not great." Rafe accepted Damian's offer of a drink and requested a red wine for Liz. Once the four of them were seated again, he explained. "They'll hold him for seventy-two hours, but unless we find something more to charge him with other than the fact he was hired by Franco to serve as his henchman, he'll be released."

"Also, we now know the Moreaus and the Champeaus are behind this little magical blackout," Liz added with a grimace. "I'm sorry my poor taste in men brought this to our doorstep."

Rafe cleared his throat.

"Oh!" Liz flushed, and it lent a pretty glow to her cheeks. "I didn't mean you, Rafe. Never you."

He covered her hand where it rested on his knee, and entwined his fingers with hers. "I appreciate that."

"Most likely, Franco targeted you, child." Alastair's sharp gazed dropped to their hands, and he didn't bother to hide his smug smile. "It's my understanding Sabrina's gift to you opened your eyes and heart to the truth. We owe her a debt of gratitude."

"We do," Liz and Rafe said in unison.

"Damian, should she ever have need of us, we will be there for her," Liz said, a solemn vow. "And for you."

The Aether smiled warmly. "I'll hold you to your promise. The time may be coming sooner than any of you expect."

"You're referring to the dark mist?" Rafe sat forward. A little voice in the back of his mind was telling him the darkness and Franco were related. Just how, he didn't know, so he wouldn't throw his suspicions into the mix quite yet. "You still have no idea what or who is behind it?"

"No. But they're persistent. I can only seem to subdue the magic for short periods at a time, a few days at most. *That* should tell you how strong it is." Damian's frown set loose Rafe's unease. If the Aether was worried, it boded ill.

Liz sat up straighter. "We won't let it touch her."

Rafe grinned at her fierceness. The flush on her cheeks this time was from indignation, and she was all the more beautiful for it. He squeezed her hand; his silent commitment to standing by her side to protect Sabrina should the need arise. The resulting smile she sent him nearly melted his heart.

Alastair cleared his throat, jolting Rafe and Liz from their wordless communication. "If both Franco and Marguerite are involved, it seems we need to take this little party to France. Or rather, you both will. The rest of us are out of commission until this is resolved."

"Not necessarily, Al," Damian protested. "I may have a spell to override all others and restore your magic. It's not exactly comfortable, but if you're game, I'll perform the ceremony."

"Do you have everything you need?"

"All but one item." Damian looked at Liz. "Any chance Nash has a Ring of Dispel? It's made of the finest silver with a Celtic cross etched on the top. In the center of the cross is a genuine nine-carat, square-cut emerald so clear and pure of color it doesn't seem real."

"I'm almost positive he's cataloged that one in our inventory books. I can call him in the morning to see what I can find out."

"Perfect. If you can obtain the ring for me, I can restore magic to the Thornes."

Rafe held up a hand. "*All* of them?"

Damian lips twisted in a mocking grin. "Yes, Mr. Xuereb. *All* of them."

"Please. At this point, I think we should be on a first-name basis. Call me Rafe." He lifted his drink in silent toast to their new friendship.

"Will the spell require the family to come here?" Alastair asked.

"No. We can go to your estate. I assume they are amassed there?" Damian casually waved a hand and topped everyone's glass.

"Yes," Alastair confirmed.

"I'll want to ward against intruders when I get there. For Sabrina's sake."

"Of course. It would make me feel better, knowing my house was protected by the Aether."

Damian snorted. "Don't suck up now, Al. You've never done so in the past."

Rafe had to laugh at the put-out look on Alastair's face. No one, besides his friend Ryker, gave him hell.

"On that note, we need to get some sleep." Liz smothered a yawn. "Thank you for everything, Damian."

"Good night, my dear."

Rafe and Liz strolled to their room, hand in hand.

"I can't wait to see him in action," she murmured sleepily.

"As in restoring magic?"

She lifted her head from his shoulder. "What else would you think I meant?"

"Action can mean a great many things," he teased with a campy leer.

She laughed, and the sound echoed softly through the long

corridor. "When I get more than a few hours sleep, you can show me all those great many things."

"You bet your sweet life I will," he promised, stopping her for a gentle, lingering kiss. "Now, let's get you to bed so you can rest up for tomorrow."

Her expression turned serious, and she stared into his eyes as if searching for the secrets hidden deep inside. He wanted to tell her not to look too closely; she might not like what she discovered.

"Thank you, Rafe. Your help means the world to me."

"I haven't done anything yet, *qalbi*."

"Haven't you?" Her gaze dropped, and she studied the top button of his shirt as if it held great interest. "If it weren't for you, I'd have made an even bigger mistake. Maybe even gotten serious with Franklin, er... Franco. You saved me a lot of grief. Now, I'm struggling with embarrassment for how easily I was duped, but it could've been much worse."

"The Franco Moreaus of the world prey on kind-hearted people, Liz. You have nothing to be ashamed of."

She heaved a heavy sigh. "I still feel like a fool. He almost brought about the destruction of my family."

"He overreached this time."

"Come. Let's go to bed, Rafe."

"It's going to be the most exquisite torture of my life, to hold you while you sleep and not make love to you."

"For me, too. But I give you permission to feel me up through the night."

He groaned and adjusted his slacks to make room for his budding arousal. "You don't play fair, *qalbi*."

"I'm a Thorne, babe. It's in our DNA to fight dirty."

AFTER LIZ AND RAFE LEFT THE ROOM, DAMIAN TURNED SOLEMN. "I'M glad she discovered Franco is a snake in the grass. I'm afraid she's not going to like what Mr. Xuereb is hiding, though."

"Is it something I'll need to kill him for?" Alastair asked casually.

"It remains to be seen." Damian stood and crossed to the fireplace, staring down at the flickering flames. "Do you know his mother is a Champeau?"

"Yes."

Damian shot a rueful look in his friend's direction. "I thought you might. Does the lovely Elizabeth?"

"It's doubtful."

He faced Alastair more fully. "Do you intend to tell her?"

"It's my hope Rafe will be honest with her." Alastair shrugged and rose to his feet. He set his empty glass on the sideboard. "I don't know how she'll react if it comes from anyone but him."

"My guess? Not well. She's already feeling betrayed by Moreau. You and I both can feel that much."

"Yes. Another perceived betrayal will not sit well with her."

"Should we talk to Rafe? Encourage him to be truthful?"

"No. I think this should play out how it's going to. If he is in league with his family, I'll destroy him."

Damian laughed and clapped him on the back. "I have no doubt you will, Al. But you should know, he *does* love her. I can see and feel that much."

"Good. I'm glad my initial impression was correct. She deserves to be happy."

"I meant what I said earlier. I owe her a debt for helping my daughter."

"Liz will never collect if she can help it. She's not wired to ask for assistance, although she gives freely of herself."

"Then I'll just have to be an adopted godfather to her without her knowing."

Alastair grinned. "Do you know how many people would crap their pants if they knew you have her back and, should they offend her, you will obliterate all they hold dear? It almost makes me want to see you in action on her behalf."

"You'll see it should Moreau crawl out of his hole," Damian promised.

"Tell me you haven't developed feelings for her, my friend."

He scowled at Alastair, irritated he even had to mention it. "Are you joking?"

"Well, I haven't seen hide nor hair of your wife. What's going on with you and Viv?"

"She betrayed me. It doesn't mean I love her less, but I can't be with a woman who would take my daughter away. One who doesn't trust me."

The compassion on his friend's face caused Damian untold embarrassment. He didn't want pity. No, he wanted his wife to love him like she had in the early stages of their relationship, before she listened to the poisonous words of others.

"Anyway, I don't have romantic feelings toward your cousin, Al. She's safe from any seduction. Although, it *is* fun to taunt Rafe."

"Oh, by all means, taunt away. He deserves a little torture for his dishonesty."

"This is why I like you. You're as twisted as I am."

Alastair chuckled again and sauntered toward the door. "I'll see you at breakfast." He turned, his face as serious as Damian had ever seen. "And thank you for what you're about to do for me. Being helpless to care for my family doesn't sit well with me. I have too many enemies."

"I know. I'd feel the same. Sleep well. You're protected here."

CHAPTER 11

*L*iz woke to the sensation of being watched. She blinked and slowly turned her head. The small figure by the side of the bed didn't move.

"Good morning, sweetheart. How are you feeling today?" she asked gently.

Sabrina hugged the tattered doll she held a little tighter and inched closer to the bed.

A glance over her shoulder showed Rafe was already gone. Liz scooted away from the edge of the bed and patted the mattress. "Want to hang with me a bit?"

The little girl nodded and climbed up next to her.

Liz propped her head in her hand and tapped a finger on the doll's frayed skirt. "What's her name?"

"Ariel."

"That's lovely." She smoothed a hand over Sabrina's dark head. "I didn't thank you properly for what you did for me. I owe you a great deal."

"Did you see the bad man yesterday?"

"I did. He's gone for now."

The girl nodded wisely, as if she already knew this to be true.

"Sabrina, will you tell me something?"

"Okay."

"Do you see the future?"

Uncertainty clouded her little features.

"You don't have to tell me if you don't want."

"Papa says I'm not 'spose to talk about it."

Liz smiled. "Then you absolutely must do what your papa says. He knows best."

"You're pretty. Like Mama."

"Thank you."

"I miss her."

"I don't see my mom as much as I'd like. I miss her sometimes, too."

Sabrina reached out and ran a small finger down Liz's cheek. "Your new boyfriend, he's nice. You should listen to him."

"I try."

"Not now. Later, when you're mad at him. You should listen, okay?"

What was she saying? Would Rafe lie to her in the near future? Was the secret she still sensed going to come back to bite her in the ass?

"Okay," she told the child. "I promise to listen." She couldn't promise to like what he would tell her, though.

A tentative smile graced Sabrina's lips and just as quickly vanished. "Papa's looking for me. I have to go."

"Will you be joining us for breakfast? I was thinking about conjuring donuts."

The haunted look left Sabrina's eyes, and her smile once again returned as she gazed adoringly at Liz. "I love donuts."

"Me, too. Do you have a favorite?"

"I like the ones with chocolate frosting."

"Of course you do, beastie." Damian's voice startled Liz, but she should've realized when Sabrina said her father was looking for her, she meant he was literally about to knock on the door.

"Damian! We were just about to come find you."

"Run along, love. We need to let Miss Thorne get dressed for breakfast."

Sabrina shocked Liz when she kissed her cheek before scurrying off.

Damian smiled indulgently as she darted by him. "Teleport, love."

The little girl disappeared.

"She's so adorable."

"Yes."

"Is it all right for her to have donuts for breakfast?"

"It is." He chuckled, and Liz felt the sound run along her nerve endings. *Holy hell.* "I'll leave you to change, my dear. Breakfast is on the veranda right off the main living room."

"I'll be along shortly. Thank you."

Fifteen minutes later, Liz stepped through the French doors leading outside. Alastair was already sipping coffee as he read his newspaper. Rafe was resting his elbows on the stone railing, a mug sandwiched between his hands. Damian held his daughter and pointed out the wildlife in the distance. It was a beautiful scene. One that should be painted or photographed for posterity. She'd title it "Warlocks in the Morning" or something along those lines. After coffee, she would probably be more creative.

"Good morning, gentlemen."

"Elizabeth!" Alastair smiled with genuine warmth. "Come, child. I have it on good authority you're treating us to donuts this fine morning."

"Yes, I promised Sabrina the chocolate-frosted kind. Do you have a preference, cousin?"

"Cinnamon crumble would hit the spot."

"I think Winnie's cooking has spoiled you," she teased.

"Indeed."

Her eyes connected with Rafe's admiring gaze across the short distance.

"Good morning, *qalbi.*"

"If I remember correctly, you are more of a croissant man."

"You remember exactly right. *Pain au chocolat*, please."

Liz closed her eyes and held her palms up. First she visualized a white platter, then she built the pastries based on their requests. She added two lemon powdered donuts for herself before she faced Damian. "And you?"

"This little miscreant is yummy enough for me." He made chomping noises and pretended he was going to bite Sabrina's neck.

His daughter's happy giggle was the purest, sweetest sound Liz had ever heard. Envy curled in her stomach. She'd dreamed of behaving that very same way with her own children someday. As yet, the fantasy of a family never came to pass.

Rafe lifted the platter from her hands and placed it on the table. When he faced her again, he spoke in a low voice, "One day, I hope to tease *our* daughter the same way."

He'd practically read her mind, or maybe the longing had shown on her face. Tears flooded her eyes, and she gave him a watery smile. She desperately wanted it, too. More than he could ever know. "I'd like that, but let's come out of this thing alive first," she murmured.

"Papa needs a donut." Sabrina cut through Liz's emotional meanderings. "He likes jelly."

"Then jelly he shall have," Liz said with a cheer-infused voice. "Raspberry or strawberry?"

"Raspberry, please." Damian swung his daughter down and set her in the closest chair. "If it's not too much trouble."

Liz added his favorites to the plate. "I believe we are the trouble. Donuts are the least I can do."

"You've added excitement to our days, my dear. Sabrina and I are happy you're all here."

Sabrina nodded even as she reached for her breakfast pastry.

Damian devoured his donut then, to his daughter's delight, gave an open-mouthed grin to show jelly-coated teeth. "Give us a kiss, beastie."

She squealed and squirmed away, laughing all the while. "Oh, Papa, you're so funny."

Liz found herself enjoying the company of the formidable Aether and his small but equally powerful daughter. If someone had asked her if she could've imagined this moment in her wildest dreams, she'd have told them no.

"Guess what?" He swiped a finger across the chocolate frosting of Sabrina's donut. The child glared at him and ran a hand over the top of her pastry, creating double the previous amount of icing.

"We are going to visit the rest of Miss Thorne's family today. You'll get to make a friend." He gave Alastair an encouraging look.

"That's right. My niece Autumn will have her daughter, Chloe, with her." Alastair folded his paper. "She's a few years older than you, I believe, but I'm confident you'll like her."

"Really, Papa? Someone like me?"

"There is no one like you, love. But yes, another witch."

"Oh, Papa!" If Sabrina looked happy before, it was nothing compared to the ecstatic glow radiating from her now.

She suddenly sobered, and her chin sunk to her chest. "What if she doesn't like *me*?"

All the adults shared a panicked glance.

Liz was the first to react. "How could she not? You're as beautiful on the inside as you are on the outside. Also, I happen to know Chloe is a lot like you. She's looking for a friend she can trust to perform magic around."

"I can show her my magic?" Sabrina looked to her father for approval.

He seemed torn before he finally graced her with a soft smile and a nod.

Tears shimmered in the child's dark eyes. "Thank you, Papa."

LATER THAT DAY, LIZ JOINED DAMIAN NEXT TO THE FLOOR-TO-ceiling windows where he watched Chloe and Sabrina play tag in Alastair's garden.

"Are you worried she'll hurt Chloe?" she asked quietly.

"Not at all. Sabrina wouldn't hurt a flea." He sighed deeply and rubbed the heel of his hand over his heart. "I find it difficult to let her out of my sight."

By Damian's deep frown, Liz could tell he was weighing his words.

"One day, my wife and I were deliriously happy, welcoming our baby girl to the world. A few years later, she disappeared with Sabrina. I lost out on three years of my child's life because I thought she might be safer with Viv and her sisters. But I missed her. Every second of every day, it was as if someone had ripped out my heart."

"What happened?"

"Someone close to Vivian planted a bug in her ear. She began to fear me. Fear for Sabrina. Then one day, she left."

"Oh, Damian, I'm so sorry."

"It's in the past."

Her voice was gentle when she said, "No, I don't think it is. You're hurting."

"I just don't understand how Viv could ever believe I'd hurt my own child. I've never laid a hand on either of them. I showered them with all they could ever desire: love, protection, gifts. And I made damned sure I was never like my mother."

The words were laced with pain, and Liz wanted nothing more than to hug him and help ease his suffering. She doubted it would go over well. Damian struck her as proud and seemed inclined to hide what he was feeling.

"How was it that Vivian allowed you to take Sabrina back?"

His face hardened to stone. The challenge in his eyes dared her to judge his next words. "When I discovered Viv lied about Sabrina's abilities, I retrieved my daughter."

Whether he'd forgotten the girl had gifted Liz with the ability to see into another's heart or not, he still put up an act. Damian made it seem as if he'd stolen his daughter, and perhaps he had, but inside, he was an open wound.

"How could you not know she had abilities?"

"A future Aether isn't like other witches. They don't develop

89

right away. Perhaps it's by the Goddess's design, so they don't throw a temper tantrum during the terrible-two stage and level an entire town. Most come into their power when they turn five or have the ability to reason."

"What about your wife? Do you think she's going through what you did?"

He closed his eyes and shifted to hide what he was feeling. The audible swallow was painful to hear. Yes, he definitely knew what his wife was going through right now.

"Damian, if I can be so bold... this war between you and your wife; it's damaging Sabrina the most."

"You know nothing!" he snapped.

The force of his anger was like a slap in the face. Her head jerked back from the surge of power focused on her. At her shocked expression, he tempered his emotions. "I'm sorry. Were you hurt just now?"

"N-no. I..." His controlled fury had stung a little, but what could she say? He wasn't the type of man who would appreciate someone delving into his affairs, regardless of how well-meaning, and she should've respected his boundaries. For the love of the Goddess, they'd only recently met. "I'm sorry, Damian. I didn't mean to pry."

He straightened his cuffs, and Liz almost smiled at the arrogant tilt to his chin. If she didn't know better, she'd swear he and Alastair were related. They were cut from the same cloth.

"You saw what is after Sabrina. Vivian can't protect her. I'm afraid if I let her know where I am, she'll steal off again, taking Sabrina with her. It would sign my child's death warrant. Until Sabrina can care for herself, she can't be out of range of my protection. Too many would use her power for their own."

"You don't owe me an explanation, Damian. I overstepped."

"Maybe I want someone to see me as someone other than a monster for a change."

She placed a hand on his forearm and squeezed. "I see a man who loves his family. A man who would help out a friend, no questions asked. You're the furthest thing from a monster as it gets."

An amused smile curled his lips. "And you're as lovely as you are naive, my dear. However, I do appreciate your well-intended words." He cupped her cheek and stared deeply into her eyes. "If you weren't in love with Rafe, and I wasn't in love with Vivian, we'd make an excellent pair."

"We'll never know."

"I believe we already do. Thank you, Liz. Your many kindnesses to us haven't gone unnoticed. I plan to give you my private number. Should you ever need anything, you call me, and I'll be there to help you. Do you understand?"

"I think so."

He leaned in close and spoke in a low tone. "When the time comes, and Rafe is ready to reveal his secret, try to maintain your cool. Listen to what he has to say without judgment, and all will be well."

"Sabrina said something similar to me this morning. I'm starting to worry."

His cool lips brushed her cheek. "Be open to what he has to say."

Liz turned her face until they were inches apart. "Should I say the same of you and Vivian?"

Sadness entered his obsidian eyes. "Maybe I'll extend an olive branch."

"I hope you do. You deserve happiness, too, Damian."

CHAPTER 12

"*Qalbi*, should I be jealous?" Although his tone was mild, Rafe couldn't disguise the unease he was feeling at seeing Damian's marked attention to Liz. The man was exactly her type, and seeing the two of them together made Rafe realize he was in no way secure about their renewed relationship. They hadn't defined anything or talked about the future. Other than to initially say she loved him, Liz was mum on the subject.

"No need." She inched back, lifted his arm, and wrapped it around her.

A relieved sigh escaped as he looked over at Damian, where he'd moved on to chat with Alastair and Nash.

Liz twisted slightly to look up at him. "You have nothing to worry about, Rafe. I promise. Damian and I have bonded over his beloved daughter. She's a darling. But he is very much in love with his wife, and I'm crazy about you."

"I wonder if there will ever be a time my hackles don't rise to see another man talk to you so intimately."

"Goddess, I hope not. I'd hate it if you lost interest."

"Rest assured, it won't happen in this lifetime or any other."

He didn't fail to note her smug smile as she faced the window.

Following her line of sight, he noticed the young girls playing in the garden.

"Marry me."

Rafe winced inwardly at his spontaneous delivery. He should've taken the time to plan a decent proposal.

"This is sudden."

"No, it isn't. I've been in love with you from our first weekend together. It's only grown stronger with time. And a Thorne only loves once. That means I'm it for you, as well."

"I accept on the condition we have no more lies or half-truths between us."

Closing his eyes, he tightened his arms around her. His happiness was great. Sealing her acceptance with a kiss would've been the proper thing to do, but he was just so damned grateful for her positive response, he couldn't move other than to embrace her tighter. Luckily, she wasn't as frozen.

Liz shifted and pressed her chest to his, her arms rising up to encircle his neck. Opening his eyes, he stared down into her twinkling amber gaze. She lifted her chin, puckered her lips, and batted her lashes. Suppressing a laugh, he brushed his nose butterfly-soft against hers.

When she frowned, he did laugh.

"I thought the standard proposal came with a kiss?" she grumbled.

"It absolutely does, but there are wide-eyed children on the other side of that glass, staring at us."

The truth of his statement was discerned with a glance over her shoulder. "Little miscreants," she muttered, stealing Damian's descriptor.

"Shall we sneak back to your bedroom and seal our bargain?"

"Hell to the yeah!" With a light wave toward the girls, Liz teleported him to her room. "Now, where were we?"

Rafe tilted her chin up and gazed down into her bright eyes. Happiness shone back at him, and he smiled his own joy. "I love you, Elizabeth. Thank you for consenting to marry me."

He lowered his lips to hers and captured her mouth in a warm, seeking kiss. Without hesitancy, she opened for him and returned his kiss with fervor. His fingers were on the top button of her blouse when a knock interrupted their celebratory sex.

"I feel like I'm being tortured," he complained good-naturedly. Or maybe not so good-naturedly. He was damned tired of waiting to be intimate with Liz again after all this time. "I forgot to tell you. Alastair called a family meeting."

Liz groaned and laughed at the same time. "The torture is mutual. Believe me." She pulled his head down to hers and ignored the second knock. When their lips parted, she said. "Tonight."

"I'll hold you to that promise, *qalbi*."

"That would be my fondest wish."

Rafe laughed when he realized she was quoting him from the night they went to Calabresi's. "Come on before whomever is banging on that door gets any more aggressive."

ALASTAIR DIDN'T MISS LIZ AND RAFE ENTERING THE LIVING ROOM LIKE secret lovers. They exchanged longing glances when they believed no one was paying attention. He gave Rafe a nod of approval when their gazes connected across the room. The couple was good for each other. He made her relax and enjoy the finer side of life, and Liz had made Rafe smile more in the last few days, since this mess began, than in all the time Alastair had known him.

"Glad you could join us. We have a ceremony to perform."

"First, I need to get to Thorne Industries to find the Ring of Dispel," Liz countered. She opened her mouth and closed it just as quickly, a dark frown tugging her brows down.

"What is it, child?"

"The wards for the business. Did anyone think to secure them?"

"Quentin and Knox took care of that the day our magic disappeared."

She inhaled and exhaled deeply, as if to banish her worry. "So

Nash's treasure room is still hidden?" At Alastair's nod, she asked, "Do I need them to bring down the wards to enter the archive?"

"Yes, Quentin should suffice." He nodded at his son-in-law. "You'll go with Liz and Rafe to help them find what they need. The rest of us will prepare for anything else Damian needs to restore our abilities. *Then* we find Franco Moreau and find out how he was able to neutralize our line so easily."

Alastair wanted to add they were more than welcome to torture the little pissant to discover the truth, but he needn't appear too bloodthirsty to his family. Half of them were still wary of him as it was. Damian didn't even *try* to hide his grin. *He* could easily discern what Alastair was thinking.

"We'll head to the clearing as soon as you return." Alastair took a brief moment to explain to Damian about the glen where they performed their more difficult spells. The ancient formations were buried, but when raised, lent to their magic. "Those with intact abilities can form a circle around the perimeter of the altar while Damian raises the stones. As soon as Liz, Quentin, and Rafe come back with the ring, we'll get started. Waiting too long makes us vulnerable."

Liz nodded after Alastair's speech and joined hands with Quentin and Rafe to teleport to the main office.

After she'd gone, Alastair pulled Damian aside. "Will this work? Or am I putting my family in worse danger by taking them out into the open?"

"It will work. Remember, my team will secure the area first while your guards follow in the rear. I doubt anyone will want to take me on, Al. Not when they would forfeit their life."

"Thank you, my friend."

***

"*WHERE IS IT?*" THE PANIC LIZ WAS EXPERIENCING RATCHETED UP HER voice by at least two octaves.

The Ring of Dispel, although cataloged, was missing from the archive room.

"It has to be here."

Rafe's calm assurance did nothing to ease her mind. He didn't realize how crazed Nash was about his possession. If he did, he'd understand nothing was ever out of place on these shelves. *Nothing.* Which meant if it wasn't where it was documented as being, it was not in the building.

They spent another ten minutes searching to satisfy Rafe, then Liz whipped out her phone and dialed Nash. "We have a serious problem, cousin. The Ring of Dispel is missing."

"How is that possible? I placed it there myself. No one but you and me has gone in that room over the last two months."

"I don't know, but it's gone. Can you find out from Damian if there is any other object he can use?"

"I'll call you right back. In the meantime, check the security tapes."

"Quentin already did. I'm afraid it's not good. There is a section of the recordings missing from the day our power went down."

"Let me guess. This happened before Knox and Quentin arrived to strengthen my wards."

"You're right on the money."

"If it wouldn't bring all the raccoons in the general vicinity to my father's doorstep, I'd swear up a storm."

Liz bit her lip to abort the inappropriate laughter bubbling up. "I'm no expert, but without your magic to call the animals, I think you're safe to swear."

"You're right! Sonofabitch!" There was a long pause on the other side of the line. When Nash spoke again, his voice was lighter. "This is one perk in this whole mess."

Her cousin disconnected when Liz told him she'd return shortly.

"I wonder if this means Franklin has the ring," she said to Rafe.

"Without a doubt. He, or someone he's working with, definitely took that ring. I wonder what else might be missing from the archives."

They shared a horrified look. "Rafe, this is bad. We have to do an inventory immediately."

"*Qalbi*, I need you to stay calm." Although his voice sounded as disturbed as she felt, Liz didn't point it out.

"I'll keep Quentin with me. You go back and gather as many family members as you can. We're going to need help figuring out what's missing. I have a sneaking suspicion it's a number of things."

"I'm not leaving you."

"Rafe."

"No. Out of the question."

"Rafe."

"Don't try to argue. I'm here to protect you."

"Rafe!" she practically shouted to gain his attention. "Quentin can guard me better than you."

"*I beg your pardon!*"

Her lips twitched at his outrage. "*Magically.* He's stronger."

Quentin chose that moment to saunter up and drop an arm across her shoulders.

"It's true. I'm the best." His tone suggested he wasn't just speaking about magic.

Liz elbowed him in the rib cage. "Knock it off. It isn't like we don't all know you're madly in love with Holly."

"It's true. My prickly pear owns my very soul."

"Gag." Outside, she mimed gagging even as she said the word. Inside, she cheered for Holly. Finding a man like Quentin was the equivalent of finding a pot of gold at the end of a rainbow. Magnificent and a stroke of massive luck.

He grinned and tugged her tighter to his side. "Don't be jealous, Lizzy. You can still look your fill."

Her laughter died the second she saw Rafe's cold face. Uh oh. Someone was *not* happy she was the recipient of Quentin's flirting. She was sure to catch Rafe's eye as she stepped out from under Quentin's casual embrace.

"Babe."

"It's fine, *qalbi*. I'll return soon. Please touch base every ten minutes or so until I get back."

When he pivoted to walk away, she ran to stop his exit. Placing one hand on his chest, she hooked the other around his neck. "I love you, Rafe. Be careful."

His expression softened as he stared down at her. "You, too." He gathered her close and rested his forehead against hers. "Please don't take any chances. If you sense any danger, you teleport to Alastair's immediately."

"Of course."

"I'll take care of her, Rafe. You have my word." All signs of playfulness had disappeared from Quentin as he made the solemn vow. "If need be, Liz can cloak herself."

"Thank you."

Rafe placed a gentle kiss on her lips then disappeared with barely a ripple.

She looked at Quentin, all business and pure determination. "Okay, so let's get started."

CHAPTER 13

*D*amian Dethridge believes it's a great idea to continue to eliminate this chapter from the series. Who am I to argue with the Aether? I'd love to know what you think of his character. Be sure to drop me a line on social media.

CHAPTER 14

*L*iz and Quentin had only made it through two shelving units before Rafe reappeared.

"Liz?" Rafe's voice echoed through the opening of the chamber.

Just as she was about to call out, Quentin clamped a hand over her mouth. "Wait."

"Liz, darling? Where are you, my dear?"

Her eyes widened. "It's not Rafe. He never uses any endearment but *qalbi*," she whispered.

"No, it's not. The energy in the building has shifted and is all wrong."

"What about the wards?"

"I left them down so Rafe and the others could return. I didn't think he'd be this long."

Liz knew true fear. Had Rafe never made it back to Alastair's estate? Was it possible he had, but then the family was attacked and incapacitated? How did their enemies know that she and Quentin were alone at Thorne Industries? Question after question tumbled around in her mind. The one she asked was, "What do we do?"

"Have a little fun."

"Oh, Goddess! I should've kept Rafe as my bodyguard."

"Oh, buck up, little Lizzy. You're a Thorne and a badass to the core."

Quentin's mini pep talk worked as intended.

She straightened. "What's the plan?"

"We're cloaked, remember? He can't hear or see us. How about we capture us an impostor?"

"You make it sound so easy."

"Easy-peasy, darlin'. Come on."

They didn't bother to creep forward, not when their movement was muffled as it was. Liz sent a silent thank you to Granny Thorne for her spell.

"Wait. Wasn't the Spear of Lugh on the list?"

"Yes. Hold still. I'll get it."

She stayed in place as Quentin went back to retrieve the spear. It had been carved by a master craftsman, who also happened to be one of the Irish gods. Rumor had it, once activated, the fiery magic could defeat the wielder's greatest enemy. Liz suspected the weapon's magic was too great for her to handle, but since Quentin descended from Zeus, she had no doubt he could bring the spear to life.

Fake Rafe continued to call to her. Anger tinged his voice. If she wasn't sure earlier, she was positive he was an impostor now. Whoever posed as Rafe couldn't enter the archives, because it was the one ward Liz had secured herself when they arrived earlier. Now, the pretender was forced to pace outside the invisible open-ing, looking for the entry.

"Got it. Now what? Plunge it into his treacherous heart?" Quentin asked, only half teasing.

"That's one option. But we need to find out answers." They moved closer to the exit. "Can you send out a feeler to see if there are any others lying in wait for us?"

"I can do better than that, Lizzy. Once we reach the opening, I want you to stay in this chamber. I'll scope out the vicinity and make sure he's alone."

"I don't think we should separate, Quentin."

"Liz? This isn't funny. Come out now!" Fake Rafe called out, his voice edging into desperation.

"I need to scope it out. If I don't, the others could walk into a trap when they get here."

She clutched Quentin's arm tighter in response. His logic was sound, but Liz hated it all the same. Finally, she nodded. "Take the spear."

"Any idea how it works?"

"I don't suppose you know the Gaelic word for ignite, do you?"

"For the love of the Goddess! Where is Spring when we need her?"

"Maybe it crosses the language barriers and will respond to Latin."

"If not, I go back to my original plan to stab him through the heart."

"Deal." She loosened her grip on his forearm. "Please be careful."

"Do I get a going-away kiss like Rafe? I mean, I'm going into battle and all."

She laughed as he had intended she should. "Go, you tool."

"You sound just like Autumn when you say that. It's creepy." Quentin gave her a warm smile that belied his words. "If something happens, get your ass out of here. Don't try to take anyone on."

Liz gave him a slight nod. The truth was, she'd try to save him if she could. He was vital to her family and—more importantly—to his wife, Holly, and his baby, Francesca.

After pausing for a long moment to study Liz's face, he shook his head. "I shouldn't have wasted my breath. You'll charge into the fray because you think it's the right thing to do."

Biting her lip to keep from laughing, she shrugged.

With a light squeeze of her hand, Quentin went out to confront Fake Rafe.

"Papa?"

"Yes, my darling beastie?"

"Liz is in trouble."

Rafe had been in the middle of informing the Thornes and the Aether of the disappearance of the Ring of Dispel when Sabrina crept into the room. His heart nearly stopped when she stated Liz was in trouble. No one questioned how she knew because Damian had informed them earlier that she was destined to be an Oracle. As such, she had the second sight and the ability to see into the future. Although, in this case, it was the present.

Her father held out his arms to her, and she crawled into his lap. She pointed at Rafe. "It's him."

"What?" Rafe hadn't meant to shout, but there was no way in hell he'd hurt Liz. It would be less painful to rip out his own heart and stomp on it. "I'd never!"

"He's there now, Papa. She needs help."

How could he be in two places?

"Is she—" Rafe's question regarding her sanity never made it past his lips. Any desire to speak was squashed when he saw the thunderous expression forming on Damian's face.

"No, she isn't, and you'd do well to mind your tongue, Xuereb."

In a move that shocked them all, Sabrina held out her arms to Rafe. With a wary look at the Aether, he lifted her until her small face was level with his.

She placed the flat of her palms on his temples. "Watch."

The scene flashed through his mind as it was unfolding. A witch or warlock pretending to be him was trying to draw Liz from the archives, only she was too intelligent to fall for it. Quentin, on the other hand, was about to walk into a trap. Ten or more henchmen had managed to cloak their presence.

Rafe handed Sabrina off to her father with a heartfelt thank you.

"We have to help Quentin," he stated with a calmness he didn't feel.

"Papa will save her," the little girl said with unquestionable assurance.

"I cannot leave you, Sabrina," Damian told her. "It isn't safe."

She patted her father's cheek like a wise old woman. "Go now, Papa. Please."

The Aether's indecision could be felt by all, and it was damned uncomfortable.

Aurora Fennell-Thorne stepped forward and clasped Sabrina's hand. "No one will touch her while I draw a breath, Damian. She's safe."

His eyes never leaving those of his daughter, he held out a hand to Rafe. "Take me to Liz."

Sabrina's sunny smile lit the room, and her happiness reached out like rays of sunshine to warm the group gathered in Alastair's study. "Thank you, Papa."

When Rafe touched the Aether's wrist, he experienced a surge of raw power. It woke his cells and made his body vibrate with pure energy. "What the hell?"

"I'm supercharging you for the fight ahead, should you need it. Take me straight into the fray."

He didn't need to be told twice, and pulling up a mental picture of Nash's office, Rafe teleported with Damian at his side. Quentin was just stepping through the opening to the archives when they arrived, but the presence of the Aether stripped his invisibility cloak. The surprise put him at a disadvantage, and the blow to his upper back sent him crashing into the wall.

"Duck and cover," Damian snapped.

What the hell he meant by that was up for interpretation, but Rafe dropped to the ground and covered his head. A radiant blue-tinged light illuminated the room instantaneously. A strong charge of electricity rocked his body, burning through his clothing and searing his skin. He couldn't contain his cry of pain. Any sound he made was mild in comparison to the terrified and tortured screams of the men around him. The exception was Quentin, who seemed immune to the bolts of lightning flying about the room.

In less than sixty seconds, Damian was squatting in front of Rafe. "I'm sorry, Xuereb. It was the only thing I could think to do in the moment. I'm going to touch you now, and it's going to hurt like a bitch at first."

The contact triggered Rafe's scream. It echoed around the cavernous office and brought Liz running. She called his name but was halted by Quentin before she could get to him. The horror in her eyes told Rafe exactly how bad he looked—a small fraction of how he was feeling. He couldn't remember ever passing out in his life, but as black spots danced in his peripheral vision, he figured he was about to experience his first faint.

Just as he thought it would be lights out, his skin began to cool and his insides no longer felt like molten lava. Rafe wanted to sob his relief. To see his skin pigment shift from crimson to its standard olive tone was disconcerting. Even as he watched, the fine hairs on his arms sprouted and thickened to pre-electrocution.

After what seemed like an eternity, Damian rose to his feet and held out a hand to help him up. Everyone studiously avoided looking at his exposed privates. Had he felt less like a lightning rod and more like a human, he'd have laughed and teased them. As it was, he barely had the energy to thank Liz when she conjured clothes for him.

He wobbled on his feet and voiced his gratitude when Damian lent him a steadying hand.

Liz hesitated only a second before she wrapped her arms around Rafe's middle.

"I'm going to have nightmares about this," she stated tearfully. "I thought you... I thought..."

"It's okay, *qalbi*. I'm all right now."

"I'm sorry, Liz." Damian touched her shoulder, and she flinched.

"You saved our lives, Damian. You don't have to apologize to me. I just need a minute to process that Rafe is alive and well. Also, that you are much scarier than I ever imagined."

"Understood." His tone was more reserved.

"How the hell did you make it through that unscathed," Rafe asked Quentin.

"I'm not sure."

They all faced the Aether.

Damian's narrowed-eyed gaze was locked on the spear in Quentin's fist. "Is that the Spear of Lugh?"

"Guessed it in one." Quentin grinned cheekily.

"There's your answer." Damian held out a hand for the weapon. "May I?"

He examined the piece, his eyes missing nothing as his fingertips traced the inscribed symbols. Under his touch, the runes glowed. "Stunning craftsmanship."

"Uh, Damian, is it meant to glow like that?"

He chuckled at Rafe's uneasy question. "For me, yes." After handing the weapon back to Quentin, he studied the bodies on the floor. "I'm afraid there's no identifying them now that they resemble burnt bacon."

Rafe felt the blood drain from his face to his toes as he took in the charred remains of the men who'd planned to attack Liz. Queasiness assailed him. "Was that how I looked? How did I survive?"

"The influx of magic I gave you before we arrived kept you alive. I hadn't intended it for that purpose, but it worked to save you all the same."

"They never stood a chance against you, did they?"

"No." The somber note betrayed Damian's inner demons. There was no doubt in anyone's mind what he was and what he could do. Rafe imagined his life was lonely as hell.

"Why don't you get back to Sabrina? We can clean up this mess," Rafe suggested to Damian.

"No. She's safe enough for the moment, and you can barely stand. If another wave of enemies attacks, I don't want to tell my daughter I failed to save her favorite person."

"Sabrina sent you for me?" At Damian's nod, Liz smiled her thanks. "We owe you both big time for this."

"You owe me nothing, and trust me, you'll prefer it that way."

The cryptic response sent a shiver of unease along Rafe's spine. He was sure owing the Aether anything would be the equivalent of selling your soul to the devil in the Christian world. You might not like what he required of you in the future.

"Rafe tells me the Ring of Dispel is missing."

Liz nodded, her concern over the absent item apparent.

"May I take a look at your inventory list and see if there may be another object that might work as well?"

"Of course. Whatever you need." Her eyes never touched on the bodies surrounding them, but instead, locked on Damian. "Do we just leave them for now?"

"Yes. It'll be hard to determine who they were if anyone else shows up." He paused as if a thought occurred to him. "Are there mortals in this building?"

Liz shook her head. "No. Nash gave them the week off with pay when this whole thing started. He was afraid they might be hurt should this very thing happen."

"Excellent. Let's see what you have on hand, shall we?"

"I'm afraid there are already a number of things missing. Quentin and I were taking inventory when Fake Rafe showed up."

Damian grinned. "Fake Rafe?"

"That's what I've been calling him mentally."

"Give me your list, and I'll save you some time."

She wordlessly reached for the clipboard on the shelf beside the archive entrance and handed it over.

The Aether simply swept a hand over the ten-page list. *"Ostendo."* He then handed the clipboard back to Liz and held up his hands, palms facing outward. His eyes took on a golden glow, and he pivoted his head from side to side. One by one, yellow lines highlighted items on Liz's inventory sheet.

"Holy shit!" Quentin muttered.

Rafe couldn't stop his racing heart. Damian made their own use of magic look like child's play.

The entire process took less than three minutes and revealed nine missing items.

Damian surveyed the list over Liz's shoulder. "These are all objects to help restore magic. It seems someone didn't want the Thornes to get their powers back."

"Fuck!"

They all looked at Liz in silent surprise.

"I'm going to rip Franco's heart out," she snarled.

Having seen how feisty she could be in the past, Rafe was the first to grin. "Welcome back, tiger."

CHAPTER 15

*L*iz's anger hadn't abated by the time she returned to Alastair's estate. A huge part of her rage was directed inward. *She* was the reason Franco had free access to do what he'd done. If she ever got her hands on that POS again, she would tear him limb from limb, patch him together, then do it again for good measure. That rodent deserved to suffer.

"Walk with me." Rafe's deep voice startled her out of her revenge fantasy.

"It's not a good time, babe."

"I think it's the perfect time. Let's take a walk."

She cast a glance around the room and noticed the watchful expressions of her family. They weren't judging her, but they damned well should be. How could they all be so understanding and kind? Another of her craptastic relationships had caused this. Tears flooded her eyes and burned behind the lids she closed to hide from the observant group around her. She swallowed hard to keep her sobs at bay.

Rafe's large, warm hand captured hers and lightly tugged her toward the French doors leading to the garden. When they cleared the exit and were out of sight of the others, he gathered her close.

"*Qalbi*, don't do this to yourself. You are not responsible for Franco Moreau's actions."

"I should've had him investigated the instant he asked me out. I could have scryed to be sure he was who he said he was. *Anything* but trust a man I hardly knew." She pulled away and began to pace.

"You trusted me when we first met," he reminded her softly.

"Exactly! And look how that ended up," she retorted.

Rafe sucked in his breath, and Liz whirled around to face him. "Oh, Rafe! I didn't mean that the way it sounded. Only that I was hurt after you left, and I knew absolutely nothing about you." She strode forward and gripped his hands in hers. "Please understand, the dig wasn't at you. It was at myself. I'm too damned trusting."

"You're perfect just the way you are, *qalbi*." He bent his knees until his face was level with hers. "Your openness is one of the things I love most about you. You're optimistic and willing to embrace life at every opportunity."

"No. I used to be that way when we first met in Paris. Now, I don't know what I am or how to be."

"Be free to be yourself with me. Always."

Her tears started, and for the life of her, she couldn't stop them. "How do they not hate me? I've made them all sitting ducks, Rafe. I've put my family in danger because of my naiveté."

"The Thornes will always be targets, Elizabeth. Your family is envied and feared because of the power they wield. You have to understand this and not blame yourself for things beyond your control."

The hand stroking her back soothed her to a large degree, but it didn't take away the ache inside her chest. "I have to fix this."

"We will. Together."

"And if Franco falls off a tall cliff without the benefit of his powers to help him teleport to safety, I wouldn't mind."

"Consider it done."

A few heartbeats passed before she spoke again. "Rafe?"

"Hmm?"

"Thank you for not giving up on me. I know I've been bitchy and reserved since we met up at Thorne Manor last year, but I appreciate that you kept trying."

He laughed softly and drew her close again. "As if I had any choice. You, and only you, hold my heart, Elizabeth Thorne. I'll love you until my dying day."

"Stick with this family, and it may be sooner rather than later," she muttered.

"You are ruining my declaration of love with your sarcasm, *qalbi*."

"Sorry. Family trait."

"Indeed."

Rafe was just lowering his head to kiss her when young, feminine giggles rang out.

"I think we have an audience, babe," she whispered regretfully.

"Mmhmm." He sighed heavily. "Tonight, I intend to kiss you senseless."

"Just kissing?"

"Are you feeling suddenly tired? Should I take you straight to bed to... nap?"

"I don't trust we won't have little gremlins spying on us," she said with a laugh. "But oh, the temptation is strong."

"You should kiss her," Sabrina instructed from her hiding spot behind a bush. "Like my papa used to kiss Mama."

Liz's smile faltered. There was a wealth of heartache in the child's words. She looked to Rafe and noted his helpless expression. He didn't know how to respond any better than she did.

Distancing herself from Rafe, she moved to a concrete bench, sat down, and called out to the child. "Won't you join me, Sabrina?"

Instead of sitting next to her, the girl climbed onto her lap.

"You're missing your mom again, aren't you?"

Sabrina nodded, her eyes brimming with sadness.

"Have you talked to your father and told him?"

"He gets angry when I talk about Mama."

Liz wasn't equipped to have this conversation. Damian had his reasons for keeping Sabrina and Vivian apart. Although she didn't agree separating a child from their mother was the best course of action, Liz owed it to him not to get in the middle of his domestic dispute with Vivian.

"He's doing what he thinks is best for you, sweetheart," she finally said. "Your papa's goal is always to protect you."

A hiccuping sob caught in Sabrina's throat, and she wrapped her arms around Liz's neck, squeezing tightly. She frowned her concern at Rafe even as she hugged the girl tight and rocked her.

"Get Damian," she mouthed.

She needn't have bothered. Damian, having sensed his daughter's upset, rushed across the garden to where Liz held the child. "Give her to me," he commanded.

Sabrina's arms tightened.

"She told me she misses her mom."

Devastation flooded his features, and Liz found it heartbreaking to witness.

He took the spot on the bench next to them. "Beastie?" The gentleness in his voice spoke of his adoration for his daughter. "Come here, my love."

Little arms tightened for an instant, but then Sabrina dove into her father's embrace.

"I want Mama."

"I know you do. When we are done helping the Thornes, we will see what we can do to arrange a visit with your mother."

She drew back, hope replacing her tragic expression. "Really, Papa?"

"Really. It's past time your mother and I had a conversation."

Only Liz heard the undercurrent in his tone. Sabrina seemed to take him at face value.

"I can give them their magic back, Papa."

"No, beastie. It'll drain you too much."

"I'm strong. I promise."

He stared down at her with a mixture of exasperation and love. "I'll tell you what. You can restore Alastair's powers. Everyone else will have to wait until we recover the things I need for a proper ceremony. Deal?"

"Deal!" she shouted happily.

"My cousin wouldn't want to put her at risk," Liz hedged.

"In normal circumstances, it would drain her, like it did when she helped you. This time, I intend to be her conduit."

Sabrina did for Alastair what she'd done for Liz; she restored his magic with the additional bonus that his abilities would be next to impossible for another witch to take away. With the exception of the Aether, only a goddess or god had the power to strip them now.

As Damian and Sabrina readied to teleport home, Liz had a tearful moment. She'd grown fond of the Aether and his pint-sized replica.

He enfolded her in a tight embrace. "Take care of yourself, Liz."

"I will. You, too, Damian."

"Should you have need of me, no matter the reason, you call me." His voice was stern like a father's, but his eyes were full of fondness.

"Promise. And it goes both ways. I'll always be there for you and your family."

Liz lifted Sabrina when the child held up her arms.

"I'm going to miss you." The girl's chin trembled.

"This isn't goodbye, you know. I'm a simple phone call away if you want a tea party."

Sabrina's eyes lit with joy. "When you stop the bad man?"

"When I stop the bad man," Liz promised.

The girl peered over her shoulder and smiled shyly at her father. "Is that okay, Papa?"

"It's more than okay, beastie." He took her from Liz. "In fact, we'll insist on it. If Liz doesn't come to us, we'll come to her. And we'll include Chloe, too. How's that?"

Sabrina wrapped her arms around his neck in such a fierce hug, and Damian's face began to flush. "I love you, Papa."

"And I love you, my little miscreant. Now loosen that hold before I expire on the spot."

She giggled and burrowed her face into the perfect hollow beneath his jawline.

Liz felt a tug at her heartstrings at the sight. Rubbing her hand on Sabrina's back, she leaned in and kissed her petal-soft cheek. "Be good for your papa, sweetheart. I'll see you soon, okay?"

"Bye, Miss Liz."

A floor-to-ceiling band of gold appeared behind Damian. He touched a hand to her cheek then turned with his daughter and walked through the opening he'd created between his home and Alastair's. The air crackled, and the portal closed with a sizzle and snapping pop.

Liz faced her family and placed her hands on her hips. "Time to get to the bottom of this mess."

CHAPTER 16

"*R*afe and I should head to France. I'm sure Franklin, er… Franco, will head back to his family's estate if he isn't there already."

"It's dangerous to confront him on his home turf, Lizzy," Quentin warned. "There's no telling how many guards he has in his employ. Also, you should see if you can determine how many of his relatives are involved in this mess and if they have his back."

"They won't be going alone," Alastair countered. "I intend to travel with them, along with a contingent of my own guards."

"I think this needs to be handled a little more delicately." Ryker spoke up, and everyone turned to listen to what the ex-spymaster had to say. "If you retaliate without proof, you'll bring down the Council on your head. The better way to go about this would be to gather evidence against Franco and whoever he may be working with. Also, it wouldn't be remiss to discover their agenda."

Liz chewed over his suggestion and silently concluded Ryker wasn't wrong. To charge in and take revenge on Franco without evidence would definitely land them in a heap of trouble. Even the head of the Witches' Council—despite her fondness for their family —would find it difficult to protect them from punishment. War, regardless of the provocation, was frowned upon in the witch community.

"Who could infiltrate Franco's home and business easily?" Rafe asked.

"That would be me." Liz met his disbelieving gaze. "He wants my magic for whatever scheme he's concocted. If I pretend to go along with it, we might get the information we need."

Sweeping a hand through his dark locks, Rafe blew out a breath. "No way in hell."

"Babe—"

"Liz, please. We haven't even had a chance to bask in the glow of a reunion, and you're asking me to sit back while you stroll into a dangerous situation that might get you killed?"

The plea underlining his reasoning wasn't hard to miss. "Okay. We'll come up with something else." She looked at each family member in turn. "Suggestions?"

Spring raised her hand from her seat on the sofa.

"Cousin?"

"Three of you have been supercharged by the Dethridges, if I'm not mistaken." Spring waited for them to nod. "Right. So I believe you're strong enough that if you utilize blood magic, you can counteract whoever is stealing and amassing ours. We wouldn't even have to leave the estate to do it."

"What would we need for a spell of that magnitude, and where would we find it?" Liz asked.

Alastair answered for her. "Actually, I remember seeing a spell in the Aether's Book of Shadows. I can call and confer with him, but I think it might actually work without the blood."

"Remember when we used the spell from the Book of Thoth to bring Mama back?" Summer cast a quick smile in Aurora's direction. "We used the boost of artifacts and the ancient magic of the standing stones."

"But there's no guarantee we could light them again," Autumn argued from the corner where she stood rocking her son. "We weren't mortal then."

Summer grimaced and nodded. "True, but it might still be worth a shot."

"How did it work?" Rafe asked.

"Each of us, along with our male counterpart, touched the symbols on the pillar corresponding to our element. It was pretty straightforward," she explained.

"So Liz and I could light the one for..." He faced Liz and frowned. "What *is* your elemental magic?"

She laughed and produces a flame with the simple snap of her fingers. "I'd have thought that was obvious when I tried to shish kabab Franco."

Rafe's lips twitched. "Right. Okay, Liz and I could light the fire symbols."

A frown drew Alastair's dark blond brows down. "Aurora and I are able to light the water. But we don't have enough couples for the remaining three elements of air, earth, and metal."

"What if we begged a favor from Isis?" Winnie suggested. "She may be willing to help in that regard."

Autumn's husband, Keaton, looked to his brother Coop. "Another option is to ask our parents. Mom's an air sign."

GiGi, who had remained quiet throughout their brainstorming session, finally spoke. "There are still members of my old coven who regularly get together. They'd be willing to help, brother. The two remaining families will have an earth and a metal elemental among them."

"We will need their male and female energies co-mingled. Are they coupled?" Alastair asked.

"When last we spoke."

"All right. Let me run this plan by Damian. If he tells me the spell will work for us, we'll gather our resources." He smiled softly at Winnie. "We'll keep a favor from Isis as option two."

The likelihood of their plan coming to fruition was slim, and Liz didn't want anyone getting their hopes up. "Should we fail to restore everyone's power, I'm reserving the right to confront Franco." She squeezed Rafe's hand. "But only as a last option."

"Well, you certainly won't be handling it on your own," Alastair assured her. "I feel confident with a few key players beside you, you'll get the answers you need."

She'd never experienced such solidarity among her family before that moment. They should all hold her in contempt for allowing Franco to get the upper hand, and yet, here they gathered, showing their support and smiling at her as if she hadn't cost them greatly.

"I love you all so much," she choked out. "Never was there a family as wonderful as this."

Autumn shifted Jolyon to her shoulder and held up a hand. "Oh, hell no, cousin! No waterworks. I'm still a hormonal mess and likely to flood this living room if I get started."

Everyone stared her down.

"Fine." Autumn sighed her disgruntlement. "We love you, too. Enough of the weepy shit, though."

Alastair tugged on his cuffs and straightened his tie. "I'll call Damian."

Once he exited the room, Aurora let loose a light laugh. "Don't think for a moment he wasn't affected, that old softie."

He popped his head back in the room and pinned his fiancée with a glare. "I'll give you old," he growled before he disappeared again. Their teasing was enough to break the somberness.

As Rafe observed the family laughing and interacting, he was struck by a deep sense of rightness. The love, compassion, and understanding this group continually exhibited were awe-inspiring. Never once had he seen a break in their loyalty to one another. This was the model he wished his own family adhered to, although they never would. The Champeaus subscribed to the "every witch for themself" motto. Any humanity Rafe had flowing through him was from the Xuereb side.

He caught Ryker's eye and gestured to a private corner of the room.

"What's up?"

"Marguerite. The other day, GiGi stated you patched things up with her. How sure are you she isn't still holding a grudge?"

His eyes following his wife from across the room, Ryker shrugged. "I can't be positive, Rafe. Marguerite seemed regretful, but it could very well have been an act on her part. Of course, she believed I was most likely going to my death for supposedly murdering Georgie Sipanil." He gave Rafe his full attention. "Why do you ask?"

"I'm surprised Alastair hasn't told you."

"Oh, he has, but I'm asking you. I'd like your take on all of this."

Rafe weighed how much to reveal. He greatly suspected Ryker knew almost everything there was to know about him, such were the resources of a spymaster. Going by a gut feeling, Rafe went with honesty. "Marguerite is my cousin. She's always been mean spirited and spiteful if she doesn't get her way." When Ryker didn't bat an eyelash at the confession, Rafe continued. "We know for sure Franco Moreau was posing as Franklin Moore to get close to Liz. We don't have exact confirmation on who his cohorts are. Like Alastair, I strongly suspect the Champeaus, based on what Franco's hired goon said. Although it's a possibility he knew who I was and lied to cause trouble."

"Al told us Isis clearly stated 'a new threat rises from the old.' He believes our problems arise from one of the older magical families." Ryker crossed his arms and scrubbed a hand along his jawline. "The Champeaus are an ancient line, like the Thornes and the Dethridges. If Alastair's right, it has to be from one of those three. It's hard to believe Damian would orchestrate this attack since he so recently helped Liz and Al. And considering all the Thornes we've contacted are affected by this, I feel they can be ruled out as well. The only remaining family would be the Champeaus."

Neither man heard Spring approach, and they both startled when she spoke. "Wrong. There were six original families according to our family grimoire." She ticked them off on her fingers as she said, "Thorne, Dethridge, Champeau, O'Malley, Carlyle, and Drake. None are as plentiful as us, or for that matter as powerful, with the exception of Damian Dethridge. Knox doesn't count, because the main source of his power was gifted to him from Isis."

They stared in amazement. Spring was like an encyclopedia of witchcraft.

Ryker was the first to speak. "I say we rule out Sebastian Drake. He's become a friend to this family. I can't imagine he'd ever strike against us. Obviously, the Thornes and Carlyles are related in some way or another. So the possible suspects are Dethridge, O'Malley, and Champeau."

"The O'Malleys lost their magic to a family feud about two hundred and fifty years ago."

Rafe shook his head in wonder. How the hell did she retain all this information?

"In that case, I suspect we can rule out Damian, too. That brings us back to our original suspects. It would make sense since the Moreaus and Champeaus are cousins. Seems old Petey might've been telling the truth after all." Rafe ran a hand along the back of his neck and wished to hell there was another. Anyone but those related to him. "They are not opposed to using black magic to get what they want."

"And what's that?" Spring asked.

Rafe shared a look with Ryker. They both knew the truth from their years working for the Council. "Ultimate control of the witch community," he finally said. "They want to be viewed with respect, but they tend to go about it the wrong way."

Ryker nodded as if to confirm Rafe's statement.

"Why? And why come after my family? It isn't as if we are heavily involved in running the Witches' Council." Spring was adorable in her confusion. Her heart so pure, it was difficult for her to imagine why anyone wanted to cause destruction to their way of life.

Knox joined their group in time to hear the last half of their conversation. "Some people have dark souls, sweetheart."

"You'll go with Uncle Alastair, Rafe, and Liz should the spell in the clearing not work?" she asked prettily.

"You know I won't leave you unprotected."

"But, Knox—"

"No." Lightning flashed outside the floor-to-ceiling windows, and the thunderous boom that followed had all the family members present turning in their direction. Knox smiled tightly and waved.

Spring buried a giggle behind her hand. "Way to freak them all out, darling."

"Yeah, sorry."

Rafe shook his head and met Liz's curious gaze from across the room. He winked to show things were truly under control.

"Back to the subject at hand. I think it might be a smart idea to see if a record exists, detailing the lineage of the original families. There could be a disgruntled family member from any of these lines, and we need to rule them out going forward." Ryker's expression was grim, and Rafe suspected he was remembering the time when a member of Alastair's own family was in league with their enemy against them.

"Do you think the Council would let us take a peek, Gillespie?"

Ryker shook his head. "Doubtful. Perhaps if we approached Georgie Sipanil separately."

"No need to bother Georgie," Spring informed them with a bright smile. "Uncle Alastair has sixteen volumes in his library. They have every recorded witch and warlock birth since the beginning of time. He once told me he started collecting and compiling more when he returned from the Otherworld."

"Clever girl." Ryker smiled his admiration of his niece by marriage. "It may take a while, but let's go see what we can discover."

CHAPTER 17

*T*heir small group poured over the books, each jotting down a note here or there in regards to the ruling families. They'd been at it for a good thirty minutes when Rafe felt a steady gaze on him. He glanced up to see Spring staring at him with a contemplative look in her eyes.

"Does Liz know?"

His heart began to hammer. "Know what?"

"Who you truly are?"

"Who do you believe me to be?" he asked softly.

Spring turned the journal in her hands toward him. His family tree was clearly on display. "Don't play games, Rafe. Your mother is Josephine Champeau." Her expression darkened. "Sister to Pierre Champeau and sister-in-law to Élise Moreau-Champeau. Élise happens to be sister to Louie Moreau, father of Franco."

Knox's head lifted the second he heard his girlfriend's tone harden, but he remained silent and watchful.

"Yes, Franco is my cousin by marriage. No, Liz doesn't know."

A gasp from behind him told him that had just changed. He closed his eyes against the sinking sensation in the pit of his stomach.

"Rafe?"

Liz stood directly behind him, but coward that he was, he couldn't turn around to face her. All he'd worked to build was about to crumble at his feet. He couldn't bear to witness her anger and suspicion, not after her sweet declaration of love.

"Can you all give us the room, please?" she asked in a dull, pain-filled voice.

With his elbows on the table, Rafe rested his chin atop his folded hands and waited. It didn't take long once the door closed behind Ryker, Spring, and Knox. Liz settled in Spring's abandoned chair and studied the chart on the page in front of her. Without looking at him, she asked, "How could you keep something this monumental from me?"

"Does it have to be?"

"Have to be what?"

"Monumental?" He dug the heels of his palms into his eye sockets and inhaled a long breath.

"Are you serious right now?"

He met her wounded eyes. "*Qalbi*, it's an accident of birth. No more, no less."

"How do I know you aren't working with him to bring down my family? How, Rafe?"

"Is that what you think of me?"

She threw up her hands. "Not before this moment, no. But what am I supposed to believe now? You lied to me."

"I didn't."

"Oh, *come on!* A lie of omission is still a lie any way you look at it, babe."

"No, Liz, it isn't." He rose and rounded the table to squat next to her chair. "I was an elder for the Council. Part of those duties included spying. It's second nature to hide who I am to protect those I care about. My relationship to Franco has no bearing on my feelings for you." He studied her closed expression and prayed to the Goddess she would understand. "Please, *qalbi*. Please know it wasn't intentional."

"At any time over the last two months I was dating him, you could've told me you were related. Honestly, the ew factor is high here. I kissed him, for fuck's sake! It's practically *incestuous*."

"Incestuous would make him your cousin, not mine." He almost laughed at her indignation. Not quite, but almost. The desire was strong when her eyes flashed fire. His gaze dropped to her mouth. "Besides, he and I aren't blood-related, and the quick pecks you gave him were not real kisses. Nothing like what we've shared."

"And what if Franco and I had gotten farther along in our intimacies?"

Again, his desire to laugh was strong. She sounded like an outraged maiden, and he knew she was far from that. He pressed his lips together and shook his head. "You were never going to get to that stage with him or anyone, *qalbi*. Remember the spell I cast to drive men away?" Rafe allowed a small smirk. "I doubled up on Franco."

"I thought that was only for Franco!" She shoved him—*hard*.

Landing on his ass, he let loose a groan.

"Oh!" Liz came out of the chair and knelt beside him. "Are you okay?"

Wrapping his arms around her, he tumbled them both onto the oversized French Aubusson rug. "I am now."

She lay beneath him with her golden hair spread around her like a halo. The deep pink of her parted lips was rivaled by the flush on her cheeks. But it was her amber eyes, so bright and focused on him, that held him captive. Had she truly been hurt or disillusioned with him, they would've darkened to a burnt umber color.

"Forgive me, *qalbi*. My family connections aren't what's important here. *You* are. If I lost your love…" He swallowed past the lump forming in his throat and let his eyes speak the words he couldn't voice.

Miracle of miracles, her expression eased, and she traced a fingertip over his lower lip. "Is there anything else I should know?"

"I'm not sure. I can't quite think when you touch me that way."

Her light laugh chased away the last of his worry. They would be all right. They had to be. Without her, life was a dull, endless stream of nothingness. Not even the spy game could keep his interest.

The amusement vanished from her face. "I mean it, Rafe. No more lies. Not on purpose, and not by omission."

"My family could very well be behind what's happening with yours, Liz. But I can promise you, I have nothing to do with any of this and knew even less than nothing prior to discovering Franco was behind it." He sat up and pulled her with him. "Marguerite Champeau is my cousin as well. She may also be involved."

"What will you do if it comes down to my family or yours, Rafe? Make no mistake, if more than just Franco is behind this, we will be at war. Whose side will you take in the feud?"

"Yours," he assured her. "Always yours."

She closed her eyes and dropped her forehead against his chest. "I'd hoped you'd say that."

When Rafe would've kissed her, a muffled sound came from the other side of the study door. "What the hell?"

"My cousins are notorious for listening in on conversations. Usually, they scry, but since their magic is gone, I imagine it's lurking at keyholes now." Liz placed her index finger against her lip and rose to her feet. As silently as a cat, she padded to the door and whipped it open.

Sure enough, three of the four Thorne sisters stumbled into the room.

"What do you busybodies have to say for yourself?" Liz's voice was as stern as a schoolmarm.

Spring and Winnie had the grace to look embarrassed, but Autumn simply shrugged and said, "Hallmark."

Having no idea what it meant, Rafe was confused when the women began laughing. He rolled to his feet and gestured to the table with a thumb over his shoulder. "Now that you're all here and apparently looking for something productive to do, how about we finish going through these books to write down possible magic-stealing suspects?"

Liz whipped back around to stare. "I thought you were positive Franco masterminded this whole thing?"

"Have you met that weasel? He couldn't mastermind his way out of a cardboard box."

She covered her mouth to stifle her amusement. When she had control, she crossed to the table and took a seat. "Let's figure out who *is* in charge."

FROM HIS VANTAGE POINT IN THE LOFT, ALASTAIR WATCHED THE NEXT generation of Thornes and their significant others where they were gathered around the gleaming hardwood meeting table in his study. They occasionally talked over each other as they learned new information. Each one excited to discover more about the descendants of the first six families.

"I suspect you know exactly who is behind this, darling. Why are you letting them waste their time?"

He glanced over his shoulder and smiled at his future bride. All these years later, and his Rorie still understood him better than any other living soul. Looking away from her delicate beauty was difficult, but he managed with a tilt of his chin toward the group. "Watch."

For a few minutes, they remained silent as they observed the others.

"What am I supposed to be seeing?"

"They are developing a camaraderie, my love. Learning to work as a unit and to depend on one another. It will serve them well after we're gone."

One of her black brows lifted, and her sky-blue eyes took on a light of curiosity. "Are we planning on dying anytime soon?"

He leaned sideways and placed a lingering kiss on her rosebud mouth. "Would I willingly give this up?"

"You had me worried there for a moment, you old rogue."

He felt his lips twitch, and he gathered her close.

She tilted her head back to study him. "Are you feeling senti-mental, darling?"

"Maybe a little." He sighed and released her to rest an elbow on the railing. "I can't explain what it was like to feel helpless, Rorie. To not have an inkling of what people were thinking or feeling. It was a wake-up call." He shook his head, but kept his gaze focused on Rafe. "I wasn't sure until today that I could trust him one-hundred percent, and I didn't like the uncertainty."

"He loves her, Alastair. He would never do anything to hurt her or, by extension, us."

"I know."

"What did Damian say about the spell from the Book of Shadows?"

"It's a straightforward ceremony for him. Apparently, he doesn't need anyone else's help to raise and draw from the magic of the standing stones. He also made sure to tell me in no uncertain terms he wasn't happy to be returning so soon since he just settled Sabrina in bed for the night."

"I remember when Summer and Holly were babies. You were a virtual bear if someone woke them after you'd put them down."

"Remember how easily Preston was able to soothe Summer when neither of us could?" Even he heard the sadness in his own voice. Goddess, he missed his brother. Sure, they'd been at odds for a great many years, but even in the midst of their war with each other, they always had each other's backs against the outside world.

"Darling, you're frightening me. First, you speak of our eventual demise, then this talk of Preston. What's gotten into you?"

"We live longer than mere mortals, Rorie. Do you ever get tired? Wonder if it's natural for us to survive to the ripe old age we do? Why are we graced with all we are when there is true suffering in the world?"

"Are you saying we've never suffered?" Her tone took on a harsh quality, and Aurora's irritation could be felt in the farthest depths of Alastair's cells. "I'll call bullshit on that. We both suffered plenty. I missed out on nearly two decades of my children's lives. And you, beyond all reason and hope, visited and cared for my shell of a body. Every bloody day of every bloody year *for all that time*. What is that if not suffering?"

"Please calm yourself, my love. I'm not ungrateful for what we have. I'm simply expressing my fatigue at yet another battle to keep it." He embraced her and chuckled when she half-heartedly shoved at his chest. "Too piqued for a little kiss?"

"You don't deserve one, you wretch. You made me believe you were ready to sacrifice yourself to end it all."

"Never. I have a healthy sense of self-preservation. Besides, you'd bring me back to kill me if I don't make good and marry you after all these years."

"Precisely." She settled her dark head against his shoulder. "Now, tell me what you intend to do to hasten Liz's and Rafe's relationship and defeat those horrid, magic-stealing trolls."

"Damian will return to activate the stones. Afterwards, it's up to us to clean this mess up."

Her worried blue eyes shifted to the group around the table below. "I worry Liz is too kindhearted to do what must be done."

"I don't. She's a fire elemental, my love. She has hidden depths."

CHAPTER 18

"*L*ook here!"

Everyone faced Spring. Her bright jade eyes were lit with excitement. "There was once a witch by the name of Isolde de Thorne."

"Oh-kaay. What does this mean to us, and why do we care?" Although her words contained a heavy dose of sarcasm, Autumn shoved a piece of paper between the pages of the tome she'd been studying and turned all her attention on her youngest sister.

"You don't understand, Tums. I've never read that name before. *Ever.*"

Rafe searched the faces around him. They all seemed to be shocked. "I don't understand."

Autumn was the first to respond. "What Witch-ipedia is trying to say, is that she has our family grimoire memorized. Everyone born to our line from the beginning of time is documented. If this Isolde de Thorne doesn't show up on its pages, she shouldn't exist."

"And yet, she does. Or did," Spring added excitedly. "Look here..." She pointed to an entry beside the name. "It has a notation in the margin. 'Enchantress.' That's it. One word."

129

Knox crowded in beside her and read the entry. "I've never heard the term used in my lifetime. What does it mean?"

"The term enchantress is used in relation to witches practicing outside the normal boundaries of magic. They pull from any source available to amass power. Think the equivalent of a female demon, or better yet, a succubus."

"Do they actually exist?" Liz asked.

"In theory. Though I've never actually read any accounts of one in my studies." Spring shrugged. "Anyway, an enchantress was known to be seductive and would use her wiles to lure in other witches and warlocks."

Rafe scratched the stubble forming on his jaw. "Then they created evil covens?"

"No. Not necessarily," Spring said. "Enchantresses were notorious for surrounding themselves with those willing to serve her—minions, if you will. These people would do anything for their queen, even at the cost of their own magic and, in some cases, lives."

"*Christ!*"

When Spring patted Knox's arm as if to console him, Rafe glanced at Liz. A troubled expression settled upon her features. "*Qalbi?*"

She shook her head and focused on Spring. "Do they have the same life span as, say, one of us?"

"No! That's the cool thing about it. They lived hundreds and hundreds of years, never aging." Spring ran a finger along the entry and tapped it. "There's no death recorded for her."

"What was her date of birth?" Rafe asked, his own unease spiking.

"April fourth, fourteen-fifty-four."

"If she was still alive, she'd be five-hundred and sixty-six years old!" Summer looked from one of her siblings to another. "If an enchantress can live hundreds of years, what happened to Isolde? Is it possible she's still alive?"

"*No.*"

Their group turned to gape at the newcomer in the entryway. Damian Dethridge had returned, and he didn't look happy.

Rafe rose because remaining seated around the Aether while the other man was standing made him uncomfortable as hell. "What do you know, Damian?"

"Isolde was my mother," he said flatly.

Mainly due to the fact that his legs didn't want to support him anymore, Rafe sat. He noticed Liz's wince at the thud his body made when it impacted the parson chair. Not an easy thing to do, considering the chair was padded.

Only Spring retained her bright-eyed curiosity. "She was a female Aether?"

"Yes. But it should be noted, not all enchantresses are Aethers. They are simply witches who crave more power than they possess. But my mother was the last enchantress of record. If another existed, she remained under the Council's radar."

Spring's jade eyes rounded in awe. "Wait! That makes you a Thorne by blood. Our cousin, if I'm not mistaken."

Damian nodded. "Technically, but many, many times removed."

"How old are you? I assumed you were around Alastair's age or a little younger."

Hearing the tremble in Liz's voice, Rafe reached for her hand and squeezed. It was disconcerting to realize they truly knew nothing about the man who'd been helping them. *Did Alastair know?*

The Aether turned his black-eyed stare on him. "Yes."

The fact Damian had seemingly read Rafe's mind with little effort was creepy as hell.

With a heavy sigh, the Aether stepped farther into the room and looked upward. All eyes followed Damian's gaze to the couple in the loft. "I suppose you should join this little party now, Al."

"You're doing so well with your explanations, Dethridge."

A half-smile curled Damian's lips. "Nevertheless, I need a drink from your private selection."

"Your wish is my command, my friend."

Looking like he'd rather be anywhere but where he was, Damian approached their table and took a seat at the far end, closest to the wall. "I suppose a lengthy explanation is in order." He held out his hand for the book in Spring's grasp. When he had it in his possession, he casually flipped back a page and read the entries there. "Hmm. Interesting stuff."

"Why isn't your name listed under Isolde's as her offspring?" Spring asked.

"I don't know. That's a question for Alastair. He's the record keeper, if I'm not mistaken."

"Uncle?"

Alastair placed a tumbler of Glenfiddich in front of Damian. "It's been in an effort to protect you. It will magically appear once you're deceased."

"Protect him?" Rafe snorted his disbelief. "Why would he need protecting, and what can be gained from the knowledge he's your cousin?"

"I believe you just answered your own question, Xuereb." Damian's brows lifted, and he silently waited for Rafe to figure it out.

"For the blood, babe," Liz inserted softly. She patted his arm then turned her attention to the two warlocks at the end of the table. "Am I mistaken?"

"No. Not at all. If it were known I was a Thorne, all of you would be in more danger than you already are at present. If enemies weren't trying to use you as bargaining chips, then they might try to empty your veins for blood magic against me."

Autumn, who had remained unnaturally silent until that moment, spoke. "Why are you telling us now? Aren't you worried about loose lips sinking ships?"

"Perhaps a little. But you all have more to lose than I do. I'm the Aether. It will take a lot to defeat me." He shrugged.

The words might've sounded arrogant coming from anyone else, but Rafe understood Damian wasn't bragging. He was simply stating a fact.

"Your gestures should've tipped me off," Liz said with a soft snort.

"How so?"

"You and Alastair tilt your heads the same way. Also, you both straighten your cuffs when you're trying to be nonchalant." She grinned. "It's your coloring that threw me off, but side by side as you are right now, the resemblance is there."

Alastair laughed and clapped Damian on the shoulder. "She's too clever by far."

"You never answered me in regards to your age. How old was Isolde when you were born? Can an Aether live hundreds of years like the Enchantress did?"

Damian's mouth twisted in a sign of distaste. "Age is just a mindset for our kind, child."

"Are you sensitive about it?"

He gave Liz a look of disgust. "You're going to badger me until I tell you, aren't you?"

"Pretty much," Rafe muttered. It earned him a poke in the side.

"I was born in eighteen-twenty. I'll let you do the math."

Shocked silence met Damian's statement. Only Alastair didn't look surprised.

"That's fantastic!" Spring broke the spell holding them still when she clapped her hands.

"I'm glad you approve." Damian gave her an indulgent smile. "So how about we work on a foolproof plan to restore your magic?"

During their brainstorming session, Liz kept sneaking glances at Damian. Finally, she spoke. "This is a shot in the dark, but do you think Franco somehow guessed who you are? Like maybe he targeted us to get to you?"

"I don't see how, but anything is possible."

Rafe gave her a considering look. "What would be his ultimate goal?"

"Remember what Petey said? He told us Franco wanted to drain us to fuel another source."

"That's right!"

"What if he meant another witch? Or perhaps an enchantress? Could another Aether exist?"

"One *could* exist—Sabrina is a prime example of two Aethers living at once. However, only one can be all-powerful as decreed by the Goddess, and they are almost always from the same bloodline," Alastair explained. "Isolde was a Thorne through her father's line, but a Dethridge through her mother's side."

"How did you come to use the name Dethridge?" Liz asked Damian, curious about the family dynamic. "Shouldn't you go by Thorne?"

"Mother was married to her second cousin, Damaris Dethridge."

"Remember, child, in those days, love matches weren't all the rage like today." Alastair smiled down at her. "The Dethridge family was extremely rich and influential at the time. As one of the founding families..." He trailed off and turned to stare at Damian. "*A new threat rises from the old.*' Could it be...?"

Leaving mid-thought, Alastair went back to the table and began thumbing through the books until it appeared he found what he was searching for.

"Spring is right. There's no death date for Isolde. I don't know how I never noticed before." His cold-eyed stare focused on Damian. "Care to explain?"

The air in the room took on a distinct chill when Damian rose to his feet. "Leave it alone, Alastair."

"I don't think so, Damian. I was a kid, but I still remember the horror stories about your mother's reign as Aether."

"The problem was contained."

There was an edgy, dangerous quality to Damian. A single glance around the others at the table let Liz know this showdown was making everyone nervous.

"Contained?" Dread entered Alastair's sapphire eyes. "Dead and contained have vastly different definitions, my friend."

It was Damian who conceded the field first. "Isolde was entombed when I was a few years older than Sabrina. It required Isis along with the strongest members from all the original families combined—from *both* sides of the veil. Isolde was nearly unstoppable."

"What was she like?" Spring, always curious, asked.

"Magnificent. A more beautiful woman, I've yet to see. She was seductive to both men and women. A terrible mother, though." Sadness flashed in his eyes just before he closed them. "I've tried to remember if there was ever more than an ounce of kindness in her heart for me. Or really for anyone. There wasn't, not that I can recall." He cleared his throat and straightened his cuffs.

"I'm sorry." Summer looked as if her heart were breaking for him. And perhaps it was. She was kindness personified. Maybe it was because she was a veterinarian and it came naturally to her, or perhaps she happened to have a heart as wide as the Atlantic Ocean, but Summer had a soft spot for wounded beings.

"It was a long time ago, dear." Damian smiled, soft and sweet, in her direction, and every woman at their table sighed. It wasn't only his mother who had the ability to seduce.

Liz idly wondered what it was like to be the recipient of his love. The intensity of his attention would probably be overwhelming. Had Vivian felt that? Was that part of the reason she'd taken off?

Across the distance of the wooden table, Damian met her thoughtful gaze with one of his own. "If you have questions, just ask, Liz."

"They are of a personal nature and have nothing to do with this discussion."

Her response had Rafe whipping his head in her direction.

She denied the unspoken question. "Not like that!"

"Where is Isolde contained, Damian?" Knox asked, helping to divert everyone's attention from Liz's burning face.

"I won't reveal the location. It's too dangerous. If someone takes it into their head to resurrect her, it might mean death to us all. Sabrina and myself included. That's a risk I won't take."

Liz leaned forward and captured Damian's eye. "I asked you earlier about the darkness we encountered at Ravenswood. Could it have to do with Isolde?"

"Saying no is foolish. Like I stated earlier, anything is possible. But I can't see how. We're talking close to two hundred years. If she isn't deceased—as I sincerely hope, then she's definitely too weak for astral projection."

"And yet, something keeps trying to penetrate the wards surrounding Sabrina," Liz said softly. Poking and prodding to get answers wasn't normally her way, but she was tired of people holding back vital information to their current circumstances. If it required angering Damian, she would, though she doubted he was the type to do more than shoot a cutting remark her way to discourage more questions.

"What would be the purpose, cousin?" Autumn asked her. "If someone knows Isolde was entombed, they would also know why. By bringing an enchantress back to life, or from the brink of death, they would risk their own lives. She'd need an immediate power infusion."

"Exactly, and having seen my mother in action, she would spare no one." Damian shook his head. "I don't know why anyone would do it."

Liz's hands tightened into fists. She had a strong sense nothing in the fiasco was as it seemed. "Franco might know."

"Indeed, he might." He nodded. "He could also lead us to whomever is in cahoots with him."

"Actually, I'm pretty positive it's the Champeaus." Alastair shrugged nonchalantly when everyone turned their attention from Damian to him. He held up a finger for each point he made. "One, there is no love lost between our two families. So it would stand to reason they might want us taken down a notch or two. Two, it's no secret their primary goal in life is to amass power, and they don't care what it costs the witch community. Three, they—"

"They are the only ones insane enough to believe they can resurrect an enchantress to destroy their greatest enemy and think they can get away unscathed," Rafe finished for him. "If they used their collective power and, with the help of Franco, targeted the Thornes through Liz, they could pull enough magic to feed Isolde what she needs to revive her."

Alastair nodded, giving Rafe an approving look. "Exactly so."

Liz's stomach dropped somewhere around her big toe. She hated the idea that Franco had used her to hurt her family. If only they were able to return to normal, then she would honor a promise to herself to never be as trusting with strangers again. She shot a searching look Rafe's way. Her gaze was met with his direct, dark-eyed stare. Was he hiding anything else, and should she take his explanation of the Champeau connection at face value? When would she stop making decisions from her heart and start protecting the family from her poor choices? She dropped her gaze and left the room.

CHAPTER 19

*T*wenty minutes later, Liz opened the door to Rafe and found a solemn, regretful man.

"Liz." His raspy tone said it all, but the worry written on his face spoke volumes. Standing back, she allowed him entry.

"Are we okay?" The hoarseness in his voice gave her heart a pang.

"I just need a little while to come to grips with all of this, babe."

"What can I do to help?"

"I don't know that you can." Upon seeing his deepening frown, she said, "The second I said yes to dinner the other night was the moment my family's collective magic disappeared. Then I find out your mother is, if not an enemy of the Thornes, certainly not a bosom buddy." She threw up her hands, unable to voice her true worry: that she was being played by Rafe. "I make poor choices. I don't know if I'm making another one."

"I see." The tone of his voice sounded as crushed as the expression he wore.

"I don't know if you do. I love you, Rafe. Wholeheartedly. And though I want to love you without reservations, I'd be lying if I said I didn't have any. Wouldn't I be a fool not to?" She took his hands and felt his inner turmoil. Had Sabrina's gift of insight actually been a curse? Because while she could experience his discontent, she had no way of knowing what caused it. Finally, she said, "It's in your nature to be reticent and hide information. You've done it your entire life, and I get that. But I'm worried. I need this ceremony of Damian's to work, and I need to know my family is safe before you and I pick up where we left off."

The weight of his searching gaze was heavy.

"I'm not rejecting you," she said softly. "I'm just putting on the brakes on our romance until this is resolved."

Still, he remained silent, and she had a very real fear that he'd wash his hands of this mess and leave them to sort it all on their own. Yet she had to believe slowing down was for the best at the moment. Distractions while the future well-being of her family was at stake could have deadly consequences.

"Don't hate me for being wishy-washy."

"*Qalbi.*" He shook his head. "I could never hate you for any reason. You hold my heart in your delicate hands. It's yours to do with what you will, but I'm trying to find a way to convince you not to send me away."

"I don't want you to go, but I keep asking myself, how does this not put you in direct conflict with your mother's family?"

"It absolutely does. However, if they are part of a scheme to hurt you, then I'm not interested in being related to the Champeaus anymore. I believed we settled this in the library earlier. What I said was what I meant." He gave her fingers a light squeeze. "The theory about Isolde's resurrection is all conjuncture at this point. One thing we know for certain, Franco is responsible for the stealing of your power. I intend to rectify that."

Unease rippled along her nerve endings. "Not alone, you aren't. If he's to be stopped, we do this together."

A sad smile twisted his lips. "How can you be certain I'm not leading you into a trap should I take you with me to France?"

"I think you know by now, Alastair and Damian would team up to kill you." She grinned to take the sting from her words. "Besides,

I'm getting a little pissy over this whole issue. I want revenge on Franco for the mischief he's caused, and I get the impression you're not a fan of his either."

"Nope. Can't stand the little toad. He's been a pain in my ass since the day we were introduced." Rafe shifted and traced a thumb over her lower lip. "Are we solid, *qalbi*? Please tell me my omission didn't bring about the end of what we could've had."

"No, it didn't. But please don't be offended if I seem suspicious. I honestly don't know who to trust at this point other than my family."

"It's late, but Alastair is determined to hold the restoration ceremony. Are you ready to lend your magic to the cause?"

"Of course. I'm going to take a bath and center myself. I'll be out shortly."

"If you need help scrubbing your back—or other parts—we can circle back around to applying the brakes to our relationship."

The gravely quality in his voice told her he was as aroused by the idea as she was. Half of her was cheering his suggestion and wondering why she was so dumb as to suggest slowing down until this mess was over. The other half threw up her hands in defeat. Cautious Liz Brain knew she didn't stand a chance of resisting when Rafe looked at her with those wicked bedroom eyes packed full of heat.

His mouth quirked as if he could see the thoughts in her brain. And maybe he could because the warmth working its way to her cheeks was a major tell.

"We don't have time." The huskiness in her voice couldn't be mistaken for anything other than desire. Every cell in her body was overheating and suffused with need for the devilishly sexy man standing before her.

He grinned. "But we have plenty of time to kiss."

"Yes," she whispered.

As he leaned forward, a knock interrupted them for the umpteenth time.

"Do you ever get the feeling everyone is conspiring against us to prevent this from happening?"

A laugh escaped her. "Do you ever get the feeling maybe this is your Karma for casting the spell against any man who wished to kiss me?"

He looked as if she'd knocked him upside the head. "I need to revisit my spell. Perhaps it's a side effect."

"Do as you will, and it harm none," they said in unison.

She nodded. "Spells can come back upon the caster threefold. You'd better find a way to fix this, or we are going to be sexually frustrated for a long time to come."

His deep chuckle made her warm. "It's first on my agenda. I can't have you sexually frustrated, *qalbi*."

"Nor do I want to be." She sighed heavily. "Should we see who is banging the door down."

"Don't mention banging when I'm hanging by a thread here."

Laughing, she crossed the room to answer her persistent visitor.

"Sorry to interrupt, but Alastair has called everyone together to head to the clearing." Holly had an apologetic look on her face while Quentin stood behind her, grinning like a demented fool. *He* had no remorse for the intrusion.

"We're on our way. Can I take five minutes to meditate?"

"Is that what they're calling a quickie these days?" he teased.

Holly lightly elbowed him in the stomach. "Don't pay attention to him. His mind is always in the gutter."

Quentin enveloped his wife from behind and placed a lingering kiss alongside the column of her throat. "Yes, it is. How can it not be when I find you so delicious, my prickly pear?"

Liz felt Rafe approach from behind. "Looks like we're not the only ones who could use more time before the ceremony," he murmured into her ear.

With a snort, she closed the door and admonished Rafe. "Don't, or we aren't leaving this room."

"That would be my fondest wish, *qalbi*."

"Oh, to hell with it!" She grabbed his face in both hands and tugged his head down.

"Now, Liz!" Holly shouted through the wooden-paneled door.

"Dammit!"

Rafe gave her a quick peck on the lips. "After," he promised. "Let's go get this over with."

"Dammit!" Liz repeated with no less heat.

———

"THE ENERGY IN THIS GLEN IS MAGNIFICENT," DAMIAN SAID. THERE was a reverence in his voice, as if he'd never seen anything like their clearing before. Liz didn't understand how a two-hundred-year-old had never been to a magical holy place.

"Do all of you feel the vibrations of the stones?"

"Only when they are awake and above ground," Alastair answered him.

Damian grunted and walked the entire circle where the enchanted pillars rested, stopping above each, closing his eyes, and tilting his head. Liz received the distinct impression he heard something none of the rest of them did. The smile on his face spoke of pure bliss, and she was loathe to bother him with all the questions crowding her brain.

"What's he doing?" Rafe had pitched his voice low so only she and Alastair could hear.

"If I didn't know better, I'd say he's readying himself to make love to the stones," her cousin muttered.

Liz choked on her laughter. Never before had she heard Alastair use sarcasm in such a way. The sound of her merriment caught the Aether's attention. He turned a sardonic grin their way.

"Patience, Al," he called.

"Tell me when you're done orgasming over this clearing, Dethridge, so we can get this ceremony started."

"Watch it, or I'll take your powers back and leave you a miserable sod for your remaining days."

"Your lovely daughter made sure that couldn't happen," Alastair retorted.

"She made sure it couldn't happen for other witches, warlocks, or Blockers. Not me." Damian grinned evilly. "Never me."

"Bloody bugger."

"Don't take this the wrong way, cousin, but I absolutely love that he gets the better of you on occasion." Liz was sure to show him her teasing smile. "It's like you've met your match."

Aurora placed her chin on his shoulder. "Some would say he met his match with me, close to forty years ago."

Alastair turned and pulled her into his embrace. "And they would be right. The perfect match for me."

"Smooth talker." But Aurora didn't look put out in the least. Suddenly, she became serious. "We need to get this over with, darling. We're too exposed."

"Noted." Raising his voice, Alastair called to Damian, who was across the clearing, absorbing whatever energy the standing stone could provide from beneath him. "We need to start, Damian."

Liz saw the Aether's shoulders rise and fall in a deep sigh. He gave the ground one last longing look.

"Just wait until they are lit with your magic, my friend."

"Take your places around the inside perimeter," Damian called to them. "Anyone whose power is intact, stay to the outside until the pillars are pulsing with life. When that happens, I want you to step inside the circle and join hands with the rest of your kin or loved ones."

Alastair directed everyone into positions as the Aether required, then took his place between Liz and Aurora outside the circle.

Damian jumped up onto the flat rock altar and spun in a slow circle, his hands raised with palms downward, parallel to the ground. There was no need for him to speak; it was as if the earth heard his intent. The ground beneath them rumbled and parted for the pillars to make an appearance. They rose faster and louder than Liz had ever seen before.

The standing stones were breathtaking. Always leaving her in awe when she witnessed their majestic beauty. Jagged formations that stood at least a story high and as thick as two men side by side. They were partially green with age. A glance showed the Aether with his head back, as if he were worshiping the night sky overhead. A wide smile seemed to cover half his face.

Talk about majestic beauty.

Liz seemed to forget to breathe as she watched him. A check of those present showed the other women did, too. Did he seduce without even trying? The longing tugging at her insides was disconcerting. All she wanted to do was go to him and kneel at his feet. A glance toward Alastair showed he was observing the process with a slight frown. Across the short distance, he sensed her regard and shot her a questioning look. With a tilt of her head toward Damian and a point of her finger toward her closest female relative, she raised her brows in question.

Silent laughter shook Alastair's muscular frame. The wide grin reassured Liz as nothing else could. She wouldn't question the odd attraction if her cousin thought it was normal.

With her focus back on Damian, Liz watched as he jumped down from the altar and moved to the nearest pillar. He ran his fingers over the largest symbol, level with his head, tracing what appeared to be a teardrop with squiggly lines below it. White light poured from every etched carving on the stone. He basked in the brightness for a moment then walked to the next rock formation and repeated the action. By the time the Aether had completed the entire circle, Liz was sure the glow could be seen from space. Someone at the NASA headquarters was freaking out right about now.

"Enter," Damian commanded.

Liz's will disappeared, and she felt compelled to move forward. Trepidation caused goosebumps on her exposed flesh. Heart racing, she crossed to stand between two family members and clasped their outstretched hands.

"Remain joined, no matter what," he ordered, and his voice was that of a God—deep and dark, reaching inside the mind as it caressed the soul.

"Redono!"

He flung his hands outward, and blue-tipped flames flew from his fingertips, followed by a cobalt-blue arc of light. It hit Autumn squarely in the chest, causing her to arch her body, her head dropping backward. Mouth open in a silent scream. One by one, Damian shot a current through those without their magic, with a similar reaction.

Because they were all linked by a magical connection at this point, Liz couldn't drop her hands even if she wanted to. The ripple of energy swept through their circle too quickly. And while she felt the initial jolt, it wasn't painful. The cells of her body absorbed the power, and her head fell back like the others, but not in agony as she feared. Instead, the surge reached in and caressed every inch of her like a lover. She released a silent gasp and shuddered at the pure ecstasy. Her eyes rolled back as her eyelids drifted shut. The desire to moan nearly overwhelmed her in its intensity. Her body tightened, and her heart raced as pleasure infused her.

"Holy hell!" Autumn shook her head and stared at the Aether in awe. "I don't know what you just did to me, but can I get another ticket for that ride?"

A bubble of laughter welled inside Liz, and she released it on the wind. The others joined in as Damian smiled in smug satisfaction.

"That, my lovelies, is what if feels like to be part of something greater. Covens of old had similar physical responses when they held ceremonies."

When the joy of the restoration spell subsided, he encouraged those whose powers had been stolen to conjure an item of their choosing. Relief flooded the faces of every Thorne present when their magic worked.

Liz imagined she could hear Franco's screams of rage from his home in France, the little peckerhead.

CHAPTER 20

*P*aris. This was the first time Liz had set foot back on French soil since Rafe had disappeared from her life years before. The magnificence of the Eiffel Tower was as she remembered and could be seen from the terrace of the penthouse suite. Such an awe-inspiring sight.

The sound of the city drifted up from below as she drank her late-morning coffee and half-listened to Rafe's conversation with Alastair in regards to Franco Moreau. She wasn't worried she was missing anything important, because any serious discussion would take place when the remaining Thornes arrived in a few hours.

Paris. The city of love.

For her, it definitely had been.

She shot a glance in Rafe's direction where he stood at the railing, overlooking the street. Did he do it subconsciously? Was he programmed to always be on alert for danger? She suspected he was. As she watched, he crossed his legs at the ankles and downed the espresso from the small cup he held. The gesture spoke of his European upbringing. Only someone who had resided in Italy would close their eyes and unabashedly savor the richness of the brew from the delicate porcelain that seemed too small for his large hands. Although his stature wasn't small and his muscles rippled with every movement, Rafe had a casual elegance about him, and it appealed to Liz on every level. If they met today for the first time, she'd still find it difficult to tear her eyes away from the stunning picture he made.

He chose that moment to look her way. The slow, warm smile curled her bare toes. Goddess, he took her breath away. His current expression was the same one she'd seen on his face when she'd first encountered him at the base of the Eiffel Tower four years ago. No wonder her head had been turned and they'd never left the bedroom! She wanted to send Alastair away and drag Rafe into her suite for a replay of those three sinfully sensual days.

His smile widened at something Alastair said, right before he laughed. The sound was rich and vibrant, just like the man himself. And although Liz didn't hear what was said, she couldn't help but smile in return. His joyful response spoke to some lonely part deep inside her. Wouldn't it be wonderful to spend her life with this man, basking in love and laughter every single day?

Yes.

His midnight eyes bore into her with such an intensity, it made her squirm where she sat. Did her face reveal her thoughts? Her eyes, her longing?

"I'll pop back by when the rest of our family arrives. Shall we have a late lunch here on the terrace?" Alastair excused himself with little fanfare and only a slight knowing smirk on his handsome face after Liz nodded absently.

"I thought he'd never leave," Rafe quipped. The huskiness in his voice sent a shiver along her spine and caressed the exposed skin of her arms and legs. "Since we never had time to reconnect last night, should we use this opportunity to do so now?"

"Reconnect? Is that a euphemism for sex, babe?"

"The party lasted well into the night, and I needed to wake early to correct my anti-kissing spell." He set the tiny cup in its saucer and placed it on the wrought-iron table. "I don't believe we had our promised kiss."

"You don't believe? As in you don't remember?" Liz leaned back in her chair and crossed her arms. "Should I be insulted?"

His deep chuckle thrilled her. "Not at all, *qalbi*. I recall every second about our time together. Both then and now."

She got the distinct feeling he was speaking about their first time in France, and not last night's party.

He stretched out a hand, and after she placed hers in his, helped her to her feet. "You should only be insulted if we *had* kissed and I didn't remember."

"Mmhmm."

"I'd like to discuss what comes next in our relationship, Liz."

The serious turn of their conversation wasn't expected, and she didn't know exactly how to respond. He'd asked her to marry him and she'd agreed, but it was on the condition he was holding nothing back. Yet he had.

"Shouldn't we hold off on important topics for when this whole mess is settled?" she prevaricated. "I mean—" Her words dried up, and her thoughts scrambled as Rafe's mouth descended on hers. Her moan may have been from the contact with his chest or from finally being able to touch him like she wanted, but either way, the sensation was delicious.

And when she had the chance to inhale a deep breath, the unique, spicy fragrance of his skin created a heady sensation and made her mouth practically water. He fed her soul, this man. There wasn't a moment spent with him that didn't make her heart whole and happy. Despite any challenges they would face, she wanted him by her side. All trust issues fell away as he took her hand and led her from the terrace toward the bedroom.

He paused halfway there as if he couldn't stand not to kiss her again, and when he lifted his head after giving into the urge, he said, "This. This comes next."

"Yeah, I'm cool with that."

His wicked grin made her knees wobbly.

"I think this is where you sweep the damsel up into your arms and carry her to bed because she's weak-kneed and can't seem to walk on her own," she said, only half teasingly.

"That would be my fondest wish, *qalbi*."

"Goddess, you say the sweetest things."

He laughed even as he bent to scoop her up. As she wrapped her arms around his neck, Liz realized there was nowhere else she'd rather be. If they could spend their remaining days like this, she'd die happy.

"What are you thinking about?" Rafe rubbed his nose lightly against hers.

"You. Me. Us—like this, forever."

"Mmm. I like the way you think."

"I missed you, Rafe."

He paused and frowned down at her. "I've always been here."

"No. I mean *us*. Like this." Placing a hand over his heart, she felt his pulse speed up. Perhaps he was nervous about the next thing coming out of her mouth, or maybe it was due to his excitement for what was to happen, she couldn't be sure. But she liked her effect on him.

"Like I said, I've always been here. I've been waiting for you to remember what we shared and reach for it again," he said softly. His cool confidence assured Liz he spoke the truth. She silently called herself all kinds of fool for rejecting his overtures over the last year.

With the utmost care, he laid her on the bed. One by one, he unbuttoned the fastenings on his shirt, exposing his beautiful olive skin. Liz's eyes trailed over the muscled contours of his wide chest and dropped to admire the rock-hard ridges of his chiseled abs. Delicious and drool-worthy. They were the only two words to describe him. There wasn't an inch of Rafe that wasn't desirable and the stuff of dreams.

As he shucked his clothes and stood naked before her, Liz got her first peek of the healed bullet hole and fought the urge to cry. No one would've known to inform her had Zhu Lin succeeded in killing him.

"*Qalbi*."

She lifted her head from where she stared at the wound to meet his warm, dark eyes.

"I'm here."

The tears fell. They reached for each other at the same time, each seeking what only the other could provide.

"I love you, Rafe. I hate the fact we lost those years."

"On this, we are in full agreement."

When she would've made short work of her clothing, he halted her hands and took over. His long, lean fingers teased the bare skin beneath her dress as he inched it upward. A warm tingling began in her thighs, and she had the overwhelming impulse to press them together, which was in direct contrast with her desire for him to intimately touch her. As quickly as she started, she wanted to put on the brakes.

Maybe he felt the tension in her body, or maybe he witnessed her brief bout of confusion, but Rafe eased his hand from beneath the skirt of her dress. "We can go as fast or as slow as you wish, Liz."

Taking his hand, she returned it to the spot he'd been caressing. "The last person I was with was you. My nerves got the better of me." She dropped her eyes and brushed the fine hair on the back of his wrists. "What if I'm…"

"What if you're what? Reserved? Rusty? Too passionate and will break me in half in your enthusiasm?"

She laughed at the ridiculousness of his statement. "I feel like I only come alive for you, Rafe. As if you're the one who wakes the sleeping beast within me, but I'm afraid of that person. She's wild and uncontrollable."

"*Qalbi*, this is not turning me off." He shifted to lift her on top of him, with her legs bent and thighs straddling his hips. "In fact, you're speaking my love language." Shifting his hips, he asked, "Can you feel what you do to me? Let your freak flag fly, I always say."

Again, she laughed. "You do not always say that."

"For sure, I will from now on."

All the tension left her body, and when he eased the side zipper of her dress down, Liz didn't object. And when he slowly peeled the straps from her shoulders, she moved to allow him easier access.

He sucked in his breath at her bared breasts. "For the love of the Goddess, you are stunning."

The skin from her chest to her cheeks warmed. Rafe chuckled even as he cupped her. "You're cute when you're embarrassed." Running his thumbs lightly over her erect nipples, he sighed. "I could lie here the rest of my life like this."

"I believe you said much the same thing once before."

"I remember. What I didn't recall was exactly how perfect the weight of your glorious breasts feel in my hands. How your skin is so petal-soft." Guiding her downward, he kissed her nipple before capturing it between his teeth for a light bite.

She bit back her moan of pleasure, and Rafe paused in his ministrations.

"Oh, no, *qalbi*. There's no holding back—for either of us."

He wrapped a hand around the nape of her neck and dragged her lips down to meet his. The contact sparked the long-banked fire inside her, causing it to rage out of control. Needing no more encouragement, Liz took charge of their kiss. Tasting him, stroking him with her tongue as she trailed her fingers up and down his penis to tease a bead of cum from its tip. She used it as lubricant for her palm to glide back and forth until she elicited a moan from him.

With a simple snap of Rafe's fingers, Liz's remaining clothing was history. She smiled against his mouth as she shifted her pelvis to rub her slick wetness along the length of him.

"Keep that up, and this is going to be the quickie Quentin was teasing us about the other night," he warned.

She giggled and began to rain light, lingering kisses along his jaw, down his neck, and across his chest. She paused here and there to flick her tongue over his nipple or to taste the salty sweetness of his skin. Along with her mouth, she explored every inch of him with her hands, needing to experience the warmth of him in a tactile way.

When she would've taken him in her mouth, he stopped her and shook his head. "Next time. Right now, I need to taste you."

Rafe flipped her on her back and went straight for the promised land at the apex of her thighs. At the first stroke of his tongue, her hips came off the mattress. On the second stroke, she cried out her pleasure. She lost count of the times he laved her core with his tongue; all she could concentrate on was the enjoyment she experienced under his skilled mouth and hands.

Her orgasm rocked her so hard, she bucked against him, chanting his name over and over like a benediction.

With her release, came the overpowering desire to have him inside her. To feel him fill her to the stretching point and then fill her some more. She rolled them to position herself on top and then eased down on his shaft until he was fully sheathed.

"Goddess!" he gasped.

And she understood the feeling. She'd have said the same if she could've formed a coherent thought at the moment. All she managed as she rocked against him was a panting plea for harder and faster. He obliged like the wonderful gentleman he was, giving his lady everything she required and more.

Liz screamed her release and gasped when he rolled her onto her back and continued to thrust. Slow, hard, fast, harder still. Over and over, never breaking rhythm until her third orgasm crashed over her. Only then did he join her, shouting her name on a hoarse, husky cry.

They lay there, locked together intimately. Neither desiring to budge an inch. Liz luxuriated in the feel of his weight atop her, cradled as he was between her thighs with her heels wrapped around his lower back.

"Can we stay like this forever?" she asked with a contented sigh.

"That would be my fondest wish," he said, then dipped his head to claim her mouth.

CHAPTER 21

"Well, someone's glowing," Ryanne leaned close to say before claiming a seat at the table where Autumn and Liz gathered.

Autumn snickered. "Yeah, unless I miss my guess, Rafe and Liz made a stop at Pound Town right before we arrived."

Liz choked. Her cousin was filterless. While it was funny at someone else's expense, at her own, it was downright embarrassing. From across the room, Rafe lifted his brows in question. She waved him off, then fanned her flaming face.

"Fess up. How was tall, dark, and dead-sexy in the sack?" Autumn prodded.

The desire to laugh was strong, but Liz finally managed to say, "I'll say one thing about it, and then you let it go. Agreed?"

"Agreed."

"Sublime and better than I remember," she admitted.

Her cousin pumped her fist in the air. "I knew it!"

"What does it say about *your* sex life when you are constantly prying into everyone else's?" Ryanne gave Autumn an arched look just before pouring the three of them wine.

"Oh, stuff it. You know you were as curious as I was."

"I totally was, but I'm too polite to ask."

"Pfft." Autumn shrugged and shot a contemplative look across the terrace. Expression devoid of all teasing, she faced Liz and asked, "Do you trust him?"

"Yes. I think if you dig deep, you do, too." She drank a small amount of the vino. "Besides, Alastair and Nash trust him, and that's the most important indication that Rafe is being truthful."

"And going forward? What does that mean for you both?" Ryanne asked.

"He mentioned marriage."

Brow furrowed, Autumn sat forward in her chair. "You don't sound enthused. Is it not what you want?"

"No, I do." Even to her own ears, she didn't sound convincing. Why was she hesitant? Liz was sure of her feelings for Rafe. Was she still clinging to the hurt from their very first hook-up? Was it the lie of omission about his mother's family? She didn't know. "I love him, and he says he loves me. Nothing he's done so far has indicated otherwise. I think I'm reticent because of Franklin, er, Franco."

Ryanne set her glass on the wrought-iron table. "Because he fooled you?"

"Maybe that's it. But I have this sick feeling in the pit of my stomach that things are about to blow up, and I don't know how to get past it."

"I had that with Keaton. It was about the time Zhu Lin tried to kidnap Chloe." Autumn gave her standard careless shrug. "It all worked out for us, and I'm sure it will for you, too, cuz. But be sure to listen to your inner voice. It won't steer you wrong."

"I hope you're right." Liz held up her wineglass. "To love and to things working out as they should."

Ryanne and Autumn repeated her toast and clinked glasses.

Liz checked her watch. "We should really get our plan ironed out for Franco and the Champeaus. Who else are we waiting on to join us?"

"Spring and Knox." Autumn tapped the screen on her phone. "They should be here momentarily."

As soon as the words left her mouth, Spring and Knox strolled through the door. Liz watched the care he gave his girlfriend; his consideration was in the small gestures. One of his large hands rested on her lower back as he escorted her to where Alastair, Rafe, and Nash gathered. Knox's attention was mostly all for Spring with the exception of the caution he paid to his surroundings. Those vivid azure eyes scanned the terrace and the adjoining buildings, missing nothing as he hovered protectively beside her.

"I don't think I've ever seen anyone as devoted as Knox," Autumn murmured. "She's his entire world, and he's hers."

"Relationship goals," Ryanne agreed.

"You both act as if your other halves wouldn't lay down their lives for you. We all know differently," Liz countered with a light laugh.

"Oh, I'm not complaining." Autumn shook her head. "What Keaton and I have absolutely works for us. I'm simply in awe of what they share. It's otherworldly."

Ryanne nodded as if she were in one-hundred-percent agreement, causing Liz to look at the couple in question. He wasn't overly large, maybe six-one and a hundred-ninety pounds, but he held himself as if he were ready for action at any minute. Knox Carlyle was a warrior in love. Or at least he was for Spring, and didn't that tug at the old heartstrings?

"I see what you mean."

Soon enough, they were all gathered around the table and were munching on the light repast Alastair had ordered for their meeting.

"What's our first step?" Knox asked.

"We've already taken it."

All heads whipped around to stare at Alastair. When everyone spoke at once, he held up a hand. "Ryker went undercover as one of Marguerite's house staff."

Autumn sat back with her arms crossed. "Jolly Ollie is in the spy game once more. I bet Aunt GiGi just *loved* that!"

A smile twisted his lips. "She might've insisted on going with him."

Spring laughed her glee.

"Are we to wait for them to report, or do we take action in the meantime?" Rafe asked.

"Always ready to delve into the action, aren't you, Xuereb?"

A sheepish expression flitted across his face as he acknowledged Alastair's question. "Sorry. Inactivity is difficult for me."

"Did you hear that? He likes to get busy," Autumn whispered in an aside to Ryanne, who clapped a hand over her mouth to stem her laugh.

Liz pinched her cousin under the table, and Alastair ignored them as if they weren't acting like a bunch of high-schoolers. "Actually, what do you say to a little game of pretend?"

Rafe sat forward. "I'm listening."

"You and Liz will pay your mother a visit at the Champeau estate to announce your engagement and perhaps mention our family's magic has miraculously been restored."

"What will that do?"

"Nothing other than stir the pot. I hope, after you leave, the key players will meet to decide on a course of action against us. It will allow GiGi and Ryker the opportunity to discover who's unequivocally involved and to overhear any plans." Alastair turned his attention to Autumn. "Since you are a master at spying through scrying, I'll assign that task to you, child. Try to break through their ward and take notes on what is said in the event my sister and Ryker are unable to get close enough."

Nash placed his hands on his girlfriend's shoulders. "Ryanne and I will cast a locator spell for the objects we suspect Franco to have taken. Once located, Knox and I will plan a little raid."

"Not without me, you aren't," Spring replied pertly.

Knox groaned, but didn't argue. They all knew he would prefer to tie her to a chair to keep her safe, but since Spring's return from her ordeal in Columbia, she refused to be coddled. Liz didn't blame her cousin one bit. Although younger than the rest of them, Spring was incredibly smart and tended to be the most skilled strategist in the group, with the exception of Alastair.

"And you, cousin?" Liz asked Alastair. "What's your next step?"

"I plan to pay a visit to the few remaining old-timers who may know more about Isolde's reign of terror. As much as I admire Damian, I want to verify he was being one-hundred-percent truthful with us."

"Who's left from when she was alive?"

"Doubtful there is anyone, but I intend to start with Georgie Sipanil. As the head of the Witches' Council, she'd at least be able to tell me what she has tucked away in her archives."

Nash grinned. "It helps that she adores you."

"Really, she favors Ryker more, but I'm sure she'll be forthcoming for me as well."

Rafe drained his remaining wine, set his glass down, and turned to Liz. "Ready, qalbi?"

She took the hand he offered. "I feel like I need a script."

"I'm afraid it will all be improv. But the general idea will be that we are popping in to ask for my grandmother's ring. I want to give it to you and design a wedding setting for it."

Although it was all for show, a part of an act to con his family, the idea of Rafe presenting her with a family heirloom melted Liz's heart.

"It won't be a lie," he said softly. "I fully intended to give it to you. Should you decide you don't like it, we'll conjure a different set."

In about a minute, she would breakdown and weep in front of their group. "We should go," she said around the emotion clogging her throat. Surprisingly, it was Autumn who shot her the understanding smile. She recognized Liz's wayward feelings.

THE CHAMPEAU ESTATE WAS IMPRESSIVE BY ANYONE'S STANDARDS. THE château put Thorne Manor to shame by sheer size alone. The dark pitched roof boasted at least eight chimneys from what Liz could see. Although it was only four stories high, fourteen matching windows ran the length of the two middle floors, broken only by a grand entryway. The uppermost floor was dotted with circular windows that reminded her of portholes on a ship. She suspected the lower floor on either side of the stone steps belonged to the basement. In the center of the rooftop was a fat, rounded steeple, reminiscent of an old catholic cathedral, with the spire topping the wide open lantern. The gated drive leading to the château was at least three-quarters of a mile long, lined with tall cypress trees.

"Holy shit! Is this where you grew up?"

Rafe smiled at her enthusiasm. "When I wasn't splitting my time with my father's family in Malta."

"I thought your mother was American?"

"Technically, she was born in the United States. It's where she met my father. But she moved back here, to the family estate, just before they divorced."

"How old is this place?"

"The building you see in front of us was constructed in fifteen twenty-four. If you squint toward the far right corner of the property, you'll see the old tower from the original structure from the eleventh century."

"It looks like it's still properly maintained from here."

"Of course. With magic, it's a simple matter to keep everything structurally sound and beautiful."

"True."

She bit her lip and fiddled with the hem of her dress. In less than five minutes, she would walk into enemy territory with only Rafe at her side. Granted, Ryker and GiGi were somewhere on the property, but who knew if they would be able to help if she wound up in trouble.

"*Qalbi*, look at me."

Tamping down her nervousness, she turned her head to meet his perceptive midnight eyes. Kindness and love shone brightly.

"It's going to be all right, Liz. I won't leave your side, and while my mother is a cold fish, she wouldn't dare hurt you. She won't take the chance of severing the last thread on our relationship."

"I wish I had your confidence, babe. Also, we strongly suspect your family of conspiring with Franco, so how sure can you be she isn't involved?"

"All the more reason for you not to wander away. Please, be sure to stay where I can get to you."

"Of course." As they approached the circular drive, she asked, "Why didn't we simply teleport?"

"There is a complex ward in place. Basically, we'd be electrocuted if we showed up on the grounds without prior notice."

Her jaw dropped. "That doesn't happen if we drive up?"

"No, for a number of reasons. They expect their employees to approach by car, bicycle, or on foot for work each day, and by the time a visitor approaches the gate, security is alerted."

"What happens if we were to simply teleport in and people were in the area? Do they get electrocuted, too?"

"This is really bothering you, isn't it?"

"I just think it's reckless to fry people willy-nilly because they happen to approach in an unconventional manner."

Rafe's booming laughter filled the cab of their car. "No one's been 'fried' in close to fifty years or more."

"How would you know? You're not here full-time."

"Touché."

When they halted in front of the main entrance, a tall, slender woman stood at the base of the stone steps. She looked to be in her mid-fifties, but the resemblance between her and her son was strong.

"Your mother, I presume?"

"Yes, that's her."

"She's stunning. And elegant. Oh, Goddess, I'm going to look like—"

He clutched the hand flapping about. "To me, you're the most beautiful woman in the world. Mother can be a snob, but you are who I choose. If it comes to pleasing my mother or pleasing myself, I will always please myself."

Rafe's words calmed Liz's building panic. "What about pleasing me?" she teased.

"I will correct my statement. I will always please myself *after* pleasing you."

"That's a whole lotta pleasing, babe."

"Did I fail to do the job earlier today?"

Heat rose into her face, and Rafe laughed when she said, "I was particularly pleased. Multiple times."

With a wide, happy grin, he lifted their joined hands and kissed the inside of her wrist. "Let's get this over with, shall we?"

CHAPTER 22

*R*afe was a lot more nervous than he let on. If anything went wrong and Liz got hurt, he'd never forgive himself. Although, he'd probably never live long enough to regret it. Between Alastair Thorne and Damian Dethridge, the worst sort of hell would be rained down upon him fast and furiously.

"Mother!" he called out and waved as he exited the car. Liz had already opened her door, but he held out a hand in support as she climbed from the low-slung sports car. The flash of thigh she exposed made him want to bundle her back inside and return to their hotel. He'd barely gotten his fill of her delectable body before the family had converged on them. At least this time, they got further than a kiss, and for that, he praised the Goddess he was able to modify the spell he'd enacted months ago.

Hand in hand, Rafe and Liz approached the steps. His mother's narrow-eyed stare was locked onto their hands.

"Raphael." The chilly tone spoke of her displeasure. Oh well, what else was new? He'd been disappointing her all his life.

"Hello, Mother."

"That's pretty formal," Liz murmured next to him right before they reached the top.

"She's a formal woman and doesn't offer a lot of warmth."

"That's what you have me for."

Rafe fought a grin and squeezed her hand.

His mother's cold, flat eyes missed nothing. *"Qu'est-ce qui est si amusant?"*

"In English, if you please."

Her brown-eyed gaze hardened. "But of course. What do you find so amusing, Raphael?"

"Can I not simply be happy to see you?" He pressed a dutiful kiss to her smooth cheek.

"Introduce me to your friend."

Rafe bristled under the order, but shoved down his irritation. It wouldn't do to show her she'd gotten under his skin, just as she always did with her domineering ways and loveless parenting.

"May I present Elizabeth Thorne?"

No surprise lit her face. The lack of expression told Rafe everything he needed to know about his mother's involvement in the Thorne's magical mishap. She knew exactly who Liz was, and while his mother may not have actively targeted them, she damned well knew someone else had.

"Ms. Thorne."

"Ms. Champeau."

He was proud of Liz's cool greeting. She'd be able to hold her own when it came right down to it. Not that he'd ever dream of leaving her alone to manage the minefield of his family, but Rafe was confident she'd remain relatively unscathed should things blow up. Liz already seemed to sense this wasn't about her and had everything to do with his horrid gene pool.

Unease swept through him. Perhaps she'd be hesitant to marry him after this meeting. Would she see this as an indication he'd be a liability in the family department? He hadn't realized he applied pressure to her hand until she brought the other up to pat his forearm. Loosening his grip, he shot her an apologetic glance.

"You have a beautiful home, ma'am."

"Yes."

His brows shot up at his mother's rudeness. Social niceties had been drilled into him since birth, by both his parents, with his mother being a harsh disciplinarian. Her departure from the norm spoke of exactly how rattled she was that a Thorne stood on her doorstep.

"I believe the words you're looking for are 'thank you,' Mother," he said dryly.

Her sneer spoke volumes. She wouldn't be corrected, not by her son at any rate.

"We've come a long way. Perhaps refreshments are in order," he suggested.

As they followed Josephine into the house, Liz cast him a questioning look. He shook his head. Later, when they were alone, he'd explain about the family dynamics. For the moment, they needed to get through the interview and score an invitation to stay the night so that they might dig deeper into the activities of Franco and Marguerite.

After they were seated in the formal sitting room, his mother rang a small bell. Liz frowned when a young French serving girl with thick golden locks stepped into the room.

"*Oui, madame?*"

"My son and his... friend would like refreshments." She tilted her head toward where they sat on the sofa. "Bread and cheese with wine?"

"That would be lovely," Liz replied with a soft smile. "*Merci.*"

The pert serving girl stopped at the door, out of sight of Josephine, and grinned, giving them a jaunty little wave. GiGi Thorne-Gillespie was in her element. Rafe had met the woman the previous year when she patched him up after his run-in with Zhu Lin. Mischievous and full of life, she was incomparable and a joy to be around. The perfect counterpart to Ryker Gillespie, spymaster.

Speaking of Ryker, Rafe suspected the gardener trimming the hedges outside the open terrace doors might be him. The man had inched closer to the room and had his head tilted to listen better. If it wasn't Ryker, then the poor gardener had neck issues. For sure,

163

his mother would never cast the man a second glance, because he was the hired help, and Josephine Champeau was above concerning herself with staff. Household affairs fell to his cousin Marguerite now.

"Now, let's get to the real reason you're here, Raphael. It certainly isn't to visit me, because you haven't been home in close to thirty years."

"There was never much of a reason to return, Mother. As I recall, you called me a terrible disappointment when last we met."

Liz placed a hand on his knee and squeezed lightly. Not missing the gesture, Josephine opened her mouth to speak, but Rafe forestalled her.

"It's not important. What I've come to say is Liz and I are engaged to be married. I'd like Grand-mère's ring, please."

All pretense at civility was lost when his mother curled her lip and turned hate-filled eyes on Liz. "*Her? A Thorne?*" Disdain dripped from her words. "You'd defile our bloodline by marrying an upstart Thorne?"

Rafe barely heard Liz's gasp over the pounding in his brain. Despite possessing a hard-edged willpower, he couldn't seem to remove his horrified stare from his mother. Yes, she'd never shown any goodwill toward the Thornes or ever expressed a kind word in reference to the family, but she was never this enraged or nasty.

"Would you care to tell me what my family has ever done to yours to deserve such blatant disrespect?" Liz's tone was coated in ice. "As far as I know, none of us have ever had any dealings with your family prior to the incident with Marguerite and Ryker Gillespie."

The gardener outside fumbled his tool as GiGi, who had returned with a tray, drew in a sharp breath. Rafe didn't dare look at either of them, or it would be a dead giveaway. As it was, he hoped his mother hadn't registered their reactions.

"Preston Thorne II was engaged to *me* when he ran off and married Rose Smythe. Your family has a long line of rapscallions and an even longer history of breaking promises."

Rooted in place at the news her father had been promised to Josephine once upon a time, GiGi eyed them in horror. Rafe felt a little horrified himself.

"Mother, that was back in 'forty-two. You can't honestly be carrying a grudge for seventy-eight years?"

Tears shimmered in her dark, forbidding eyes, and Rafe received his answer. *She most definitely was.*

"I'm sorry that particular family member broke a commitment to you, but I'm his distant cousin at best, Ms. Champeau, and he's long-since deceased. It has no bearing on my feelings for your son."

Josephine jerked her head and settled her fierce stare on Liz. "You will not marry my son!"

"Begging your pardon, madame, but you don't get to decide who he marries."

"I—"

"Liz is the woman I choose, Mother. There will be no argument. If you provide the ring, we'll be on our way."

"My mother's ring will never touch her finger," Josephine snapped.

When Rafe stood to argue, Liz clutched his hand and drew him back down.

"I understand your feelings, Ms. Champeau. Your mother's ring is sacred to you and must hold great sentimental value. Rafe and I will design a different one."

"You know nothing, you little tart!"

"Enough!" Rafe barked. Surging to his feet again, he drew Liz up with him. "You will not insult her."

"Did you know she was dating your cousin Franco only last week? You dare come here with a woman who played whore to another man, then have the gall to announce your engagement?"

"I never slept with Franco. We—"

Rafe held up a hand. "You don't need to explain yourself, *qalbi*. We both know the truth." He turned back to his mother. "Franco isn't the man you believe he is. He's a liar and has been draining the Champeau estate for years. All to fund his many failing businesses and dig himself out of trouble with the cartel. You're a fool if you trust him." He guided Liz around the coffee table and headed for the door. "I suppose this is our final goodbye, Mother."

"It's not as if you've ever been a son I can be proud of."

LIZ DIDN'T KNOW WHAT HAPPENED. ONE SECOND, SHE WAS IN FULL control of herself, and the next, she was all up in Josephine's business. "You shut your foul mouth, you heartless bitch!"

The other woman stared at her as if she'd grown two heads. Her mouth opened and closed like a trout out of water, struggling to breathe.

"Don't you ever—and I mean *ever*—talk about Rafe like that again. He's all that is good and kind in the world. He's intelligent, brave, and he's a thousand times the person you or your precious Franco will ever be."

"How dare you!"

"Oh, I dare. I dare a great many things." Fire flared in the palm of her hands, and she lifted them in a show of rage. This appalling excuse for a mother had some nerve. Talking down to Liz was one thing, but belittling the man she loved was quite another.

"Liz!"

Rafe's concern penetrated the fury pounding in her brain.

Snuffing out the flames, she leaned in closer to Josephine. "You should realize what you've done just now. You've not only lost your son, you've lost any access to the children he and I will have. Stay in this mausoleum and hold your bitterness tight, lady. I hope it keeps you warm at night."

"Let's go," Rafe said curtly, and with a hand on her elbow, he escorted her to their car.

His stone-faced countenance made her worry she'd gone too far. "Rafe? Babe?"

"Not now. We need to get out of here."

Without another word, she climbed into the passenger seat and buckled her seatbelt. She worried she'd crossed a line for which he couldn't forgive her. Nobody appreciated when you told their mother off.

When they were a half-mile down the road, he pulled the car to a stop and faced her. She belatedly registered he'd been too upset to use a seatbelt himself.

"You were magnificent back there. No one has ever defended me so passionately before. *No one*," he said gruffly.

Relief surged through her. "She was wrong, babe. And when I think about the emotional abuse you must've suffered at her hands growing up..." Words failed her, and she wanted to sob for the lonely little boy he must've been. "I'm sorry, Rafe."

"*Qalbi*, please. Please don't cry for the past." He unhooked the seatbelt holding her secure and wrapped one of his large hands gently around the nape of her neck. "Don't waste a single tear on her."

"Not on *her*," she cried softly. "For *you*. Only for you, babe."

Without any fanfare, Rafe produced a handkerchief and dabbed at the tears trailing down her cheeks. "I don't deserve your tears either."

"Too bad. You're getting them anyway," she retorted with a sniff.

The smile starting on his sexy-ass mouth chased away the last of her sadness.

"Did you see her face when you called her a 'heartless bitch'?" He chortled. "I thought she would have a stroke on the spot."

"I'm glad you think it's funny. I almost torched her."

"I've never seen you so fierce or so beautiful. I wish I could've captured the moment and frozen it in a picture forever."

"You're twisted."

"Perhaps a little," he agreed. "I guess your cousin GiGi and Ryker got quite the show."

She laughed. "Yes. Autumn will be cross she missed all the drama."

"Your confrontation with the matriarch of the Champeau family will go down in the Thorne Chronicles, to be read about for generations to come."

Suddenly, she couldn't joke anymore. "I understand what you were trying to say in Alastair's study, Rafe. The accident of birth." She caressed his beloved face. "Any reservations I had about us are gone."

His wide, engaging grin stole the oxygen from her lungs. "So you'll marry me for real?"

"That would be my fondest wish."

WITH SHAKING HANDS, RAFE DUG INTO HIS PANTS POCKET AND PULLED out the ruby-and-diamond ring that had once belonged to his grandmother, and presented it to Liz.

"What's this?"

"Grand-mère's ring."

"How... what... how did you get this?"

"GiGi slipped it into my hand as we were walking out."

"I don't know how I feel about this, babe. It seems to come with so much hatred."

"No, it comes with great love. Grand-mère was the most incredible woman I knew. Her ring was always intended for my future bride. That's you." He eased it onto her finger and ran his thumb around the band. The gold contracted to fit snugly. "Mother never had a say as to Grand-mère's will, and I'm sure it's why she was livid when I asked for it."

"Well, that and the fact that Preston II screwed her over. Can't say I wouldn't have been a little pissed if it had happened to me."

"I thought GiGi was going to drop the tray when Mother mentioned her father."

"No kidding! Talk about a shock. I'm sure she'll have a lot to discuss with Alastair when she returns to the hotel." She held up her hand to admire her new ring. A slow smile bloomed upon her face, spreading wider with each passing second. "Your grand-mère's ring is stunning."

He gazed down at the square-cut, two-carat ruby ring framed by smaller diamonds that lent to the majesty of the piece. "Grand-père created it for his bride. He always said her eyes shone like the most brilliant jewel when she looked at him."

"Oh, Rafe! What a lovely sentiment!"

"I've never seen two people more in love. I'll also never understand how they had a daughter with such ugliness in her heart for everyone." He shook his head at the morose thought. Now wasn't the time to spoil his proposal with gloomy memories.

Placing a hand on either side of his face, Liz leaned in and gently kissed him. There was a softness to her amber gaze when she said, "Maybe Josephine's bitterness is understandable. For as deeply and as passionately as your family loves, maybe Preston's betrayal was more than she could bear and turned her heart to ash."

"Perhaps," Rafe conceded. The knowledge of his mother's broken engagement cleared up a lot of the questions he'd had in the past. Why she couldn't seem to love him was the biggest. "It must be why my father divorced her so early into their marriage."

"How sad."

"Yes. He is a good man."

"I figured there was a fifty-fifty chance he was. You had to get your charming personality from one of them."

He laughed at her cheeky response. "Let's go back to our hotel room and celebrate our engagement in style."

"My thoughts exactly, and we both know how much you love the way I think."

CHAPTER 23

"What did you find out, child?"

Liz took a sip of her morning coffee and checked to be sure Rafe was out of earshot before she answered Alastair. "That Josephine Champeau is the absolute worst sort of human being."

"Ryker and GiGi briefed me last evening on the argument. I was also informed you not only held your own, but you gave her what for."

"She's a piece of work. Who tells their son he's a disappointment? Especially a guy as amazing as Rafe?"

Alastair lifted her hand to examine the ruby stone. "It's a beautiful piece."

Warmth flooded her as she looked down at her new engagement ring. "I loved it the minute he showed it to me. It was his grandmother's."

"My sister said she had quite a time, appropriating it from the safe."

As she imagined her cousin's antics, Liz laughed. "She's reached hero status in Rafe's eyes."

When the smile left Alastair's face and his expression turned serious, she took a deep breath. "Out with it, cousin."

"He's a good deal older than you, child."

"I'm well aware."

"Do you have reservations about the age difference?"

"I didn't until this moment. Is there something I should know?"

"Not at all. As far as I know, he has all his teeth."

She couldn't curb her smile. "He's a good man, Alastair, and I love him."

A slight frown came and went between his brows in less time than it took Liz to register his reaction. "I'm glad you found someone worthy of you, child."

"He is, isn't he?"

Confidant sapphire-blue eyes met her concerned gaze. "He is."

A sigh of relief escaped her. She hadn't realized she was holding her breath until he answered. It wasn't as if she needed Alastair's approval, but she trusted his judgment. If she was wrong about another man, she might just lose her mind. "Thank you."

"I just needed to make sure this is what you want."

"It is." She sat forward in her desire to relay what she was feeling. "My world is brighter with him in it. He reminds me that life isn't all business, and encourages me to have fun. I feel things so much more with him."

A blinding smile lit Alastair's face. "Good, because you deserve the best, Elizabeth. Always remember that."

Her tears blurred her vision, distorting his handsome face. "Thank you for always being kind to me, my mother, and my brothers. After Dad died... after... well, I know what you did for us, and I can never repay you."

"Your father was my friend. I regret that I couldn't save him during the war."

"Mom said he'd been imprisoned with you in Zhu Lin's dungeon. Did my dad suffer?"

Pain flashed in Alastair's eyes before he blinked to clear away his strong, immediate reaction. But he was too late to hide the truth. "I'm sorry."

"That wasn't on you. The witches' war took many lives. I remember him as a kind and loving father."

"He talked about you, your brothers, and your mother. During." He loosened his tie, as if it suddenly felt too tight. "He was so proud of you kids."

"How come you never told me before?"

"It was my mission to forget. Rorie is helping me deal with the memories instead of trying to lock them away."

Liz covered his hand with hers. "I cannot imagine the trials you faced, nor do I want to. But I'm glad you're with us, and I feel better knowing my dad had you to keep him company in the end."

Alastair closed his eyes, swallowed hard, and nodded.

Looking away, she gave him time to compose himself. The timing was good for them both because Rafe ended his call and joined them.

He leaned down to kiss her cheek, then took a seat beside her. "Coffee?"

"Please."

"Who was on the phone?"

He wore a look of one disturbed. "Marguerite."

Liz paused mid-pour to stare. "Why did she call you?"

"Seems she's concerned about the goings-on at the château. Grand-mère's ring went missing, my mother is having a meltdown, and two of the staff up and quit this morning." He picked up his cup and saucer and toasted her. "I say a job well done on our part, don't you?"

Laughter bubbled up and out. "I can just imagine your mother's face!"

His deep chuckle spoke to the part of her seeking revenge against his iceberg of a mother. A thought occurred to her, and she addressed Alastair. "Did you know Josephine was engaged to your father?"

"GiGi informed me last night." He stilled, and his contemplative gaze swept back and forth between her and Rafe. "You realize this changes things, Xuereb?" Alastair said solemnly.

"How so?"

"Your mother has the motive to steal our power."

"She wouldn't."

Liz didn't speak, but she wasn't as confident as Rafe that Josephine wasn't behind their misfortunes. She met Alastair's thoughtful stare. As she was about to comment, her phone rang. The caller ID showed Damian's name.

"Damian? Hey—"

"The darkness attacked Sabrina again this morning. Twice."

"Holy shit!"

"Precisely. What have you discovered?"

"Unfortunately, very little. I—" She stared down at her phone. "He hung up."

The air around them crackled, and a brilliant yellow light indicated an opening portal. Damian stepped through with his tearful daughter wrapped tightly in his arms.

"This stops today," he stated without ceremony. "Will you watch over my daughter?"

When the Aether asked you a favor, you agreed. To garner his displeasure was unthinkable. Liz nodded. "Of course. Tell me how."

"Keep her here with you while I have a talk with Franco Moreau." The emphasis on "talk" said Damian was going to do much more.

"I'll go with you," Rafe offered.

"Fine, but I leave now."

"Don't you need to scry to find out where he is?" Liz asked quietly as Damian handed her Sabrina.

He ran a hand over the black coffee in Rafe's cup. An image of Franco kneeling in a temple was reflected back at them. Only Alastair didn't look surprised the Aether could use a cup of coffee for a scrying mirror.

Damian's vicious curse caused the hair on Liz's arms to stand on end. His displeasure turned the very air around them heavy even as the sky darkened. "He's at Isolde's old temple. The bloody fool is trying to resurrect her on his own." With a growl low in his throat, he stepped through another portal. The sizzle of the rift sealing up was instantaneous.

"So much for you going with him." Liz's gaze ping-ponged between Rafe and Alastair. She covered Sabrina's ears. "He had murder in his heart. One of you needs to find him, like yesterday."

"Does anyone happen to know where Isolde's temple is located?"

"Spring might have an idea." Alastair pulled her contact information, called her, and quickly explained the situation. After he disconnected, he stood. "Her best guess is England." A contemplative frown tugged his brows together.

"If I tell you where, will you save Papa?"

Liz met Sabrina's stark stare. Her heart contracted at the fear she was witnessing. Knowing what it was like to lose a parent at a young age, she was compelled to say, "Yes, sweetheart. We'll do what we can, but you need to tell us all you know."

"He's going to kill that man."

Rafe bent his knees to make eye contact with the girl. "We're not going to let that happen."

"No, he's going to. But if he does, she'll drain his powers to free the evil one."

Insides cold with fear, Liz said, "Sabrina, sweetie, you need to tell us where your papa went, right now."

"I don't know the name, but I can take you."

"No!" Rafe ran a shaking hand through his hair. "No. We are *not* taking her into a dangerous situation."

Alastair held out his hands, palms up, and a burst of light had them all shielding their eyes. When they dared look again, he had a pair of shackles in his fist. "We don't have time to waste. Sabrina, take us to your father, child." When she looked from Liz to Rafe to Alastair, he gave the girl a warm smile. "You can do it. All you have to do is visualize the room where your father is, just like when you teleport from room to room at home."

"I can open the door like he did," she said softly.

"You mean the portal he went through?" Liz asked, shifting Sabrina's weight in her arms.

"It's easy." Real enthusiasm colored her voice.

Liz didn't know whether to weep or cheer. They were relying on a six-year-old to take them to a place none of them had ever been, where the Aether was likely to murder them all slowly and painfully for endangering his daughter.

"We don't have a choice, Elizabeth," Alastair said softly. "If we do nothing, Isolde will wake and destroy us all."

"How do we know? I mean, her time entombed could've mellowed her out, right?"

"It could also have made her even more deranged than before." He squeezed her shoulder lightly. "If Isolde was so out of control that a goddess needed to take action, it was bad."

"Then we should petition her to help." *Anything* other than take a child into battle with the people who stole their power to begin with.

"They can't steal your power again, Miss Liz."

"From the mouths of babes," murmured Alastair.

Still, Liz was torn. In the end, the pleading dark eyes of Sabrina tore at her conscience. If they did nothing, and Damian suffered the loss of his magic—or worse, died—after all he'd done for them, she'd never forgive herself. "Take us to him, sweetheart."

"YOU BLOODY IMBECILE!" DAMIAN INFUSED HIS VOICE WITH ALL THE fury he was experiencing. The current rippled between him and Franco Moreau, knocking the man sideways. Wariness flooded his face, but Franco continued to speak the spell.

"Stop! This is your one and only warning, Moreau."

Still, Franco chanted. All the while, he sat back on his heels and stared in terror at a spot behind Damian.

Turning in a slow circle, Damian sent out a feeler. Another, darker energy, was present, but it lingered in the air, never touching down in one place. Was it his mother? Had he been too late to stop the damned fool trying to resurrect her? There was only one thing for it; he must prevent her from waking, or they were all doomed. There would be no shoving her into the box a second time.

Almost two hundred years ago, Damian had stood next to Nathanial Thorne on the hill overlooking the containment ceremony. Isolde's destructive rage was unlike anything he'd ever witnessed before. In the end, it had taken a goddess, a god, and the most powerful witch families, both living and dead, to come together to stop her.

Now, left with no choice, he gathered all the elemental magic available to him and stepped into the circle Franco had created. The other warlock's eyes burned with a fanatical light, and he rocked back and forth on his knees, hands clasped in front of him, as he spoke the forgotten language of the gods. The pleading light in his eyes was off-putting.

A tingle started in Damian's lower extremities, but he ignored the sensation and closed the distance between him and Franco. Placing his palm flat on his enemy's head, Damian shot his power into the man's skull, short-circuiting his brain's wiring and frying his neurotransmitters. Franco's scream ricocheted off the stone walls, making his excruciating pain known. Damian didn't stop, because Franco began to chant again. *As if he were compelled to!*

The tingling shifted into Damian's torso, and it became difficult to take a deep breath. Blood vessels burst in Franco's eyes, and the sclera turned from white to garnet. The tear ducts dripped blood, and it ran down his gray cheeks to drip onto the floor.

The second the first droplet hit the ground, the temple came to life. Stones rumbled, and ancient symbols flared brighter than the sun. Franco crumbled at Damian's feet, his sightless eyes locked onto a phantom only he'd seen before death embraced him.

Damian swayed as a sharp, excruciating pain rocked through his skull. Disoriented and discomfited, he grabbed his head and crashed to his knees. A female's wicked laughter rang out, and for the first time in his life, he knew real fear. He could feel the steady drain of his power as the room put off enough light to sear his skin. With the last of his strength, he attempted to crawl toward the circle's edge. If he could cross the border, he could break the spell sucking away his life force.

"Bloody hell," he ground out between pants. The crushing pain in his head was about to cause him to black out. If that happened, he was done.

Across the room, his daughter appeared, and he had a second of joy before he registered she should be as far away from Isolde's temple as she could get.

"Go," he mouthed over the deafening rumble of stones. Instead, she ran directly for him, and Damian was sure his heart was going to stop beating in his chest as she crossed the line to grab his hand.

Her little body jerked, and the color on her face drained away drastically.

"Go, beastie, hurry now," he rasped out.

"Not without you, Papa," she screamed over the ear-piercing hum of magic filling the room, although she did back across the circle's border.

"Sabrina, I'm ordering you to go!" he roared, using the last of his strength.

"No, Papa."

Liz and Alastair were next to them in an instant, and they gripped his arms to drag him across the circle's border. They rolled him onto his back because he was incapable of movement even if he could drum up the energy.

With his very last breath, he ordered, "Get her out of here, goddammit!"

CHAPTER 24

*O*nce Rafe registered the magic of the circle hadn't stopped with Franco's death, he swiftly traversed the corridor of Isolde's temple, looking for another threat. Franco's face had been frozen in fear, and that might have been because he saw the devil in the form of Damian, but Rafe very much doubted it. The little weasel had been staring toward the east wing of the building until his collapse.

He caught sight of a woman in black just as she ducked around a corner. The click of her heels on the stone indicated she was moving at a fast pace. The only reason she would run was if she'd seen and recognized him. From the back, Marguerite and his mother were roughly the same size. But based on the rhythm of her rapid walk, Rafe suspected he knew exactly who had manipulated Franco.

Utilizing Granny Thorne's cloaking spell, Rafe concealed his presence and muted any sound he could possibly make, then high-tailed it after Josephine. He shoved aside his inner turmoil and feelings of betrayal. What had he expected from her when she admitted how much she hated his future in-laws? She'd never been much of a parent to begin with, other than to drill manners into him, making him unfailingly polite so as not to embarrass her among the elite crowd. Later, when this mess was over, he'd examine why she still had the ability to cause him endless pain.

His mother paused to listen. Lips curled in a self-satisfied smile, she held up the paper she tightly gripped and began to voice the hand-written words. If memory served Rafe, they were exactly what Franco had been repeating in the circle when they arrived.

The ground beneath him shook, and Rafe cast an uneasy glance at the stone ceiling above him. Dust particles showered the area, and he tried to subtly shift so it wasn't obvious the dirt wasn't hitting the ground directly.

Josephine's head jerked sideways as if she sensed she was no longer alone. Cunning lit her eyes, and her sinister smile was awful to behold. Had she always been so evil and he failed to recognize it? Had her various disappointments in life turned her heart to stone? Perhaps the ugly nature of her personality was what drove Preston II away, and not his unfaithfulness.

"I know you're here, Raphael. I can feel your presence." She pivoted slowly in each direction. An animal sensing danger.

He dropped the cloaking spell.

"Always doing the Thornes' bidding, like a good little soldier." She sneered when she saw the magic-suppressing shackles dangling from his hand.

"This has nothing to do with the Thornes and everything to do with the destruction you are about to cause the witch community. If you resurrect the Enchantress, she might never be able to be contained again. The devastation she rendered the first time around hurt real people, Mother." Appealing to her softer side was a gamble because Rafe doubted she had one, but anything was worth a try.

Her eyes turned positively feral as her lips curled back into a snarl. "You don't get it, Raphael. You're soft—like your father—with little understanding of what it takes to maintain our name. Our reputation. Our lifestyle."

Latching onto the one thing that seemed odd in her little speech, he asked, "Lifestyle?"

"Yes!" she spat. "Do you know what it costs to keep the château running?"

His head jerked in an involuntary negative response.

"Of course you don't, because you never cared enough to ask or to be part of our family. To be part of something greater."

"Mother, if you were hurting for money, you could've always told me. I would've given you whatever you needed."

"She is too prideful."

Both Rafe and his mother expressed their surprise for the newcomer. Marguerite stepped from the shadows and approached Josephine. "Isn't that right, Auntie?"

Although he'd had no doubt he could've taken his mother should she attack, Rafe was a little leery of two. Bottom line, he wanted to be able to subdue them without seriously hurting or killing either woman.

"You!" Josephine scoffed, giving Rafe the first indication they weren't a team. "You are a waste of good air. Always flitting around, living the high life. Society's little darling."

He risked a glance to register his cousin's reaction. Her stone-cold countenance told him nothing. Was this an act to throw him off guard?

"Franco admired you, Marguerite, but instead of using and guiding him, you rejected him at every turn. His continued failings were all in an effort to impress *you*."

A memory came back to Rafe. One of Franco trailing his captivating cousin, and Marguerite reading him the riot act, telling him to bugger off because he was no better than the slime train of a slug. More than once, Rafe had caught Franco rifling through Marguerite's room, touching her things and sniffing her clothing. The guy had been a creepy little fucker from the get-go.

Marguerite's solemn-eyed expression bothered Rafe. He'd failed her. Left her alone with a pervert and a deranged old woman who always belittled those around her. As best he could, he tried to relay his apology with unspoken words. Now was not the time to verbally express his regret.

She gave a slight nod of understanding, and turned her attention back to Josephine. "The game is up now, Auntie. You've been caught out."

"No!" With a frantic shake of her head, his mother lifted the crinkled spell in her hand. "Only one more step, and she's awake. She'll reward me for releasing her from her prison and for delivering the family responsible for putting her there."

"You're wrong, Mother," Rafe said softly. "She'll kill you for your power. She'll kill each and every one of us without prejudice or reason. Her sanity will be even more questionable this time around after two hundred years of isolation."

"You'll see. I can restore the family name again. We will be revered."

It wasn't a stretch to see his mother was on the same playing field as Isolde had been. What must it take to send someone so far over the edge?

"No, we will be reviled, and disgust will drip from everyone's voice when they speak the Champeau name," he corrected. "Because by resurrecting the Enchantress, you resurrect an evil so great, it will decimate families... *again*."

"*I will have my fortunes restored!*" Her scream echoed off the walls and brought more dust down on their heads from the ancient ceiling overhead.

Sweat beaded Rafe's brow, and his cousin didn't look particularly thrilled at the idea of a cave-in either, as was obvious by her wary look up.

"That weasel Franco! He stole from our coffers to fund his ridiculous business ventures. He's cost us everything." A villainous smile formed on her thin lips and sent a chill down Rafe's spine. "But I had the last laugh, didn't I?"

"What did you do, Auntie?" his cousin asked in a soft, non-threatening tone. "How did you get your revenge on Franco?"

"I persuaded him to channel the Thornes' magic to wake Isolde de Thorne. The fool thought he could do it, too, but it wasn't him who took their power." Her evil glee was directed at Rafe. "You did."

His ability to inquire as to her deeds died away, and all he could do was stare at this twisted stranger in budding horror.

"I can't fix him," Sabrina cried.

Liz gathered Damian's daughter to her and stared at Alastair, helpless, as the girl began to sob. It wasn't difficult to see the deep emotion from the two of them was crippling him, and he closed his eyes against their grief.

"Take her home, child. Back to Ravenswood. I'll follow shortly with Damian."

"No! No!" Sabrina frantically fought to escape Liz's embrace; shoving, squirming, and anything else she could do to wiggle free. "No! I can't leave Papa. I can't, or he'll be gone for good."

"Sabrina, sweetheart, I need you to calm down," Liz ordered in a firm, no-nonsense tone. "We cannot help your father if you're hysterical, and you're our best chance to revive him." She smoothed back Sabrina's black hair and gently brushed the tears from her cheeks, praying all the while the girl could really do it. "My cousin is an empath. Do you know what that means?"

The girl nodded and cast a worried look his way.

"He's feeling what we are, but amplified because of where we are. This is a magical place meant to kick things up. You and I have to put our feelings on hold so we can help Alastair fix your papa."

Again, the child nodded.

"Thank you, Elizabeth."

"No problem, cousin." She avoided looking at the center of the circle. Franco's bloodied face was a gruesome sight and the stuff of nightmares. Positioning herself to shield Sabrina from the scene, Liz got an up-close-and-personal view of Damian's still body. She inhaled a shaky breath. Seeing him practically lifeless made her want to vomit what little breakfast she'd had time to consume. "Tell me what we need to do."

"I'm not entirely sure," Alastair admitted quietly as he felt for a pulse in Damian's neck.

Sabrina caught their attention when she asked, "Do you have Grandmother's note?"

"What note, child?"

"She sent you a note before she was put under the garden by Isis. It will help you save Papa."

His eyes narrowed, and Liz had to wonder to what Sabrina was referring.

"Are you sure she sent it to me? I wasn't born when she was entombed."

"I see it in my head. She was talking to Nathanial."

"Nathanial?" He scratched his head and gave her a considering look. "The only 'Nathanial' I know was our great-grandfather, who lived at Rēafere's Fortress."

"No, sir. It was you." Sabrina spread her arms, offering one hand to Alastair and one to Liz. "Watch."

A vision of what Liz assumed was the past took over her mind.

A black-haired woman with obsidian eyes fisted her hair at her temples and viciously tugged at her scalp. She shook her head and muttered, "Shut up! Shut up! Shut up! Shut up!"

As suddenly as she'd been swept into her episode, she stopped and looked at the writing desk a few feet away. A snap of her fingers started the writing tools moving, and the pen worked furiously over the paper, ending with a swish and a dot, then dropping onto the wooden surface.

"Deliver yourself to Alastair Thorne," she said aloud.

The parchment rolled itself into a tight ball and disappeared in a light puff of dark smoke.

The next scene flashed to her speaking with a young man with an uncanny likeness to Alastair. The challenge between the two was unmistakable, altered only by a young black-haired boy, who flung himself into the Alastair lookalike's arms.

A sharp pain followed on the heels of the vision Sabrina had gifted them with. Liz, much like the black-haired woman, gripped her head in her hands and applied pressure in a misguided attempt to rid herself of the discomfort.

The instant Sabrina trailed her fingers over Liz's brow, the pain disappeared as if it had never existed. "I'm sorry, Miss Liz," she whispered tearfully. "I didn't mean to hurt you."

"You didn't know, sweetheart. Keep in mind for the future; your level of magic can have a powerful effect all on its own."

"I'll remember."

"I know you will. You're a clever girl." Liz faced Alastair and noted the contemplative expression he wore. "Who do you suppose got the parchment, cousin? Unless I'm completely ignorant of our family history, you weren't born yet."

"I wasn't, but Nathanial *Alastair* Thorne was. We're almost identical in looks. Isolde may have confused the two of us in her mental state."

"Our great-grandfather, of course!" She snorted. "And *almost* identical? You were his damned twin."

"I need to go to Rēafere's Fortress to see what I can discover, but I can't leave you here alone without protection for you or the girl."

"Sabrina, where do we need to help your Papa? Here, or can it be anywhere?"

She pulled away from Liz and rested her cheek over her father's heart.

"I think she's going into shock," Alastair said in a low tone so only Liz would hear.

"I don't know where we are, but I can take a picture of this place and send it to Nash or Knox. They can be here instantly."

"I doubt your cell phone would work here, child. I suspect this temple, like the clearings at my place and Thorne Manor, will block the signal. It's the strong energy."

"Then go and hurry back. Between Sabrina's abilities and mine, I challenge anyone to fuck with us."

"No one would dare, if they saw the fierceness of your expression, Elizabeth," he assured her. His tone was dry as dirt, but wry humor lurked in the quirk of his lips. Alastair helped her to her feet and led her out of range of Sabrina's hearing. "If you have to leave Damian to his fate, do so to protect her. I've known him my entire life, and I can assure you, he'd want her taken to safety."

"Understood. Hopefully, Rafe will be back soon. Now get going."

CHAPTER 25

"*M*e?" Rafe managed to choke out.

"Oh, yes. Elizabeth Thorne was always irresistible to you, wasn't she? It only took a little blood magic to make you my tool, just like Franco."

He turned horror-filled eyes toward Marguerite, and she returned his stare with a shocked look of her own.

"How?" he barked when his power of speech returned.

"Your blood and mine are the same, Raphael, or did you forget?" She shrugged, and her smile grew crafty. "As for Elizabeth, Franco arranged to have a wineglass break in her hand one evening during dinner. He helped her clean up the wound and brought me my prize."

Rafe stared at his mother like he'd never seen her before, and perhaps he hadn't. Yes, she'd always been reserved while he was growing up, sometimes harsh in her criticism of him, but never in his wildest dream had he ever imagined she could be so cold-blooded and evil.

"You knew I loved her, and you put a spell on me to destroy her and her family? Your own son?"

"You were a sniveling baby from the beginning. Nothing much has changed."

His brain refused to catch up with the present. All his memories of the past rearranged themselves to show his mother in a worse light. The stones around him shook again.

"Rafe? Cousin? You need to calm down."

His gaze collided with Marguerite. "What?"

"You're going to bury us alive with your emotions," she stated slowly and softly, as if talking to a wild beast.

He glanced up as more dust fell down upon their heads.

Goddess! She was right. He was an earth elemental, and his strong reactions were causing the stones to shift. Until now, he'd believed it was the magic his mother was performing—and maybe it initially was—but the current rumbling was caused by him and his feelings of disbelief, betrayal, and rage. Essentially, Marguerite was saying, "calm the fuck down, or you'll trigger an earthquake to kill us all."

Rafe sucked in a deep, cleansing breath.

Finally, a few key incidents clicked into place. "Just so we're clear here. You used blood magic against Liz and me. The moment she agreed to have dinner with me, this whole spell went into effect." He began to pace as he spoke his suspicions aloud. "When that happened, the Thornes lost their magic."

"Yes. She was never going to resist you for long. A Thorne only loves once. Using her own magic against her was a simple matter."

He suspected as much. A Champeau wasn't strong enough on their own to drain a Thorne. But using Liz's magic to drain her own powers was exceedingly clever on Rafe's mother's part. "You already knew, other than another Thorne, the Aether was the only one who could remove their abilities without black magic and that the Thornes would immediately turn to him to accuse him or beg for his help. Either way, you were golden."

"Maybe you aren't as brainless as I believed."

He ignored his mother's jibe and continued. "The attacks on his daughter were designed by you. Because she is a Thorne, too, you could use blood magic to target her even knowing you'd never be able to actually hurt her." He paused, piecing the rest together.

Frowning, he glanced back the way he'd come. Then the reasoning became clear. "Of course," he muttered. "By attacking Sabrina and riling Damian, you were assured he would retaliate. You already knew we'd found out about Franco."

Rafe shook his head at her cunning. "That poor bastard never stood a chance. What did you do, bind him to the temple so he couldn't move when Dethridge came to call?"

Her self-congratulatory smirk told him she had.

"I almost feel sorry for him."

"Don't you dare!" She shook her head and forced out a long breath. In a calmer, cooler voice, she said, "He got what he deserved. He defiled our family name with his underhanded practices. My idiot brother believed Franco had a keen mind for business. Pierre left him in charge of our estate, which the imbecile ran into the ground." She shook in her rage. "The bank foreclosed on the château this morning." Angry tears flooded her eyes. "I didn't even know he'd taken out a second mortgage on the place. I thought the land was the one thing Franco couldn't touch. Yes, the finances, but I foolishly believed my home was secure."

Rafe looked at Marguerite and nearly smacked himself on the head. "It's why you called me this morning. You thought I could step in to save the estate."

"Yes." She gestured to the temple around them. "I didn't know about any of the rest of this, and I only recently discovered Franco had ruined us. I thought perhaps you could calm Aunt Josephine and figure a way for us to save our home."

He sighed heavily. "Mother, why didn't you simply call me. I get you detest me, but you know I would've stopped Franco."

"Men have always ruled my life. First my father, my brother, then your father, finally Franco. I'm more intelligent than all of you combined."

"Not so much if you believed attacking a powerful family, antag-onizing the Aether, and bringing the Enchantress back from the grave was a brilliant idea." His voice rose with each word until he was shouting. The echo of his voice was painful on his eardrums. Rafe didn't care. "Damian killing Franco triggered some type of chain reaction, didn't it? How do we reverse it?"

"You don't." Josephine laughed with evil glee. "You can't. This is Isolde's temple, Raphael. She brought her victims here to drain their power and feed her own."

"Is that what you are attempting? To feed your own with Franco's?"

"How ignorant you are! Not Franco's and not my own."

"The Aether!" Marguerite and Rafe gasped out in unison.

He'd heard enough. His instinct was screaming at him to finish this and find Liz.

"I can't leave you loose to create more havoc, Mother. Come with me now, and we'll figure this mess out. Perhaps we can find a way to hide you from Damian." Why he wanted to protect her was a question of his sanity. He'd be putting a target on his own back. All for a woman who hated him and everything he represented.

"Damian?" She scoffed. "Damian Dethridge is dead, boy. Didn't you see the stones light? That was the last of his life force. It's directly connected to his power. Remove the magic, kill the man."

The blood drained from Rafe's face, and he felt positively light-headed. "Mother, the Aether is for balance. Without him, the magical world will be chaos. He's who the Witches' Council turns to when all else fails."

"Now, they'll turn to me."

"No, they won't. You'll be dead because, if you've succeeded in raising Isolde, she won't honor a pact between you. She's a monster and will bleed your magic dry."

Finally, some of what he was trying to impress upon her must've sunk in. She paled slightly and looked at Marguerite, who nodded her agreement with Rafe's assessment. Panic and an emotion remarkably similar to fear flashed upon her aristocratic features and vanished just as quickly. Josephine Champeau was old-school. She believed in herself, her family name, and her ability to beat the rest of the world into submission. Lifting the paper, she opened her mouth to finish the resurrection spell.

Rafe dove for her.

The blast of a gunshot reverberated off the stones with a deafening effect. He ducked, but not before witnessing his mother's blank-faced stare of death as she crumpled to the ground. Marguerite didn't miss. The smoking gun, proof of her crime. Although, when he had longer to process what just happened, he would most likely conclude she'd done mankind a favor and not murder.

"I'm sorry, Rafe," she said softly. "I'm so sorry."

The ground around them shifted and shook.

"You have to get out of here, cousin," he warned.

"Come with me to safety," she urged.

"I can't." He staggered to his feet and balanced a hand on the vibrating wall. "I have to get to the Thornes. To Liz. But you should go." A large chunk of the ceiling crashed beside her, and Marguerite jumped in fear. "Go. Now."

"Not without you. Let's find your lover and get the hell out of here."

In silent agreement, they ran down the temple corridor to where Rafe had last seen Liz. When he found her, she was slowly twisting this way and that as if to keep an eye on all the passageways. Little Sabrina rested with her eyes closed and her head on her father's still chest. A heartbreaking sight. Not to mention terrifying, with the illuminated pillars behind them.

"*Qalbi*, we need to leave. Right now. This temple is coming down."

"We can't. Sabrina needs the spell Isolde wrote to reverse this." The dawning panic in her eyes tore at his insides.

"It's too late for him," he said, regret heavy in his words and heart.

"You and Marguerite go. I can't leave her, and she won't leave him."

Then he understood. Even if she wanted to, Liz wasn't going to try to remove a baby Aether from her father. The kid had enough juice to fry anyone who tried. Yet, as kind and caring as she was, Liz wouldn't leave her alone to die. Fear danced along his spine and tickled his nerve endings.

"All right. Then you and I wait with her."

"No, Rafe. You need to go." She rubbed the left side of her chest. The tears in her eyes spoke of the emotional toll this was taking on her. The idea of them parted forever was hurting her, and one he didn't wish to entertain.

"That's not going to happen, *qalbi*. Where you go, I go. If this is our final resting place, then so be it." Where his bravery came from, he didn't know. Because had it been anyone else, he'd have cursed them for a fool. But he couldn't leave her, and he didn't want to live without the one person who made him feel whole.

"Can the three of us shore up the walls, until Alastair returns?" Marguerite asked, dodging another section of falling stone and crowding closer to Rafe in her nervousness.

"We can certainly try," Liz said feelingly. "Uh, anyone have any clue how?"

As suddenly as the rolling earthquake started, it stopped. Silence reigned and left a ringing in Rafe's ears. He dropped his gaze to the child. She stared back at him with eerily calm eyes.

Liz squatted beside her and touched her shoulder. "Was that you, sweetheart?"

A single nod was her answer.

"Thank you, Sabrina."

The girl nodded once more and shut her eyes.

"I think she's keeping his body in stasis," Marguerite said in a hushed voice.

"I'll be damned. I think you're right."

"Handy kid to have around."

"You have no idea."

Rafe moved away to sit against the inside of the exterior wall in order to keep watch over their small group. Resting his head back against the rock, he thought about his mother and all the pain she'd wrought. A better son might grieve for her, but he wasn't. Never was it more obvious than when he'd stayed away for the last thirty years. His father would need to be informed when this was all said and done. Perhaps he'd want some type of ceremony honoring her life. Rafe felt bad for his dad because, once upon a time, he'd been in love with Josephine.

The sight of Sabrina clinging to her father tugged at Rafe's heartstrings. Theirs was a parent/child love as it should be. Not how his dysfunctional relationship with his mother had been. He swiped at his eyes, finding it odd they came away wet. He frowned at the dampness on his fingers, unable to comprehend the tears. For sure, his mother didn't deserve a single one. But maybe the little boy inside him still needed to grieve. Not for the woman, but for what the woman should've represented.

He made a silent vow to his unborn children. Never would he abuse their trust. Never would he not show them, every single minute of every day, they were wanted and loved. Turning his gaze to Liz, he smiled. She was fierce when it came to the protection of Sabrina. Sometime in the near future, he hoped she'd be his wife and that they could create a small family of their own to care for and spoil.

Rafe closed his eyes to visualize their perfect family, keeping an ear tuned to any potential threat.

CHAPTER 26

*A*lastair sorted through the papers in the study at Rēafere's Fortress, searching for anything resembling the note he'd seen in the vision. Nothing. Wanting to swear up a plague of locusts, he nevertheless refrained.

"Well, Nathanial, you could certainly stand to help a descendant out, old boy," he said aloud.

As soon as the words left his mouth, a light appeared on the far side of the study and floated around a small antique chest on the top shelf of the ornate thirteen-feet-tall bookcases.

"If that's a sign, I'll take it with a hearty thank you from me to you."

Alastair crossed to the shelves and, with a flick of his wrist, brought the library ladder sweeping to his side of the room. Once he reached the top shelf, he scooped up the small chest and climbed down. It was only when he'd set it on the four-foot, circular table in the center of the study, that he realized he didn't have a way to open the lock, because in all of his searching, he hadn't seen a key. Of course, Nathanial wouldn't make it easy to delve into his belongings. Alastair's brother, Preston, would've tried his lock-picking skills at this point.

Looking skyward, he called out half-jokingly, "Isis, I don't suppose you want to send my brother to me for this one, hmm?" He hadn't expected an answer, but in the span of an eyeblink, Preston was standing before him.

"You rang?" Preston's droll tone was music to Alastair's old ears, and he found himself choking on a mix of happiness laced with sadness.

"Brother," he said gruffly. "I've missed you."

"I've missed you, too, Al."

They embraced for a long minute, neither wanting to lose the contact.

Finally, Preston patted him on the back. "Well, this is getting awkward."

He startled a laugh from Alastair, who released him with a hard squeeze. "Of course. My apologies for crying on your pretty gray suit." With a gesture to the small, jewel-encrusted chest, he asked, "Any idea how to open this thing? I think it contains a spell I need."

"Think? You don't know?"

He grimaced. "Our great-grandfather liked his secrets."

After lifting the box, Preston turned it this way and that, looking for what Alastair assumed was a false bottom. His brother's dark auburn brows collided as he studied it.

Alastair found himself grinning. Preston was always in his element when he discovered something old with a bit of mystery attached. "Why did she send you?"

"She seems to be over her pique regarding the Book of Thoth spell to raise Rorie." Preston shot him a mocking smile. "Or maybe she felt sorry for you fumbling around without the brains of the family to help you."

A bark of laughter escaped him. Damn, it really was great to have his brother here, if only for a brief time. "I'll have to thank her profusely for your services when next I see her."

"She'd like that." He set the box down. "There's no key for this lock."

"Yes, I know. I've been all through this place."

"No. I mean, there is literally no key that exists to open it. See the runes here?" Preston pointed to the small marks encircling the lock. "These hold the directions to open it."

Alastair lifted the box to study the marks. "They're different than anything I've seen before. I don't know how to read them."

"Damian's daughter will know."

He ran a hand through his hair. "I'd almost forgotten the urgency as I basked in how good it felt to see you again, little brother. I should get going."

"It's all right, Al. This won't be the last time. Do what you must to bring the Aether out of stasis. Isis is on your side."

"Thanks, Pres. And thank our beloved goddess when you return, won't you?"

"Of course." They shared a long, solemn look. "I wish things were different, brother. I wish I was at your side, fighting the good fight. More than you can possibly know. Thank you for taking care of my girls and seeing to their happiness."

Tears burned behind Alastair's lids, and all he could do was nod. Damn, he was feeling the maudlin old fool, lately. All he wanted was his family around him for whatever remaining years he had left.

Preston embraced him one last time. "Don't forget to take a pin or lancet with you. I believe that lock calls for a drop of Aether blood, but I can't be sure."

Before his brother could teleport back to the Otherworld, Alastair clasped his forearm. "Pres? Are you... happy?"

"I'm not unhappy, with the exception of how much I miss all of you. Isis's consort is not a bad job." Preston's bittersweet smile turned mischievous. "Oh, and I've met someone. She refuses to give me the time of day, but I think I'm wearing her down."

Alastair chuckled. "I have no doubt she'll throw herself in your arms—sooner rather than later."

"We are of the same mind, brother."

And then he was gone. The smile slowly fell from Alastair's face as he looked at the empty spot where Preston stood seconds ago. "I love you, Pres."

Liz eyed Rafe where he sat against the wall. His eyes were closed, and deep emotion tightened the lines around his mouth, and it didn't take a genius to guess the reason for his turmoil.

Sidling up to Marguerite, she touched the other woman's shoulder. In a voice pitched for her ears alone, Liz asked, "What happened with Rafe's mother? I'm assuming she was the one behind this."

"She was." Marguerite looked over her shoulder at Rafe. "The betrayal on his face was difficult to witness."

"And Josephine?"

"I shot her through the heart."

Marguerite had said it with such dispassion, Liz found it difficult to wrap her brain around her lack of reaction. She must've picked up on Liz's disbelief because she said, "My aunt was like a rabid dog in recent years. As time went on, she snapped and snarled at anyone who tried to get close. I began to watch her in earnest about a month ago when I caught her conversing with herself."

"Yet you never told Rafe?"

"He hadn't been back in almost three decades, Ms. Thorne. How was I to know if he even cared?"

"If you knew him at all, it would be obvious he does," Liz snapped.

Marguerite studied her through narrowed eyes. Finally, she nodded. "Perhaps. But our family was never like yours. There are at least ten Champeaus who live on the estate. Nine of which don't care about anything or anyone other than the next society function. And while it's a simple matter to conjure basic needs, it's a little harder to maintain the finances for such a large estate. Especially when the property is listed in government records, and taxes need to be paid, or when the staff needs to collect their paychecks."

Some of the anger Liz was experiencing left. Rafe's cousin wasn't to blame for Josephine's unstable mind or her inability to love her son as a mother should. "I'm sorry. I didn't mean—"

"You did, but I accept your apology. Your deeper feelings are based on your love of Rafe, and I'm glad. He's been lonely a long time."

Her attention drifted back to him, only to find Rafe staring back at the two of them. His expression was stark, and Liz wanted nothing more than to run to him and wrap him in her arms. One hand dangled over his raised knee, and dejection hung over him like a black cloud. He probably saw himself that way.

"She cursed you both with blood magic, you know."

Liz whipped her head back around and gaped at Marguerite.

"I'll let Rafe explain, but you'll need to make sure you find a way to kill the spell, so it doesn't affect you both moving forward."

"Thank y-you." Suddenly cold, Liz hugged herself and rubbed her arms. "Is the temperature dropping in here?"

Alarm lit Marguerite's classically beautiful face. Her air of detachment disappeared as she puffed out a breath. "I'm about to make the understatement of the year and say that can't be good."

In preparation to conjure a coat for Sabrina, Liz held out her hands.

"Don't!" Rafe barked and surged to his feet. "Something dark is here. I can feel it pulsing and moving underground."

"The Enchantress?" she whispered, as if by saying it softly, she wouldn't be overheard by anyone other than them.

"It's coming for Papa."

"What is? What's coming for him?" Fear curled in Liz's belly and made her queasy as hell. What the hell could want Damian's body so badly?

"It's a death dragon." Sabrina's small voice shook, and she clutched her father tighter. "It wants to eat Papa's soul."

"That's all we need right now." Rafe swore under his breath. "We have to go, Liz."

Marguerite nodded in agreement, shifting back and rubbing her hands together. "I've never heard of a death dragon, but it seems pretty serious."

"Sabrina? Can we fight it off?"

"They don't like fire."

"It's convenient I'm a fire elemental, then, isn't it?" She tried to act cheerful, but the other three looked through her pretense.

"Actually, I'm a fire elemental, too," Marguerite added. "You, me, and Rafe will form a triangle around them."

"Should we create a circle of protection? Do you think it will help?" Liz asked, taking up a position at Damian's head.

Rafe gave her a shrug. "Couldn't hurt."

"It won't help, Miss Liz." Sabrina sat up and looked around the chamber as if seeing it for the first time. "It comes up through the ground. We have to lift Papa."

"Levitation is my party trick. I've got this." Liz, in no way, had this. Her poker face needed work if the roll of Marguerite's eyes was any indication. Poor woman probably saw her brain with that one. "What? You never played Light as a Feather as a kid?"

A distinctive, animalistic growl echoed around the room, and the dirt floor beneath them shifted and bucked like a wave from the sea. The continuous motion sent Liz crashing to her knee. The sound unnerved her, and she wasted no time as she shoved her hands under Damian's stiff body. "Sabrina, support your papa's head, sweetie."

Rafe mimicked her action, and Marguerite latched onto Damian's ankles.

"Dear Goddess, hear our plea,
assist us in our time of need.
His body make as light as air,
keep him from the death dragon snare."

Sabrina actually giggled at the ridiculousness of Liz's impromptu spell, triggering a snort from Rafe and another "are you for real" reaction from Marguerite. But luckily for Liz, the spell worked, and Damian's body lifted from the ground to float waist-level.

"What do we do with him now?" Marguerite asked. "We can't hold him suspended like this forever. There's no way to even know if what's after him is a death dragon. Why are we taking direction from a young child?"

Frankly, Liz didn't care for Marguerite's superior attitude. "She's a baby Aether. She *knows* things. If she said a horde of earthworms was heading for us, I'd listen and take precautions."

"A group of earthworms is called a clew, not a horde."

"This is why you don't have any friends," Liz retorted.

The other woman stiffened and looked down her perfect, aristocratic nose at Liz. "I have friends." But she didn't look convincing.

The air around them grew heavy and sizzled just as Alastair stepped through a rift. His brows flew skyward as he took in the scene. "Dare I ask?"

"Death dragons," Rafe supplied helpfully with a dry look at Liz.

"Look, if the kid said they exist, I believe her," she growled.

Alastair nodded and moved forward to join them. "They absolutely exist." He lifted a small jeweled chest. "Back to why I was gone, I believe I found what we're looking for."

"Thank the Goddess," Liz murmured under her breath. She met Sabrina's serious, dark gaze. "What's next?"

"We have to put Papa in the circle to give him his magic back."

"Then that's what we'll do."

CHAPTER 27

*T*ransferring Damian to the magical circle Franco had initially created within the confines of the pillars was a simple matter after the four of them coordinated their movements together. Walking should've been a simple matter of one foot in front of the other, and although Damian's body was lighter thanks to Liz's spell, it was still like moving a bulky piece of furniture.

Rafe nearly tripped over Franco's corpse, but Alastair stepped in to save the day and rolled the body out of the way. One would think the sight of so refined a man squatting to shift a body would be odd, and they would be right, but still, Alastair did nothing more than dust his hands off and straighten his cuffs as if disposing of dead people was an everyday occurrence.

Once they stepped into the circle, the pillars lit a second time, and the ground outside the circle rippled in a constant wave around the perimeter.

"It wants Papa," Sabrina told them.

Rafe heard the fear in her voice and wished he knew what to say to comfort her. "Can we set him down now, or can it cross the line?"

"We can put him down," she confirmed.

Alastair tugged his slacks up and squatted down next to her. "I need to prick your finger, Sabrina. I believe it's the only way to open this box. Will you do that for me?"

The girl took the small chest from him and turned it this way and that in her curiosity. When she was satisfied, she returned it to him.

Alastair removed a small pin from his suit jacket and held it up. "Would you like to do the honors, or shall I?"

"You do it."

Grasping her tiny hand in his, he shifted her fingers to access her thumb. Alastair caught her eye and made a funny face in what Rafe assumed was a distraction. She smiled, and Alastair pressed the sharp tip into her flesh. A small bead of blood appeared, and he guided her thumb to the lock. When she placed the pad of her thumb against the mechanism, the runes on the box began to glow a soft gold, and the small click sounded loudly in the cavernous chamber.

Alastair removed the scroll, untied the ribbon, and unrolled the paper to read. With a grin for Sabrina, he said, "Clever girl. I think this will work to bring your papa back to us."

The beatific smile Sabrina gave him was a sight to behold. Never had Rafe seen such adoration for another person. It was as if she viewed Alastair as a god among men for his pronouncement. "Thank you, sir."

"You can thank me when this is over by not letting your papa murder us for bringing you here in the first place." He pulled a comical face to soften his words, but the rest of them understood the seriousness of what he was saying.

Rafe prayed Damian didn't wake killing-mad. They'd all seen the result on Franco's face.

"Okay, it says here we need to take a small bit of the Aether's blood and apply it to the largest rune symbol on each of these stone."

"That doesn't sound wise." Marguerite had broken her silence and looked around skeptically. "It's never good to use blood magic if it can be avoided. Who wrote the spell?"

Dread began to build inside Rafe. Where had Alastair gotten a spell to revive the Aether? "No idea."

"The Enchantress wrote it before she was entombed. As if she had a vision of what was going to happen. But what if she's trying to pull a fast one?" Liz bit her lip. "Like now that her temple has drained his magic, his blood will be the final step to wake her. I really don't care for this plan."

Sabrina began to cry, loud gut-wrenching sobs. Before any of them could react, Alastair scooped her up and kissed the crown of her head. "Shush, little one. We're going to help your papa." He tilted her chin up with one finger and met her troubled gaze. "If you tell me this is a good plan, then we'll do it."

She wrapped her arms tightly around his neck and buried her face against his throat. For a long moment, the two of them stood locked together, with Alastair rubbing small circles on her back and crooning to her in words so low, none of them could hear.

Rafe had never witnessed this softer side of Alastair. In fact, he'd have said it didn't exist. All he'd ever known was the hard-edged warlock who frightened everyone who came in contact with him. But apparently this was the Alastair that the Thorne family saw in rare moments. The man who would smite the most deadly of their kind to protect what was his.

Never had Rafe admired him more. What might his life have been like if he had a family like Liz's? He cast a glance toward Marguerite, and the longing in her eyes matched what was in his heart. They had both been robbed by being born to the Champeau line. Reaching over, he gave her hand a light squeeze. Surprised, she met his steady understanding gaze then contracted her hand within his in response. Theirs would be a better relationship moving forward.

"The death dragon is getting violent, cousin," Liz said gently. "We need to speed things up."

"Are you ready to continue, child?"

Sabrina drew back and stared into Alastair's concerned sapphire eyes. Finally, she nodded. "When Papa wakes, he's going to be so mad."

"I'll deal with your papa." He winked before setting her down. "He likes to bluster, but he's a big softie."

Clasping his hand, Sabrina tugged him toward Damian's body. "Please help him."

"That's the goal." He knelt beside the Aether's still form and pricked his index finger. "Liz, I need you to lift Sabrina up to apply the blood. No one else touches these stones."

Squeezing a few drops on the girl's index finger, he gave her a light push in the direction of the first pillar. As instructed, Liz lifted her to within reach of the rune etched into the stone. It seemed Sabrina knew instinctively to trace the symbol because it began to hum at the same time it illuminated. They repeated the process for the seven pillars. The buzzing sounded like a thousand bees and set the death dragon to growling beneath ground.

"What's next?" Rafe shouted over the noise.

"Next, I etch the runes in Damian's chest."

Rafe practically swallowed his tongue. The idea of carving up the Aether's chest made him lightheaded. This did *not* seem like a finely tuned plan. If Damian woke furious and in pain, it didn't bode well for the rest of them.

"I need the four of you to step out of the circle now. This part is dangerous."

He wanted to argue with Alastair that the dangerous part would be *after* Damian came back to life. Instead, he bundled the women and Sabrina out of the inner temple. They huddled against the exterior wall and watched the older warlock from a safe distance.

Alastair conjured a knife and proceeded to use the tip to copy the runes from the stones. One by one, the open marks on Damian's chest began to glow, and the blood seemed to dissolve under the heat of the light radiating from his skin.

Liz's complexion had taken on a green tinge, and unable to watch the entire process, she buried her face against Rafe's shoulder. Taking the cue from her, he lifted Sabrina and positioned her to rest her head on his opposing shoulder and to turn her face away from the scene of her father being cut up.

After all seven symbols were replicated in the Aether's flesh, Alastair rose and left the circle.

"What now?" Marguerite asked in a shaky voice.

"Now, it's Sabrina's turn."

Liz's head whipped up, and she pinned Alastair with a glare. *"What?"*

Rafe almost laughed at her mama-bear stance.

Lips twisted with amusement, Alastair shook his head. "Perhaps I should clarify."

"Please do, cousin."

"Sabrina needs to read the spell. She's the only one with the power to resurrect her father." He lifted the child from Rafe's arms and set her on her feet.

Squatting down to eye level, Rafe asked, "Can you read, Sabrina?"

Worry clouded her eyes as she shook her head.

"Plan B. How about one of us speaks the words, and she repeats them?" He looked over his shoulder at Alastair. "Does that work?"

"I believe it will." His reassuring smile was directed at Sabrina and did the trick. Hope flared on her little face, and she headed straight for her father.

"I'm ready, sir."

The words were in Latin, but the girl had no difficulty parroting whatever Alastair said. With each line uttered, the air became thicker and created its own windstorm. Dust kicked up around the outside of the circle, and Rafe shielded his eyes against the grit.

"Holy shit!" Liz gasped.

He peered around his hand to see a web of lines illuminate from beneath Damian and run to each of the pillars. The death dragon groaned one last time and seemed to quiet forever. Rafe was sincerely grateful they never witnessed that monster rise from beneath the earth. He wasn't sure his old heart could take another shock.

"I think it's working," Marguerite said softly. "Should that child glow like that?"

"Alastair?"

"I'm not certain. This is new for me, too." The grim expression on his face was a deeper reflection of his thoughts. "I think I should pull her out."

Liz stopped him with a hand on his arm. "Not you, cousin. If those stones are designed to remove power, you can't lose yours. I'll go."

Right when she intended to step across the border, Sabrina held up a hand to stop her and shook her head. Rafe felt as torn as Liz looked. Leaving a young child in the center of such a tempest didn't sit well with any of them.

"Papa, wake up!" Sabrina shouted. "Papa! Please!"

The Aether's lids popped open, and he stared unseeingly at the rock ceiling above him.

Rafe's heart sunk.

Clutching his arm, Liz let loose a small sob.

Sabrina shouted over and over, trying to get through to her father. It didn't appear to be working, and Rafe could feel the child's pain as it permeated the air around them.

Without warning, Alastair crossed the line and knelt beside his friend. He unknotted his tie and ripped it from his neck then unbuttoned the top three buttons of his dress shirt. Just as Rafe was going to question Liz as to what the hell Alastair might be doing, the warlock wrapped his large hand around the pendant at the base of his throat. He laid a palm flat over Damian's heart, then closed his eyes.

"Wake, Damian. It's time to come back to your daughter."

Tears streamed down the little girl's face as she sat by her father's head and stroked his hair.

"Wake, my friend. You're needed here."

The Aether blinked once. Then again. Suddenly, he opened his mouth in a silent scream, his back arching as a thin column of blue light poured out of his mouth toward the sky.

"What the hell is happening?" Marguerite asked. Never had Rafe heard her so nervous.

No one had an answer for her, so they remained silent.

The beam of light cut off, and Damian's eyes shut a final time. The room was cast in semi-darkness.

Sabrina flung herself over her father as Alastair sat back on his heels.

Rafe was stupefied. Frozen with his shock, he could only stare on in horror. It appeared their ceremony had failed spectacularly, and they'd managed to kill the Aether.

CHAPTER 28

From outside his body, Damian observed Alastair and Sabrina perform the ceremony to revive him with detachment. He *should* feel upset on his daughter's behalf, but a numbness had settled in his soul, and he couldn't find the energy to fight the beckoning darkness and its promise of restful sleep. Exactly two hundred years he'd survived, only to be tricked by an unscrupulous woman with a grudge. Goddess, he was tired.

"Papa, wake up! Papa! Please!"

The words came to him as if from a great distance, but he responded to the urgency behind them. He slammed back into his body with a force that stole his ability to breathe.

"Wake, Damian. It's time to come back to your daughter. Wake, my friend. You're needed here."

The area over his heart burned where Alastair touched him, and his skin felt as if it were on fire. He opened his mouth to cry out against the pain, but no sound emerged. His body arched up and bucked, trying to dislodge what was left of his soul. There may have been sweet relief in letting go, but Alastair had somehow tied Damian's soul to his body. There was no escape. The light faded from the room, and he closed his eyes, grateful the ceremony had ended. Perhaps now he could sleep.

"Take the child and head to my estate," Alastair said roughly.

But his little beastie had latched on and refused to be budged.

"Sweetheart?" Liz's voice cracked as she addressed Sabrina. "Sweetie, I need you to come with me. We can't stay here anymore. It isn't safe, and your papa would want us to protect you."

Sabrina's small, ravaged voice said, "I can't leave Papa. The death dragon will get him."

"No, it won't, child. I'll see he's cared for. Go with Liz and Rafe."

"Please tell me that care comes with a damned glass of water, Al," Damian pushed out through cracked lips.

"Papa?"

He lifted his lids and stared at his determined little savior. Tears clung to her long dark lashes, and her little button nose was bright red from crying. "You just can't stay where you're supposed to, can you, beastie?" He softened his words with a loving smile.

"Oh, Papa!"

The impact of her forty-pound body on his aching chest made him grunt.

"Same old, Damian. You live for the drama of a grand entrance." Alastair helped him sit up. "Welcome back, my friend. Enjoy your nap?"

"I could've used a few more hours." He cradled his daughter close and glanced around at all the relieved faces. "How about we blow this joint? This place gives me the creeps."

Liz laughed even as she wiped tears from the corners of her eyes. "You missed the real excitement. Apparently, there's such a thing as death dragons."

A shudder swept his body. *Death dragons.* He hadn't heard mention of one since he was roughly Sabrina's age. They had populated the ground beneath this temple, waiting impatiently for his mother's scraps. "Yes, they are ugly little fuckers that feed on the souls of the dead, but they also like to chomp on their remains at the same time." He kissed the top of Sabrina's dark head. "Thanks for sparing me that, love."

"You're welcome, Papa."

Damian's attempt to stand with Sabrina wrapped around him, clinging to his neck, was aborted, and he fell back on his ass. "You're going to have to let go, beastie. I'm as weak as a newborn kitten."

Liz opened her arms, and his daughter was happy to dive into her embrace.

"Thank you," he mouthed to her from behind Sabrina.

Her Madonna-like smile reminded him of his wife. *Vivian.* He'd thought of her in the moments he lay dying. Their failed relationship was his biggest regret. If he had it to do over, he would try harder to convince her to stay. Pride be damned. A visit to her home was in the near future.

When Alastair cleared his throat, Damian grinned. "Sorry, Al. I was woolgathering. We're going to need a portal. Care to whip one up?"

"I'll do it," Sabrina volunteered. Already, he could see the strain performing the blood magic had done on her, but he couldn't deny her this one last thing.

"Of course, beastie. You're the best at portal conjuring of anyone I know. Will you create a door to take us all home?"

"To Ravenswood, Papa?"

He started to say yes, but then shook his head. "No. Let's go back to the hotel in Paris. Then we'll detour to see your mother."

Her dark eyes rounded and tears, shimmered on her lower lids as her lips trembled. "Really?"

"Really."

When they were back at the hotel, Rafe filled them in on Josephine's involvement and her subsequent death at his cousin's hand. No one was surprised she'd concocted such an elaborate scheme. Especially not Liz, who had been on the receiving end of that woman's hatred. Everything made so much more sense after learning Franco was a pawn.

Liz's only remaining concern was if the curse Josephine had placed using the blood magic would continue after her death, and whether she and Rafe needed to delve deeper into the removal of the spell, as Marguerite suggested. Again and again, her eyes drifted to where he silently sipped his wine. The melancholy surrounding him wasn't disguised as well as he probably thought it was. She wanted nothing more than to bundle him away from the crowd and soothe his hurt.

Having grown up in the loving bosom of her relatives, she could only imagine how lonely and dysfunctional his upbringing had been. Any child of theirs wouldn't spend a day wondering if they were loved.

As if he sensed her focus, Rafe glanced up, and they locked gazes.

"I love you," she mouthed.

His lips quirked in a small, sad smile.

When he didn't respond in kind, she wondered what could possibly be running through his mind. Nothing good. The barrier he was erecting would be difficult to breach if he was left to his own devices much longer.

She rose to go to him when Damian stepped in her path for his final goodbye.

He grinned when she contorted to see around him, and she had to smile when she realized she'd done a one-eighty. Just a few days before, she was trying to see around Rafe to take in all Damian's deliciousness, and now, she was consumed with the love of her life.

"Thank you for all you've done for my family, Liz. It's a debt I can never repay."

"It could be argued I was the cause of all your problems."

With a shake of his head, he said, "No. The problems were from an overreaching witch who felt she had the right to meddle in the lives of others for her personal gain."

"I'm glad you see it that way, Damian. I'm also glad you decided not to flay me alive for taking your daughter into such a dangerous situation."

"Now that you mention it…" But he winked to show he was kidding. "Sabrina is headstrong, and she had a vision of what was to come. There was no stopping her, Liz. I'm grateful she had you to watch out for her."

They hugged.

Liz was happy to see Damian had regained his strength throughout the day because apparently you can't keep a good Aether down. After a lengthy phone call to his wife, he'd stated he fully intended to honor his promise to Sabrina to visit Vivian. Liz hoped he was able to work out the problems in his marriage. Both he and his daughter deserved a better hand than they'd been dealt.

As for Liz, she was happy to have her family's magic restored and to have everyone survive this last ordeal in one piece. She was hesitant to even think about peace and quiet for the Thornes at this point. The last time she'd had a similar thought, hell broke loose.

Ryanne tried to capture her in a conversation, but Liz waved her off with a smile. She wanted to find Rafe and make sure he was okay. When she looked up from the hug she shared with Damian, Rafe had disappeared, and worry was nagging her hard. Something was off with his behavior.

A quick search of their hotel room showed all his personal items missing. She tried his cell phone but was sent immediately to voicemail.

"Rafe," she said to the empty room. "Please don't do this to us."

Moisture built behind her closed lids, and she feared she would break down and cry copious amounts of tears if he chose to exit her life again. Why hadn't he stayed to discuss the problem? For that matter, why not tell her what the problem was to begin with?

Three hours later, he still hadn't returned her call. With a heavy heart, she curled up on the bed they'd shared and pulled his pillow to her, inhaling the lingering scent that was his alone. It was awful how closely this moment resembled that morning four years ago when she woke alone and heartbroken. Hugging the pillow tight, she gave way to her exhaustion and drifted to sleep.

RAFE WANDERED THE HALLS OF THE CHÂTEAU, IDLY TOUCHING OBJECTS he remembered from his childhood. No obvious changes had occurred during the centuries his family owned this place. But now, when he looked closer, he could see the ravages of time. Why hadn't Mother used magic to restore these things? She'd had it within her power to do so. Maybe Marguerite would help him solve the mystery of his mother's downward spiral and determine what the catalyst had been.

He felt a deep kinship with Damian at the moment. Both their mothers had gone insane. Both needed to be put down like rabid animals. Both men had kept their feelings bottled up until the right woman came along. And they both adored Elizabeth Thorne.

His phone rang for the fourth time, and he let it go to voicemail. Even though he didn't bother to check the caller ID, there was little doubt Liz was the one calling. Thorne Industries had yet to be reopened, and he rarely received calls from the Witches' Council since they'd parted ways. He supposed the mighty Alastair might be calling, but he was too emotionally drained to care who might be on the other end of the line.

Currently, he had nothing left to give, and he wasn't ready to rehash the day's events with anyone. Liz, being the kind-hearted woman she was, would understand and allow him this time alone without taking him to task for abruptly ducking out.

The air in the drawing room thickened, and an atmospheric change occurred, indicating an incoming witch. Only three people had the ability to teleport in without finding themselves fried to a crisp. Two of the three were now dead. It could only be Marguerite.

"I thought you might be here."

He shrugged, not looking at her. "Where else was I to go?"

She laughed lightly. "Anywhere else. Your father's place. Liz's hotel room. Your apartment in North Carolina. Literally anywhere."

"True." He snorted and turned around. "Why are *you* here?"

"I live in this old mausoleum."

"Why not sell it?"

"Because it's yours now, Rafe."

His jaw practically scraped the marbled floor.

"You didn't know you were next in line after Franco?"

"No." He couldn't seem to wrap his brain around his inheritance. "Why the hell would it come to me? Mother hated me."

"It was outlined in Grand-père's will. That predates anything Josephine would've had drawn up."

"I don't want it, Marguerite. This place holds nothing but bad memories for me."

"With Liz, you can make new ones," she said softly. "You could have a half-dozen little ones running about."

He strolled around the room, thinking about the possibilities, before focusing his attention on her. "And you? What would you do if that happened? Would you stay on?"

"Where else would I go." She released a bitter little laugh. "Franco burned through all our funds. There is nothing left. We owe too many creditors."

"I still find that difficult to believe. What of the mills or shops?"

"Sold or dismantled. And before you ask, the last of the farmland not entailed to the estate was sold off about ten or eleven years ago."

"And Jean-Paul?" He mentioned the Champeau estate manager, hoping beyond hope Franco hadn't sacked him.

"He passed away about two years ago." She grimaced and waved a hand around, gesturing to the house. "This place needs a cash infusion, and someone with a strong business sense."

"Can I access the records?"

"We can try." She pivoted on her heel to go.

"Marguerite."

She cast him a curious look over her shoulder.

"I want you to have this place." When she frowned, he quickly added, "But only if you want it. I'm sure it'll be a headache to manage, but if you're willing, I'll give you what you need to restore the place."

A genuine smile lit her face. The first real emotion he'd witnessed in as long as he could remember. "I'd like that."

"Do you know why mother never used her magic to restore this place?"

"I believe she didn't want to give Franco any reason to sell off the antiques. If he believed everything was worthless, he'd leave the château intact." She touched a hand to his arm. "Your mother was wily, Rafe. She knew how to manipulate. Even you."

"Me?"

"You don't think she knew that by sending Franco to kindle a romance with Liz, you would make your move? She knew you loved her and only needed to be prodded into action. That's why she put the blood curse on you."

He scrubbed his hands up and down his face. "I keep asking myself what kind of mother does that to her own son."

"And what have you come up with?"

"Nothing. I don't see how anyone would do something of that nature to their child."

"She was never mother material, cousin. Josephine never had the capacity to love."

"Was it because of Alastair and GiGi's father, Preston II?"

"Perhaps. Their relationship was long before I came into the world. And while she never had nice things to say about the Thornes, I thought it was jealousy for their successes. She never spoke of her engagement to me."

"Thank you for being forthcoming, cousin. Let's take care of matters around here so I might put this all in the past."

CHAPTER 29

*T*wo days passed with minimal communication from Rafe. The first night he disappeared, it was roughly eleven hours before he finally texted Liz. The message had been straight-forward and simple.

"I need to take care of a couple of important matters. I'll be in touch in a few days. xo - Rafe."

Of course, she'd been understanding. As the third day grew later and morning faded to afternoon, Liz grew annoyed by the continued silence. The damned man had contacted her more when they *weren't* a couple than now when they were supposed to be in love. Ignoring her didn't bode well for their future.

When she hadn't heard from him by noon on the fourth day, she resigned herself to the fact he was no longer interested in her or deeper issues were at play. She prayed to the Goddess it was the deeper issues and tried to maintain a positive outlook. More than once, she reminded herself he was a stand-up kind of guy. It hadn't helped.

Because Paris without Rafe was a major letdown, she checked out of her hotel to return home.

On the morning of the fifth day, she called for the third and final time only to get Rafe's voicemail again. She didn't bother to leave a message, because she wasn't a complete idiot and knew how to take a hint.

How he could do this to her after proposing was beyond Liz's scope of comprehension. The heartache this time around was worse than anything she'd ever experienced in her life. If she thought she'd been hurt four years ago, it was nothing compared to this utter devastation. It was tempered only by the slow, burning anger beginning to build.

On the sixth day, she aborted what was left of her vacation and returned to work.

Nash greeted her as Liz stepped into his office. "Welcome back. It's been a madhouse here without you. I hope your time with Rafe was worth the stacks of paperwork on your desk," he teased.

The humorous light left Nash's eyes as he studied her face. Hiding from an empath was impossible, and Liz didn't bother to try. He was most likely picking up on her self-loathing and crushing hurt.

"You and Rafe weren't together all this time? Or did you break up in the last day or so?"

"He disappeared the day we revived Damian, and he hasn't bothered to..." She swallowed. With a deep, fortifying breath, she continued, "... he hasn't bothered to return my calls or texts after the first night."

A dark frown tugged at Nash's blonde brows. His confusion was understandable because they'd all trusted Rafe to be a good guy and not an asshole. When Nash would've spoken, Liz waved off any well-meaning advice. "Let's move on to a different topic, shall we? Did you ever locate the missing artifacts?"

He was hesitant to speak, and she shot an exasperated glare his way.

"Yeah, um, Marguerite brought them all back two days ago," he finally admitted.

"And?"

"She said Rafe found them in a hidden room of the château. He wanted to be sure they were returned to us asap."

"Well, that's a plus."

"Liz—"

"Please don't, Nash. I'm trying to control my anger, but if it's too much for me to be around you like this, I can take off for a bit longer."

They tabled any discussion of Rafe and moved on to current business affairs. Liz took a walk around the complex to check in on their staff and catalog any issues the employees may be dealing with. They all greeted her like a long-lost sister, and it took away a small measure of the sting from Rafe's behavior.

As she was shutting down her computer for the day, a shipment of roses was delivered to her desk. For a moment, her heart stuttered in her chest at the stunning arrangement. Two-dozen blood-red roses with the tiniest buds of baby's-breath she'd ever seen. She snatched up the card.

"Dearest Liz, Sabrina and I humbly request your presence for dinner tomorrow night at Ravenswood. - D."

Tears filled her eyes, but she roughly swiped them away before they could fall. She refused to allow herself to give in to the disappointment riding her hard. How foolish to believe Rafe would go through the trouble when he couldn't even manage a text.

Grabbing up her phone, she searched through her contacts until she found Damian's number. Without a second thought, she shot him a text, accepting his invitation.

"Wonderful. No need for formal attire. My little beastie has requested burgers, fries, and milkshakes, so we've decided to make it a casual night."

Liz smiled at the image of the stylish Damian in casual clothing. Another text dinged her phone.

"Sabrina would like to know if you would be so kind as to extend the invitation to Chloe?"

After she agreed, she signed off, caressed a velvety rose petal, and stuffed her electronics into her bag. The idea of going back to her place by herself caused her stomach to flip. A split second later, she was on a call with Piper, her closest cousin and best friend.

"Hey! I was just thinking about you," Piper said. Genuine warmth flooded across the wire and almost sent Liz into a tailspin of tears.

"What are you doing tonight? Any plans?"

"Not a one. Josh canceled on me last minute. Again."

"Does he take off after he tries to kiss you? Like he's got somewhere more important to be?"

Piper laughed. "What the hell are you talking about, Liz?"

"Nothing." Ugh! Everything reminded her of Rafe. She needed to get a grip. "What do you feel like for dinner?"

"Calabresi's sounds good. It's close to your place, right?"

The old ticker spasmed, and Liz wished she could rip her worthless heart right out of her chest. She infused cheer into her voice. "Yep!"

"Liz, you okay?" The heavy concern Piper expressed caused another pang. Apparently, Liz overdid it on the pep.

"I will be." She glanced at her watch. "I can be there in about twenty. Does that work for you?"

Twenty-two minutes later, the two women were standing next to the hostess's podium. "I suppose we should've called for a reservation," Piper said in an aside to Liz.

Just as she would've responded, a deep, familiar voice drifted to her ears.

Rafe.

Liz pivoted in time to see him exiting the office with a short, stout man who could only be Gianni.

Of all the gin joints in all the towns in all the world...

She had to walk into Rafe's.

Quickly turning her back, she said, "Piper, do you mind if we go? Maybe order a pizza and grab some wine. It's better if—"

"*Qalbi.*" The sinfully intimate pitch of his voice made her stomach hurt. She wanted to teleport the hell away as fast as she could, but she couldn't expose what she was to so many non-magical patrons.

Piper's golden-eyed gaze locked onto her face. "We can still go, cousin."

Her use of the word "cousin" firmed Liz's spine. She was a Thorne, dammit. And Thornes had inner cores of steel. Fixing a cold smile on her face, she turned to confront Rafe. She hadn't expected to see the love radiating from his midnight eyes, and the deep adoration shining back at her gave her pause.

He lifted the bags in his arms. "I just arrived back in town an hour ago and had Gianni prepare a special meal for us." Glancing between the two women, he said, "There's more than enough, Piper, if you care to join us."

Piper cleared her throat, and for that, Liz was ecstatic because she couldn't have voiced a response to save her life. He disappeared for nearly a week and had the nerve to believe he could show up with a gourmet meal as if everything was still the same? Assuming she'd fall right in with his plans?

Fury exploded in her brain, and of its own volition, her fist flew out with the force of a jet-propelled rocket and impacted with his gut. The bags dropped to the floor, and Rafe bent double, coughing and gasping in an attempt to catch his breath.

"How about you shove that in your pipe and smoke it, you ass?" she snarled. Liz was halfway to her jeep when she realized she'd left Piper gaping in the restaurant foyer.

The rapid clicking of heels on cement came to her, and she exhaled her relief that Piper had the presence of mind to follow.

Unfortunately, the second set of footsteps registered as she spun back to apologize to her cousin.

Liz couldn't recall seeing Rafe as enraged as he was in that moment.

"Want to tell me what the hell that was all about?" Rafe bit out.

"Not right now. Maybe I'll text you in eleven hours or so and drop a cryptic message. Perhaps, after you call me once or twice with no response from me, you'll figure it out."

Understanding dawned, and his anger drained away. "You're upset I didn't touch base every day," he concluded.

"I didn't know if you were alive or dead, Rafe. I get one stinking message eleven hours after you disappear without a word then radio silence for the next five and a half days."

"It didn't occur to me you'd worry, *qalbi*." And it honestly hadn't. For the year he'd worked for Thorne Industries, he came and went with hardly a ripple. Communication was always sparse, and he had no reason to believe Liz would see this last trip of his any differently. Except she had, and he was an idiot.

"Unbelievable," she muttered.

"How about I leave you two to sort this out," Piper said in a gentle, soothing tone. "It sounds like you have a lot of catching up to do."

"No. I don't care to hear anything the King of Disappearing Acts has to say. Let's go, Piper."

"*Commoro!*" Rafe barked out in his panic.

He reached out an arm to support her when her upper body swayed precariously.

With a shriek of outrage, she shoved at his chest. *"Did you just freeze me in place?"*

A fiery red lit her irises, and Rafe knew he was about five seconds from being burned to a cinder like the time Damian had fried his ass in Nash's office. "I panicked," he admitted. "You were about to walk away—"

"You'd best remove that spell, or I'll torch your ass. They'll see you burning three counties away."

The wind picked up around them, blowing her golden locks around her head. The trees bent, and a flash of lightning streaked across the sky. The resounding boom of thunder followed seconds later.

Rafe voiced his awe. "Goddess, you're incredible."

"And that's my cue to leave," Piper said brightly. "Word to the wise, cousin, contain your power in public. You're drawing a crowd." An engaging grin took up nearly half her face. "Also, if a man risked life and limb to keep me at his side and tell me I'm incredible, I'd listen to what he has to say."

With a wink and a wave, she sauntered to her vehicle.

When she opened the door to a nineteen-sixty-eight Ford Mustang GT390 fastback, Rafe lost his ability to speak.

"Now you're going to stand there and drool over my *cousin?*"

"Not the woman. The *car.*"

The throaty sound of the engine roared to life, and Rafe never had such vehicle envy in all his life.

"*Rafe.*"

He snapped his head around to meet Liz's narrowed-eyed gaze. Her growl rivaled that of the Mustang. She pointed down at her feet, then placed her fists on her hips.

The two of them were at a crossroads here. If he released her, she'd take off and never give him the time of day again. If he didn't, he stood the chance of her turning him into a flaming pile of dog doo.

He crossed his arms and scratched the length of his jaw. "You're going to have to promise to hear me out, *qalbi.*"

"I can promise I'll murder you in your sleep if you don't release me in two seconds."

The urge to laugh overwhelmed him, and Rafe failed spectacularly to hold it back. He loved her feistiness. She, however, didn't find the situation nearly as funny. In fact, retribution burned brightly in her eyes. As abruptly as his humor took hold, it dissipated.

Rafe snapped his fingers to release the magical hold. "For what it's worth, I initially left to get my head on straight. My mother's death... My reaction was worse than expected."

She crossed her arms but remained where she was. A measure of her fury had melted away. "Why didn't you return my calls, Rafe? Why ghost me as if I meant nothing to you?"

"Like I said, it never occurred to me that you'd be worried after my first text. But when Marguerite and I reworked the wards on the château, the magic short-circuited my phone. I figured I'd pick up another one when I returned home." He continued in the face of her silence. "I travel for Thorne Industries constantly, Liz. You know I don't always check-in, but I *always* return. I thought it was understood I would this time, too."

Her full lip was caught between her white teeth, and Rafe figured she was chewing over a decision to forgive or not.

"I love you, *qalbi*. I believed we had an understanding. We committed to building our lives together. I didn't take that lightly." He shifted closer and used the knuckle on his index finger to nudge her chin upwards. "I'm sorry I hurt you. And from here on out, I can assure you, I will never take off again without telling you where I'm going first. Should I fail to check-in at least twice a day, I give you permission to torch my ass, as you so dearly want to at the moment."

Her lips compressed, and she closed her eyes. For a second, Rafe feared he'd crushed any affection she held for him. Then her eyes opened wide, and her love was shining bright and bold.

"Goddess, I feel like a fool. I'm so sorry, babe. My insecurities got the better of me. After everything... I suppose I thought you'd figure all this..." She gestured between them. "... was too much work."

"You can't get rid of me that easily. I would've haunted the hallways at work, continuing to plague you and beg for your affections."

He rested his brow against hers. "Liz Thorne, would you care to have dinner with me tonight?"

"I would."

Rafe shifted his head enough to claim her lips. The kisses started out as soft, lingering caresses but moved to a passionate embrace. The taste of her made him want to bundle her up and teleport home. He lifted his head to draw in a lungful of air. "It's only been a week, but I missed this."

"Me, too."

The slight frown hadn't lifted from Liz's brow, and Rafe figured they should address whatever else was bothering her. "*Qalbi*, tell me the last of your concerns."

"Why did you stay away so long?"

"The morning I left, you and your family were having a celebration of sorts. Not that I blame you. The Aether was alive, the bad guys conquered, and magic restored." Attempting to find the right words, he looked off in the distance, not seeing any of the surrounding scenery. Finally, he settled on, "The gaiety was too much for me right then. As unfeeling as my mother was, she was all I had."

"Why didn't you tell me? I would've gone wherever you wanted. Helped you mourn."

"I don't know that I was in mourning, per se, but I wasn't happy either. As far as taking you with me, I didn't plan to be gone so long. I'm not sure if you noticed when we visited, but the château was falling into disrepair."

"I did, but with all the other things going on..." She trailed off and shrugged.

"Right. So when I returned, I questioned Marguerite. Apparently, I was the heir to the estate, but all I inherited was a headache."

"So you were taking care of business matters?"

"Yes, and seeing to the transfer of the property to my cousin, so she always has a home. Of course, we were also on a treasure hunt to find the artifacts Mother and Franco stole."

She smiled softly and clasped his hand, lacing their fingers together. With a light tug, she led him back toward the restaurant. "You had a busy week. Now, I feel doubly bad."

"You were the best part. All I knew was that I wanted to finish as quickly as possible to return to you." He held the door open for her to enter. "I never wanted any more ugliness to touch you, and I felt dragging you with me to the estate would do that. You didn't need reminders of how poorly Franco and my mother treated you."

"None of it would've mattered as long as we were together, babe. This whole experience taught me as much."

"Forgive me?"

"Only if you'll forgive me."

He grinned and lifted their joined hands to kiss the inside of her wrist. "There's nothing to forgive."

Gianni spotted them the second they stepped into the foyer. He held the takeout bags from earlier. "I thought you might be back for these." After he handed them off, he turned to Liz. "You must be the fiancée I've heard so much about." Gianni shot a wry look Rafe's way. "I'll admit, after she delivered that magnificent blow, I thought you might have lied about your engagement."

Liz pulled a long gold chain from inside her shirt. It looped through the ruby engagement ring Rafe had given to her. "No lie. Just a simple misunderstanding on my part."

"Good," Gianni stated firmly. "There is no better man than Rafe Xuereb."

"I quite agree," she said, giving Rafe a soft look. "I said much the same thing not that long ago."

"Good. Now, come. You'll use my office." Gianni winked. "I believe you will find my recipe book will come in handy tonight."

EPILOGUE

One week later…

*a*s Mackenzie Thorne traversed the pebbled paths of the Drakes' garden, she turned her face to the sun. The beauty of the fine English day wasn't lost on her. Unlike her small home-town back in the States, the weather here tended to be cooler, and at times, overcast. Because Sebastian had a last-minute phone call he needed to make, he'd encouraged her to entertain herself for a short while. Now, as she waited for Baz to join her for their picnic, she explored the estate's extensive grounds.

"Beautiful," she murmured to herself. "I could live here forever."

At the end of a northbound walkway, tucked behind an over-growth of trees and rose bushes, she discovered a dilapidated garden gate, with a handful of symbols carved into the wooden framework. The grass around the entrance had turned to a dingy yellow and was on the verge of dying.

Because the gate had an antiquated lock that required a skeleton key, Mack figured that she wasn't getting in that way anytime soon. Her cousin Preston had taught her to pick locks for fun when she was a small child. But she hadn't retained anything but the basics. As rusted as the keyhole looked, she doubted the mechanism inside could be moved without a barrel of lubricant.

"Well, hell."

Stepping back, she eyed the height of the wall, judging it to be a good eight-feet tall. She could levitate, but if a non-magical human happened to be present and glancing out the window, they'd get a shock for sure. Of course, she could get around that with Granny Thorne's cloaking spell, but then Baz wouldn't find her. She grinned at the mental image of him walking right past her. What fun could be had lifting his kilt to discover what he did—or hopefully didn't—wear underneath.

Her best plan to scale the wall was the oak tree on this side. It would allow Mack to look like a normal, everyday mortal—albeit a crazy one—climbing a tree should anyone happen upon her. Unfortunately, there were no low-hanging branches to grab onto. With a quick look around, she swirled her hands in the air and created a thick, rope-like vine to aid her.

"Perfect."

As she wrapped her hand around the climber, a shiver of awareness teased along her skin. She almost backed away, but when no immediate vision of the future appeared to her, she shrugged off her unease. In mere seconds, she was at the top of the wall, peering over.

The sight filled her with sickening dread. The other side of the garden wall was nothing but a wasteland of dead foliage. Any grass had long-since shriveled and died, and the remains of trees were blackened and bare. It was as if a fire had swept through, and she'd have believed it to be so if it weren't for a single rose bush flourishing at the center of the deadened ground.

The bush was no more than three-feet high, but it had runners along the ground in every direction. Long, fat vines unlike any rose bush she'd ever seen. But it was the sight of the roses themselves that chilled her. They were a black so void of light, they looked like mini black holes dotting the landscape.

She shifted her grip on the wall slightly and peeked over the edge, straight down. Even as she watched, the runners grew in length and started climbing the brick wall faster than Mack would've thought possible without magical intervention. The thorns were at least three inches in length. The tips looked wicked and threatening.

She knew she was being fanciful, but so much death and darkness was off-putting.

"What the bloody hell are you doing?" boomed a furious voice from below her.

Mack almost lost her grip on the wall and wet her pants from fright. She'd have grabbed her pounding heart if her position wasn't so precarious.

"Dear Goddess, Baz! You nearly gave me heart failure." She peered down at him, and in doing so, missed the fact the rose runner had reached the top of the wall.

"Mack, *look out!*"

She whipped her head around in time to see the vine poised to shove one of those three-inch spikes directly into her neck. Throwing up a hand to protect herself, she deflected the plant's trajectory, but not without injury to herself. Her palm now sported a deep gash, and blood flowed freely, dripping down the garden-side of the wall.

The rose bush apparently wasn't done with its attack on her person, and coiled up, arching like a viper ready to strike.

"Let go, Mack. I'll catch you," Sebastian shouted up. "Now!"

As the vine came at her a second time, Mack released her hold on the wall, calling her air element to her to slow her descent and not be such a burden to Baz when he caught her. She was exceedingly glad when the wind kicked up. Only a few weeks ago, her magic had been on the fritz. Even with the air as a cushion, Sebastian grunted at the impact.

He stood her on her feet and gave her a single, hard shake. "That garden is forbidden, Mackenzie. Do you hear me? *Forbidden.*"

Never had she witnessed such a strong reaction in another person, and she'd seen everything from fear to fury to murderous rage. Where his strong emotion came from was anyone's guess. "I'm sorry, Baz."

"You don't understand the dangers it holds." The fingers gripping her shoulders dug in on the word "dangers."

"Baz, please calm down." Although she could've easily broken his hold with magical force, she realized he needed the physical contact. Not to intimidate, but to intimate. To stress the importance of his worry.

She stroked his exposed wrist. "Please."

As if he'd woken from a dream, his wide-eyed gaze locked onto where his hands clutched her. His chin jerked as if that sight shocked him. One by one, Sebastian's fingers loosened. "I'm sorry, Mack. Please forgive me."

"There's no need. We both got a scare."

"Every time I turn my back, you find something to get into." The heavy irritation in his voice was based on his concern for her safety —Mack was wise enough to recognize that much.

"I like to explore. It's one of life's little pleasures."

He lifted her hand to examine the wound. "And this?" he asked dryly. "Is this one of your life's little pleasures?"

"Comes with the territory," she teased.

The sight of his pale face as he stared down at the scratch gave Mack a little pang of conscience. "I didn't mean to frighten you, Baz. I'm truly sorry."

He met her steady gaze, and in his dark, soulful eyes, she saw worry.

"Baz? What is it?"

Glancing up toward the top of the wall, he grimaced. "We shouldn't be here."

"What is this place?"

"The garden of death."

"That's terrifying," she quipped, only half-joking. With a look back at the gate, she noticed the pale glow of the symbols. "Um, Baz?" She pointed. "Has that ever happened before?"

"*Fucking hell!*"

ON THE OTHER SIDE OF THE WALL, THE BLOOD FROM ITS VICTIM trailed down the considerable length of the rose climber. When it got to the ground, the liquid re-formed into droplets and ran toward the base of the bush, picking up speed as it neared the center of the garden. From there, it was sucked into the roots and converged to tunnel through the poisoned soil until it connected with the six-by-three, Carrara marble casket located ten feet below the ground's surface.

The earth rumbled at the receipt of the nutrient it so craved —*magic!*

In the cold interior of her coffin, the Enchantress rested in a forced stasis. But the moment the blood drops fell upon the sigil etched into the stone lid, she opened her obsidian eyes, waking from her one-hundred-ninety-two-year slumber.

FROM THE AUTHOR...

Thank you for taking the time to read **MOONLIT MAGIC!**

Be sure to join my mailing list for news on current releases, potential sales, new-to-you author introductions, and contests each month. But if it gets to be too much, you can unsubscribe at any time. Your information will always be kept private. No spam here!

www.tmcromer.com/newsletter

Join my Facebook Reader Group. While the standard pages and profiles on Facebook are not always the most reliable, I have created a group for fans who like to interact. This group entitles readers to "fan page only" contests, as well as an exclusive first look at covers, excerpts and more. Cromer's Carousers is the most fun way to follow yet! I hope to see you there!

www.facebook.com/groups/cromerscarousers

ALSO BY T.M. CROMER